ROBIN HOOD YARD

October, 1938: Johnny Steadman, investigative journalist, is called to the scene of a gruesome murder — a man has been tied to his bed, mutilated and left to bleed to death. This is the second time the killer has struck, and it won't be the last. Together with D.C. Matt Turner, Johnny tries desperately to find a link between the victims. When the next Lord Mayor of London is subjected to a vicious anti-Semitic attack, Johnny begins to wonder if the two cases are connected. Against a backdrop of escalating violence in Nazi Germany, he uncovers a shocking conspiracy that could bring the United Kingdom to its knees. But will Johnny live to tell the tale?

ROBIN HOOD YARD

MARK SANDERSON

LARGE
PRINT

First published in Great Britain 2015
by
Harper
an imprint of HarperCollins*Publishers*

First Isis Edition
published 2016
by arrangement with
HarperCollins*Publishers*

The moral right of the author has been asserted

This novel is entirely a work of fiction. The names, characters and incidents portrayed in it are the work of the author's imagination. Any resemblance to actual persons, living or dead, events or localities is entirely coincidental.

A catalogue record for this book is available
from the British Library.

ISBN 978–1–78541–136–6 (hb)
ISBN 978–1–78541–142–7 (pb)

Published by
F. A. Thorpe (Publishing)
Anstey, Leicestershire

Set by Words & Graphics Ltd.
Anstey, Leicestershire
Printed and bound in Great Britain by
T. J. International Ltd., Padstow, Cornwall

This book is printed on acid-free paper

To Curtis, Lucy and Jack

I had not thought death had undone so many.
                        T. S. Eliot, *The Wasteland*

FOREWORD

The bomb was in place. For the umpteenth time he checked his pocket watch. Two more minutes . . .

The Lord Mayor's coach — a fantasia in red and gold — emerged from Prince's Street by the Bank of England and turned, groaning on its leather straps, towards Poultry. The Lord Mayor, leaning out of the window, doffed his cocked hat to the dignitaries assembled under the portico of his new home, the Mansion House. The ostrich feathers on his hat rippled in the chilly breeze.

The cheering crowds that packed the pavements did nothing to scare the horses. Pairs of mounted policemen protected the coach at the front and rear. The floats that followed were also mainly drawn by horses, whereas others relied on another form of horsepower. It was one of these that stalled. The actors portraying Sir Francis Drake and his fellow bowlers staggered as the truck coughed then lurched to a stop.

The theme of this year's show was physical health. Everywhere banners proclaimed FITNESS WINS! Dancers, boxers, golfers and rowers continued to demonstrate their moves.

The plaster of Paris mountain being climbed by the alpinists started to emit smoke. Johnny watched in disbelief. No one climbed an active volcano.

1

The army jeeps and wagons of the auxiliary fire brigade rolled on. They were on parade, not on duty.

As soon as a gap appeared in the procession, Johnny pushed through the crowd lining the route and crossed Cheapside.

He weaved his way through a maze of penny-farthings, unseating a couple of the riders. Their companions, cursing loudly, wobbled precariously but somehow remained upright and continued to pedal. Some of the spectators started to boo.

A few members of a marching band, distracted, fell out of step. The loss of rhythm was accompanied by an unscored clash of cymbals. The catcalls got louder.

One of the police outriders craned his neck to see the cause of the commotion. Calling to his colleagues, he turned his mount around and headed towards Johnny.

The Lord Mayor, arm aching from waving to his devoted citizens, stuck his head out of the left side of the coach. Below him, on a painted panel, Mars, god of the City of London — and not, as many assumed, Mammon — pointed to a scroll held by Truth. What was going on?

A ginger-haired man was being dragged to his feet by two policemen. He seemed to be unconscious.

Beyond them, outside St Mary-le-Bow, a float was engulfed in flames . . .

PART ONE

Royal Exchange

CHAPTER
ONE

Friday, 28 October 1938, 9.05a.m.

The call came as he flung down *The Times* in disgust.
The Tories had won the Oxford by-election, albeit with
a halved majority. Quintin Hogg, the triumphant
candidate, claimed the result was a victory for Mr
Chamberlain and a vindication of the Munich
Agreement.

The "Thunderer", which had revealed itself to be a
proud organ of appeasement, made much of the defeat
of A. D. Lindsay, the Independent Progressive candidate
and Hogg's only opponent, even though the Master of
Balliol College had been supported by such dissident
Tories as Winston Churchill, Anthony Eden and Harold
Macmillan. Most of the other newspapers, including
Johnny's own, the *Daily News*, chose to highlight the
fury and disappointment of Edward Heath's student
Conservatives who had campaigned under the slogan,
"A vote for Hogg is a vote for Hitler."

He grabbed the receiver. "Steadman."

"What's wrong now? Lost a shilling and found a
sixpence?" Matt could usually tell how he was feeling.

"Bloody Tories."

"Never mind them. They don't mind you." Matt
wasn't interested in politics. Johnny, who took every

5

opportunity to needle high-hatted right-wingers, opened his mouth to protest but got no further. "Get yourself over to Crutched Friars. We've got another body."

He took a taxi to Fenchurch Street. Crutched Friars ran below the station. Plumes of steam and the sounds of shunting filled the smoky air.

Detective Constable Turner was standing on the corner of Savage Gardens. The sight of him always made Johnny smile. Although in plain clothes, Matt looked every inch the policeman. His recent promotion to the Detective Squad had nevertheless cost him the rank of sergeant. They shook hands.

It wasn't unusual for Turner to tip him off. They had known each other for a quarter of a century. The bonds forged in the playground of Essex Road School for Boys had only tightened as they'd jumped through the hoops of the adult world. They had been through a lot together, learning the hard way that it wasn't what you knew but whom. Their careers had become almost as intertwined as their emotions. Two sets of eyes were better than one.

Matt led him downhill to where a towering uniformed cop stood guard outside the open front door of a soot-encrusted terraced house. The sentinel's disdainful glance made Johnny feel even shorter than his five feet six. His flippant "Good morning!" received only the slightest of nods. Reporters, no matter how useful they often proved, were generally looked down on.

Low voices could be heard in the basement but Matt ignored them and climbed the uncarpeted staircase to the top of the building. Johnny, somewhat out of breath, grasped the peeling balustrade. Its sea-green paint matched the greasy walls. A filthy gas-cooker took up most of the tiny landing.

"Too many gaspers," said Matt. The champion boxer never bought cigarettes but was not above cadging them from others.

It was brighter up here. Through the open window of the living room Johnny could see the site of the Navy Office in Seething Lane where Samuel Pepys had worked and, in the distance, the tower of St Olave's where he had worshipped. Johnny was a dedicated diarist too.

However, Dickens was his greatest literary influence. He instantly recalled the passage in *The Uncommercial Traveller* in which the author had dubbed the church St Ghastly Grim. Its gateway, which bristled with iron spikes, was decorated with skulls and crossbones.

Once again the body was in the bedroom. Johnny braced himself. The naked victim lay spreadeagled on the bed. His wrists and ankles were tied to the iron frame. The mattress was black with blood.

A flashbulb popped. Its sizzle brought back unwelcome memories. Johnny, trying to block them, nodded to the photographer.

"As you can see, his cock is missing." Matt might as well have been talking about a tooth. "The amount of blood suggests it was amputated while he was still alive. In other words, he bled to death."

"Who is he?" Johnny opened his notebook.

"Walter Chittleborough. A clerk at the Hong Kong & Shanghai Bank in Gracechurch Street."

"He's pretty beefy for a pencil-pusher."

"Didn't do him any good though, did it?"

"The killer must have had great strength to overpower him."

"Perhaps. But can you see any signs of a struggle?"

There weren't any. A shaving brush, cut-throat razor and toothbrush were lined up on the glass shelf above the sink. A pair of striped pyjamas was neatly folded on a chair. One suit, three collarless shirts and a Crombie hung from wooden hangers on hooks. Johnny eyed the luxurious overcoat with envy. Winter was not far away.

"Have you got an age for him?"

"Twenty-four — but that's to be confirmed."

"Any family?"

"A sister in Bristol. We're trying to contact her."

"Who found him?"

"We did. The bloke in the basement called us. He had a key but the door was bolted from the inside."

"Fingerprints?"

"Dabs are on their way."

Johnny walked over to the window. "Was this open when you found him?" Matt nodded. Johnny stuck his neck out. It was a long way down. The area railings grinned up at him. "Is there an attic?"

"Indeed. The access hatch is on the landing." Matt, trying to suppress a smile, waited for the inevitable question.

"So how did the killer get away?"

"Who knows? Why not give Freeman Wills Croft a tinkle?" Matt was not a great reader — he relied on Johnny for literary knowledge. The real world was more interesting.

"We don't need him. It's obvious. They went up the chimney."

Ironic applause broke out behind him. Detective Sergeant Penterell filled the door frame.

"Very good, Steadman. You ought to be on the stage."

They had met before. In Johnny's eyes the ambitious fool had done nothing to deserve promotion.

"You should know by now that murder is not a laughing matter." Johnny glanced at the gagged and mutilated corpse again. Its young, firm flesh was already mottling. He hoped it had experienced pleasure as well as pain.

"Indeed," said Penterell. "That's why you shouldn't be in here." He sniffed the cold air as if searching for clues. "Turner, escort your friend off the premises."

"That won't be necessary." Johnny winked at Matt. "I'm sure you need his help more than I do." That wasn't necessarily true. "Besides, you can't stop me talking to the other residents."

"They've gone to work," said Penterell. "Now fuck off."

The two cops waited until they could hear his rapid footsteps on the stairs then went straight over to the fireplace.

Instead of leaving via the front door, and giving the bouncer in blue a second chance to look down his nose at him, Johnny walked through the narrow hall and down another flight of stairs to the basement.

A fat man sat smoking at the kitchen table.

"The door was open."

"I've made enough bleeding cups of tea. If you want one you'll have to get it yourself."

His head, encircled by receding hair, resembled a partly peeled boiled egg.

"Make a fresh pot, should I?"

"Don't go to any trouble on my account. Who are you anyway?"

"John Steadman. *Daily News*. I take it you're the landlord?"

"Nah, I'm 'The Wacky Warbler'. *Cwooorrr!*"

Johnny was not a fan of Joan Turner. Impressionists left him cold. Professional parasites, they fed off other people — just like journalists. When it came down to it they were all in the same business: entertaining the masses.

Johnny refilled the kettle and set it on the range where a vat of soapy water burbled away. He leaned closer. What was *that*?

"It's the only way to ensure they're clean. Can't live without my long johns."

Johnny stepped back in disgust. *Ensure?* Johnny suspected that, behind the scruffy appearance, there lurked an educated man.

The fatty stubbed out his cigarette and punched his chest in a vain attempt to silence an evil cough.

"I wondered when you lot would get here. How much for an exclusive?"

"Tell me what you told the police and I'll let you know, Mr . . . ?"

"Yaxley. William Yaxley."

"How long has Walter Chittleborough been your tenant?"

"I've been through all this already. I'm not a bleeding parrot."

"So I hear. Your mimicry would be a lot better. Start squawking. If one of my rivals turns up you can kiss goodbye to any chance of remuneration." Johnny offered him one of his own Woodbines.

"Ta muchly. Wally moved in about a year ago. Before that he'd been in digs in Whitechapel."

"Hardly worth the effort." The Ripper's hunting grounds were only a few streets away. "Previous address?"

"If I did know I've forgotten."

"Did he have a girl?"

"I'm sure he did — but rarely more than once. He wasn't courting, if that's what you mean."

"What sort of chap was he?"

"An ordinary chap. He worked hard, liked a pint and was mad about football. Never missed a Hammers match. Spent more time at Upton Park than here."

Soccer bored Johnny. One-on-one contests — battles of body *and* mind — were more exciting than team sports. The glory to be achieved was greater too.

"How would you describe his personality?"

"We weren't close. We didn't socialize."

"Moved in different circles did he? Try." So far Humpty Dumpty was not getting a penny.

11

"Unassuming, undemonstrative — unless he was stinko . . ."

"How d'you know if you didn't socialize?"

"We bumped into each other on the doorstep a few times. You hear everything down here." He glanced at the ceiling. "The more beer he'd had, the heavier his tread."

"Very well. What was the other adjective you were going to use before I so rudely interrupted?"

His interviewee watched him waiting, pencil poised.

"Unintelligent." He smirked. "A bathetic climax. Sorry."

"So am I. Nice oxymoron though." Humpty was playing with him, trying to distract him. What was he hiding?

The kettle lid rattled as the water reached boiling point. Johnny's blood was not far behind.

"And the other tenants? Did Wally socialize with them?"

"Not so far as I know. The Sproats on the ground-floor have a six-month-old baby. The wailing never stops."

"Seems pretty quiet now."

"He works at the Royal Mint. She's a cleaner. Leaves the brat with her mother in Shoreditch during the day."

"Do the people above them complain about the noise as well?"

"Mr Tull is deaf as a post. Lucky old sod. You won't get anything out of him." He blew a stream of smoke towards the range. "The tea won't make itself, you know."

12

"So who completes this happy household?"

"Rebecca. Beautiful Becky Taylor." He sighed. "She knows what Wally was like — inside and out, if you get my drift. She's some sort of secretary at Grocers' Hall. Talk to her."

"I will." Johnny slipped his notebook into a pocket. "Thanks for your time. Shouldn't you be at work as well?"

"I am." He hauled himself to his feet. "Looking after this place is an endless job. There's no clocking off here."

He rinsed out the teapot and spooned in four heaps of Lipton's. It seemed there was no clocking on either.

"Who owns the house?"

"I do."

Johnny, while Yaxley's back was turned, slipped out of the kitchen. He was halfway up the stairs before the landlord noticed.

"Oi! Steadman! What about the money?"

"Send me an invoice."

Even if the sluggard were to submit one he would see that it was never paid. Instinct told him Yaxley had concealed more than he'd revealed.

CHAPTER
TWO

The first body had been found on Monday in Gun Square, actually a gloomy triangle off Houndsditch. Jimmy Bromet, nineteen, was a waiter at the Three Nuns Hotel next door to Aldgate Station. He, too, had been tied to his bed and emasculated, but not castrated. No one in the lodging house had a heard a sound.

On his way back to the office Johnny made the cabbie take a detour. Although entirely surrounded by banks, Grocers' Hall, off Prince's Street, had its own courtyard. Two covered entrances allowed vehicles to drive in and out without the irksome task of reversing. A polite but obdurate doorkeeper informed him that Miss Taylor had arrived late for work. Consequently she would not be available until this evening. And livery companies were supposed to be charitable institutions.

"Undemonstrative? Fifteen letters." Tanfield, a junior reporter, had a strange knack of determining the length of a word no matter how long.

"We'll never know how long Chittleborough was though, will we?" said Dimeo. The deputy sports editor was obsessed with physical attributes. "What d'you think the killer does with the trophies?"

"I loathe to think," said Johnny.

"Yet you must find out, Steadman, post haste. It is what you are paid to do."

Gustav Patsel's wire-rimmed spectacles glinted in the milky midday sun. Tanfield and Dimeo returned to their desks. "Pencil", as the news editor was ironically known, had never been popular but, since the invasion of Czechoslovakia, anti-German feeling was at an all-time high. The ever-hungry Hun's waist had its own policy of expansionism.

"Perhaps they're turned into sausages," said Johnny. "You'd know more about that than me. Frankfurters, bratwurst, knackwurst . . ." Dimeo disguised a cackle with a cough.

"I want a thousand words on the two murders by four o'clock," said Patsel. "They are obviously the work of the same degenerate." He was about to say more when Quarles, his long-suffering deputy, handed him a sheet of yellow paper. The bulletin did not contain good news.

Johnny watched Patsel resume his throne in the centre of the newsroom and pick up a phone.

"What's so important?"

"Goya and El Greco are following in the footsteps of Rembrandt and Rubens," said Quarles.

The central rooms of the National Gallery in Trafalgar Square had been closed for more than a month. Rumour had it the priceless paintings were being stored somewhere in Wales.

"They and their curators clearly don't have much faith in old Neville," said Johnny. "I wish Pencil would pack up and leave."

15

"He'd rather be interned than return to the Fatherland — and who can blame him? Pressmen are even less popular over there. At least we try to tell the truth."

"Are we interested in birching? There's another demonstration planned for this afternoon. It might be lively."

"No. Given the whole country is in danger of losing their skins, you'd think they'd have something better to do. Concentrate on the murders. See if you can find anything that connects the two men."

Peter Quarles was the main reason why Johnny was still at the *Daily News*: without his frequent, good-natured interventions, Patsel and his star reporter would have come to blows. The editor was not blessed with a sense of humour. He found Johnny's wit and disregard for authority difficult to take. Quarles, though, had learned to handle — and respect — Johnny's wayward talent.

Johnny, keen to hear more, rang Matt but was told D. C. Turner was still out of the office. The press bureau at Old Jewry, headquarters of the City of London police, promised to relay any developments in the double murder case. He wouldn't hold his breath.

Apart from the manner of their deaths, there appeared to be nothing to link the cases. Bromet had lived on the first floor; Chittleborough on the third. Had the two bachelors known each other? Bromet had no criminal convictions. Did Chittleborough have a clean record too?

16

Matt would have no difficulty in answering the second question. He was invariably quick to acknowledge the part Johnny had played in his promotion. Although unofficial, their collaboration in several headline-hitting cases had boosted both their careers. The lifelong friends made a good team. That didn't mean they always saw eye to eye.

Lizzie jerked awake. The glowing coals shifted in the grate. Lila Mae, Johnny's god-daughter, slumbered on in her arms. It was natural for the child to fall asleep after being fed, but not for her. Still, in more ways than one, breast-feeding took it out of her.

She'd been dreaming again. The same silly dream. Walking down the aisle, carrying her bouquet of lilies of the valley — she could smell them now — and coming to a stop beside the man who, instead of being blond like her husband-to-be, had copper-coloured hair. Both Matt and Johnny had been in love with her — Lizzie knew, at least she hoped, they still were — but she was beginning to wonder if she had chosen the wrong man.

She'd seen less and less of Matt since he'd joined the Detective Squad. There was no doubt he was a devoted father — he adored Lila Mae, even if he was hopeless at changing nappies. However, after the birth, Matt had seemed to lose interest in her. A distance crept between them and, unless she was mistaken, it was, like Lila, growing by the day. It was almost as if she'd served her purpose by producing a baby. When Matt did pay her any attention — usually on a Saturday night, after a bout of boxing and boozing — it felt as though he was acting out of duty rather than desire.

Could you suffer from postpartum depression fifteen months after the event? It was unlikely. She had been down in the dumps for a couple weeks in September last year — when the prospect of caring for such a helpless, relentless bundle of need had become over-whelming — but the feeling had passed. Resentment at being trapped, being a prisoner of her all-consuming love for Lila, had given way to resignation and, eventually, a newfound resilience.

She was proud of the fact that she'd regained her slim figure — well, almost — but why had she bothered? No one else saw her. Men rarely gave more than a glance to women pushing prams. She missed the admiration she'd attracted while working in Gamages. Her parents had been right when they'd said such a position was beneath her. Their darling daughter was not meant to be a salesgirl, yet they'd been perfectly happy when she'd left the department store to be a housewife and mother. They seemed to have forgotten she had brains as well as beauty.

She didn't feel clever today though. She felt grubby, distracted and disappointed. She kissed Lila on a chubby pink cheek; sniffed her silky fair hair. Her whole world had shrunk to this infant. She owed it to herself not to drown in domestic drudgery. She couldn't go on like this.

She got out of the armchair and lay Lila down in her cradle. The baby whimpered and waved her arms but

18

did not wake. Lizzie, watching over her, sighed deeply. It wasn't only nappies that she had to change.

He didn't light the paraffin heater even though the cold gave him goose pimples. Perhaps it wasn't the pervasive underground chill. Perhaps it was nervous anticipation.

The vat squatted on the workbench. He wouldn't peep inside it again. The contents made him gag. The thought of touching the thick, foul liquid made his stomach lurch. Sweat beaded his broad forehead.

The bottles were lined up waiting. He put on a pair of cotton gloves, picked up the first one and turned the spigot.

Nothing happened. Then, just as he was about to turn off the tap, a black trickle quickly became a torrent. He grinned with relief. He'd soon be done.

The expected knock on the cellar door came at the exact appointed time. That was encouraging. He paid the pair of toughs and pointed to the crate.

"Remember, gentlemen, if you do it right, I'll give you the same again."

"Piece of cake," said the older one, licking his lips. His accomplice hoisted the crate on to his shoulder with ease.

"We're going to enjoy this."

CHAPTER
THREE

He finally got through to Rebecca Taylor at four thirty as she returned from the canteen. Reporters didn't get tea breaks. A trolley came round on the hour, every hour. The women who pushed it, each of them wearing what seemed like the same floral apron, were a valuable source of gossip about the goings-on in Hereflete House.

They knew what the seventh floor had decided before anyone else.

It was too late for the early edition — he'd already filed his copy — but it didn't matter anyway.

"I can't talk now. Besides, the detective told me not to speak to the press at all." Johnny liked her voice. She sounded like Jean Arthur.

"What was he called?"

"Parnell, Pentell, something like that."

Close enough.

"Penterell. Don't worry about him. He's a dolt."

"I don't want to get into any trouble."

"You won't. You have my word."

"Are you in the habit of making promises you can't keep?"

"Meet me after work and you'll find out. What time d'you finish?"

"Half past five. Don't come to the reception. Wait for me outside."

"I don't know what you look like. How will I recognize you?"

"Keep your hair on! I know you."

He lit up and, slowly exhaling, stared at the massive blank walls of the Bank of England: unscalable, unbreachable, very unfriendly. Prince's Street had seemed to be one of the most boring thoroughfares in the City until the discovery of the London Curse a few years ago. The lead tablet, inscribed on both sides in Latin, declared: *Titus Egnatius Tyranus is hereby solemnly cursed, likewise Publius Cicereius Felix.* Empires rose and fell but human nature remained the same. Had the two dismembered men also been cursed?

"You look exactly like your photograph." Johnny laughed. Miss Taylor looked nothing like Jean Arthur but she was still a dish.

"Is that a good or bad thing?"

"Good, I reckon. You're famous for not misleading your readers."

She was only partly right. There were times when he felt it necessary not to tell the whole truth. He did his best to protect his sources and the innocent. Then again, as PDQ was fond of saying — Peter Donald Quarles's initials gave him the inevitable nickname "pretty damn quick" — what is not said can be just as revealing as what is.

"I'm not famous. I'm simply good at my job."

Now it was her turn to laugh. "Such modesty!"

"Indeed. I've got a lot to be modest about."

They went to the Three Bucks round the corner in Gresham Street.

"What can you tell me about Walter Chittleborough?"

"Not much, I'm afraid. He seemed a decent enough chap to begin with, but I was wrong."

She took another sip of beer — a surprising choice of drink. He'd had her down as a G&T sort of girl. He waited for her to break the silence.

"I shouldn't have given in. He'd been asking me out for months but I wasn't interested."

"Why did you?"

"I thought he'd leave me alone if I gave him what he wanted." Johnny's eyebrows shot up. "Don't look at me like that. You're no different. Men are only after one thing. Go on, I dare you. Tell me you'd say no."

Once upon a time he'd have answered her by kissing her on the lips. They were so red they scarcely needed lipstick. He was no stranger to brief encounters, but as he got older — thirty-one now! — he hankered after something more meaningful. Besides, he'd been in love with someone — someone he couldn't marry — for years.

"You're a knockout girl, and I admit I'd like to get to know you better, but what's the hurry?"

"Haven't you heard? There's going to be another war. We might all be dead by Christmas."

"Let's concentrate on those who are already dead. Who'd want to kill Chittleborough in such a horrid way?"

"Me, for a start."

"Don't say things like that. I thought you wanted to keep out of trouble."

"I do — but Wally had it coming. He was handsome on the outside, ugly on the inside. He had a sick mind."

"In what way?"

She shook her head. Her black curls gleamed in the gaslight. "I'd rather not say. It's not important."

"Of course it is!" Was she insane? "What did he do to you?"

"Nothing."

"So why did you reject him?"

"I didn't! He rejected me."

"I find that hard to believe."

"Stop flattering me."

"I'm not." Was he? "Why would he reject you after pursuing you for so long?"

"Pillow talk is dangerous."

If he pressed her further she would clam up altogether. He tried a different tack.

"Did you ever meet any of his friends?"

"No. He didn't go out much during the week. His pacing up and down, up and down, drove me mad. I was planning to get out from underneath him."

"And yet you didn't hear a thing last night."

"Not after I went to bed. I was listening to the third act of *Carmen* from Covent Garden. I think Renée Gilly is marvellous. It finished at five to eleven."

She met his gaze as if challenging him to contradict her. He remained silent.

"I'm still going to move out, even though he's dead." She sighed. Out of relief or satisfaction? He couldn't tell. "I don't feel safe. I'll never spend another night in Savage Gardens."

"You can stay with me if you like." The words were out before he could eat them.

"Now who's in a hurry?" She smiled. Her eyes were almost maroon. "I'm going to stay with my brother in Tooting."

"Good for you. Call me if you think of anything else." He handed her his card. "You'll feel a lot safer when the killer's in custody."

"Perhaps. Thanks for the drink."

Johnny drained his glass and got to his feet. They shook hands. He watched her walk quickly out of the pub, aware of other eyes — those of half-cut bankers, brokers and jobbers — examining her assets. Miss Taylor was too much of a catch to let slip through his fingers. He must find a good reason to see her again.

"Hello stranger!"

It had been over a year since Cecil Zick — brothel-keeper, pornographer and extortionist — had seen his fellow purveyor of smut, Henry Simkins of the *Daily Chronicle*. It was not a fond reunion.

"Don't be like that, darling. We make a good team."

"Keep your voice down." The wooden walls of Ye Olde Mitre were thin but Zick, a stickler for keeping up appearances, still went to the trouble of hiring a private room. "What brings you back this time?"

"Herr Hitler. I don't trust a word the ghastly man says. The sooner someone exterminates the jumped-up little man the better. In the meanwhile I'm going to hide behind Britannia's voluminous skirts."

"Where exactly?"

"I'll let you know soon enough. Everything's almost ready. The show must go on."

"If word gets out, you'll wish you were in back in Potsdamer Platz."

"I know. I know. That's where you come in."

"What's in it for me?"

"Whatever you wish. A new pair of balls?"

"Very droll. It's always someone else who pays the price, isn't it? You've a remarkable talent for survival. One of these days your luck will run out."

"Not if I can help it." Zick coughed discreetly. "I was sorry to hear about your little accident . . ."

"It wasn't a fucking accident. It was deliberate!"

A psychopath — an amateur surgeon who abjured the use of anaesthetic — had deprived Simkins of his crown jewels the previous summer. If it hadn't been for Steadman, his arch-rival, he'd have lost a lot more.

"Yes, indeed. You do understand it was impossible to visit. Let me make it up to you. Can you still . . . ?"

"Rise to the occasion? No — but there are other sources of pleasure."

"Indeed. I should know. However, let's not forget that pleasure doesn't equal happiness."

"That's rich, coming from you."

"Revenge can be almost as satisfying as sex. The longer it's deferred, the more glorious its consummation."

"So that's what you're after."

"Detective Constable Turner is not a man for letting bygones be bygones." Zick put down his glass and, as if the champagne had turned to battery acid, grimaced. "I hardly touched his wife. How was I to know she was pregnant? I only detained her so that Turner would do what was required. Once again he represents a serious impediment to my business plans."

"What's it going to be then? Bribery or butchery?"

"Much as the latter would be fun, the former would be more expedient."

"Why not have a word with the Commander?"

"The less he knows the better."

"At the risk of repeating myself: what's in it for me?"

"Don't you want to get one over on Steadman?"

"He saved my life!"

"But not your balls, alas. And it seems that's not all you lost. Where's the Machiavellian streak that's got you this far?"

"I don't have to prove anything to you. He did set me up though. Have you still got the photographs?"

A couple of years ago both Matt and Johnny — on separate occasions — had been drugged and molested while a camera recorded the criminal depravity. So far they had succeeded in preventing the attacks becoming common knowledge.

"*Bien sûr, mon petit choux.* I knew it would be a mistake to destroy them."

"So you didn't keep your word?"

"You saw me burn the negatives, didn't you? I recall how pleased you were to be able to tell Steadman the good news. Didn't get you anywhere with him though, did it?"

Simkins scowled. "Get on with whatever it is you want to say."

"Be like that then. Our old friend Timney, hearing that I'd returned to the Smoke, crawled out from whichever stone he was hiding under and made himself available to me. I was delighted when he told me that — against my direct orders — he'd kept a copy of the negatives. That's why I need you. Steadman is the simplest way to put pressure on Turner."

"You mean blackmail him."

"Such a nasty word." He waved his hand as if to disperse a bad smell. The ruby on his finger flashed in the candlelight. "Still, it worked last time — if not quite in the way we'd hoped. I can't approach Steadman, but you can. Tell him the truth — you need his help."

"To do what? He's not a fool."

"You'll think of something."

"And if I don't?"

Zick got to his dainty feet. "Remember what a sticky end is? You used to like nothing more."

The champagne — still in its glass — smashed against the door. Wisely, he'd waited until his nemesis had gone.

CHAPTER
FOUR

Saturday, 29 October, 10.15 a.m.

The first report came in shortly after ten o'clock. Others soon followed. Five banking houses had been attacked: N. M. Rothschild & Sons, Samuel Montagu & Co., M. Samuel & Co., Seligman Brothers, and S. Japhet & Co. All of them were Jewish. Bottles of blood had been flung against the walls of the noble institutions.

The attacks couldn't have happened at a better time. Johnny was making little headway with the double murders. Everything was too clean. Matt had wearily informed him that Chittleborough had no criminal record and the only fingerprints found in the flat had been his. No one had seen or heard anything strange on Thursday evening. The killer had shown a clean pair of heels.

"Someone's not happy," said PDQ. "Perhaps they're blaming the Jews for dragging us — kicking and screaming — towards war. They get blamed for all sorts of things."

"Perfect scapegoats," said Johnny. "But Chamberlain's flying to Munich this morning. Third time lucky."

"I hardly think so, Steadman," said Patsel. "Such — how do you say it? — yo-yo diplomacy is bound to fail.

It demonstrates weakness, not strength." He appeared gratified at the prospect.

"There's been another one." Tanfield, who had the desk opposite Johnny's, brandished a telegram from Reuters. "The next Lord Mayor's been hurt."

Mansion House Street was to the City what Piccadilly Circus was to Westminster. It was the very heart of things, where no less than eight arteries met, and as such was usually clogged with traffic. On the map it resembled the head of a splayed octopus with one limb shrivelled.

Johnny stopped the taxi by the monumental headquarters of the Midland Bank. Lutyens had a lot to answer for. The naked boy wrestling a goose above him was a jocular nod towards the building's location: Poultry. Ten years on, only the southwest corner, regularly lashed by rain, retained a hint of the Portland stone's original whiteness.

Outside the Bank of England a City cop in reflective white gauntlets waved him and Magnus Monroe, a staff photographer, across the road. The Royal Exchange lay in the fork between Threadneedle Street and Cornhill. The Duke of Wellington and Copenhagen — cast in bronze from captured French cannon — gazed down at him with sightless eyes. The City thrived on making the man in the street feel small.

The Exchange had closed — or been closed — early. One of its constables — instantly recognizable in his blue-and-gold uniform — stood talking to a City cop beneath the portico. As soon as Johnny started climbing the steps, he raised his stick. Johnny kept going.

"Thus far and no further." The bumptious beadle attempted to block his path.

"John Steadman, *Daily News*."

"Sorry, sir. The Exchange is closed."

"I can see that. Let me pass."

He was tempted to knock off the beadle's cocked hat. The old man — who had the power to arrest and detain him within the Exchange — waved his stick at him. Pop! Magnus set to work. It was always good to illustrate the risks a fearless reporter faced as he went about his business. The old soldier turned his attention to the photographer. As soon as he took his eyes off him, Johnny headed for the doors.

"Going somewhere?" The long arm of the law felt his collar. It wasn't the first time — nor would it be the last.

"Yes."

"No." The constable let go of his collar but only to pluck the hairs on the back of his neck.

"Ouch! Fuck off, Watkiss." They had met before. The Square Mile often felt as small as a bear pit or bullring. "Still a plain bogey, I see. You must miss Sergeant Turner."

"Not as much as you."

"He'll be here in a minute."

"Really?"

Johnny nodded. Several of his competitors were piling out of taxis. "Do me a favour — keep that lot out."

30

"What's in it for me?"

"I'll put in a good word for you."

"Go on then — and mind that you do."

He pushed open the heavy swing doors and made a beeline for the man sitting on a bentwood chair in the middle of the empty courtyard. It was pleasantly warm beneath the glass canopy but a metallic tang hung in the air. The antique Turkish pavement was splotched with blood.

"It's not mine — at least, most of it isn't." Leo Adler tried to get up but his legs gave way. A concerned minion dabbed at the cut on his forehead. "Let me be!"

"John Steadman, *Daily News*."

The cop interviewing one of the gathered witnesses turned round but said nothing.

"How d'you do?" They didn't shake hands. "Not fond of bankers, are you? I must say, I enjoyed your exposure of that wicked boy's scam."

A post-room worker had been removing foreign stamps from envelopes and selling them. As the recent pepper scandal had demonstrated — an attempt to corner the world market in white pepper had floundered because the perpetrators failed to realize that black pepper could be turned into white — there was no shortage of crooks in the City. However, it was generally those at the bottom who were caught. Those higher up the ladder remained at large. In Johnny's eyes, anyone in pinstripes belonged behind bars.

"A reporter is only as good as his sources."

"Much like a French chef!"

"What happened? Why aren't you taking this seriously?"

"It's nothing. A rough-looking gentleman sprayed me with blood then threw the bottle at me and scarpered. Fortunately, it didn't smash. I saw stars for a minute but I'm right as rain now."

"Red rain. Why blood?"

"No idea. Perhaps he was a communist protestor hell-bent on keeping the red flag flying. We'll probably never know."

"What did he look like?"

"As I said, rough. Not the type generally seen round here."

The mayor-in-waiting gestured at the arcades that lined the court where commodities had been bought and sold for centuries. There were other exchange nearby: the Corn Exchange in Mark Lane, the Baltic Shipping Exchange in St Mary Axe, the Metal Exchange in Whittington Avenue, the Wool Exchange in Coleman Street, the Rubber Exchange in Mincing Lane and, of course, the Stock Exchange in Threadneedle Street.

The motto of the City of London was *Domine Dirige Nos* — "Lord, guide us" — but it might as well have been *Quid pro quo* — "something for something" — or "anything for money": timber, minerals, coffee, sex, information or access.

Magnus, the archetypal shutterbug, came beetling towards them. No doubt he'd slipped Watkiss a oncer to let him in. If Steadman's profession was asking, Monroe's was taking — usually without permission.

Mouths opened in protest were more dramatic than thin-lipped smiles. Adler, though, was only too happy to oblige. No wonder he'd been elected Lord Mayor. His regular, tanned features represented the acceptable face of capitalism — even if he was Jewish.

Johnny had read interviews with the second Jew destined to become Lord Mayor of London. The first, David Salomons, had been elected in 1855. City folk, pragmatists par excellence, were less vocal in their anti-Semitism than some of the population. The size of a man's fortune was more important than the size of his nose.

"You must have heard about the other attacks," said Johnny. "They can hardly be a coincidence. This seems like the start of a hate campaign. It must be personal, anti-Semitic. You're the only person to have been attacked."

"I've just come from Rothschild's in New Court." St Swithin's Lane was less than a minute's walk away. "It won't take long to clean up the mess."

"Rothschild," murmured Johnny. "Red shield."

"What's that?"

"Probably nothing. I was thinking aloud."

"Come off it. Next you'll be saying that murder spelled backwards is *red rum*."

"Why would I? I like crosswords but no one's been murdered — not here anyway. Are you sure you haven't a clue as to who's responsible?"

"If I had, they'd be under arrest already."

Johnny believed him. After "The Silent Ceremony" at the Guildhall on 9 November — during which the outgoing mayor would hand over the sword, sceptre, seal and list of Corporations to him — Adler would be the Chief Magistrate of the City.

"Such publicity is bad for business," he continued. "The sooner it stops, the better."

"Why talk to me then?"

"Your opposition to the bowler-hat-and-brolly brigade is well known. If you say it's nothing but a stunt, people will believe you. Outside the City I don't have much clout."

Johnny was flattered but not convinced.

"Adler. That's a German name, isn't it?"

"Yes. My grandparents were German, but both my parents were British. It means eagle."

"Perfect for a high-flier."

Adler's laughter echoed round the Exchange.

"I need a drink. Care to join me? It's almost midday." He got to his feet and, this time, stayed upright. "Are we done now, Sergeant?"

"Yes, sir, if you're sure you don't want to go to Bart's."

"Quite sure. I've had worse bumps. Got a thick skull. Let me know when you catch the blighter."

It was all right for some. Lesser mortals would have been obliged to make a statement at Snow Hill police station.

Adler, having dismissed his entourage with reassuring noises, led them out of an exit at the rear of the building and thus avoided the scrum waiting at the front. Johnny was delighted. Monroe went off to develop his prints while he and Adler crossed the road

34

and entered the maze of alleys that zigzagged between Lombard Street and Cornhill. Thirty yards down Birchin Lane they turned left into Castle Court.

The George and Vulture was one of Mr Pickwick's favourite haunts.

"He dined here with Sam Weller," said Johnny.

"I don't have time to read for pleasure."

"But you do read the papers."

"Lord Beaverbrook, Viscount Rothermere and their cronies are powerful men. It's not called the press for nothing. If they want something, they can exert great pressure."

"Even they can't stop a world war though. They're more concerned about their livelihoods — the supply of newsprint — than the lives of their readers."

"Agreed," said Adler. He sipped the fine claret. "There'll be no shortage of news though."

"There will. Dora will see to it." The Defence of the Realm Act was introduced in 1914. "The government is bound to tighten its grip on the flow of information."

"The Nazis are fond of censorship as well," said Adler. "The problems facing Jews in Germany are far worse than leaks suggest. They're now being rounded up and expelled to Poland. Not only men of working age but women and children too."

Johnny had long campaigned for the *Daily News* to highlight Hitler's atrocious treatment of the Jews. However, he was a crime reporter. Foreign news was not his concern. Patsel dismissed such reports as gross exaggeration, propaganda spread by embittered refugees.

Fleet Street preferred to reflect public opinion rather than change it. Britannia ruled the waves but her citizens were insular in outlook. There was enough suffering at home without worrying about Johnny Foreigner. Only last week the *Daily Telegraph* had run an advertisement for typists with the proviso that "no Jewesses" need apply.

"Why d'you think Hitler hates Jews so much?"

"Fear. Paranoia. Perhaps he's secretly afraid there's a tincture of Jewish blood running in his veins. Self-hatred is even more corrosive." He sighed. "It's easier to blame other people for your own weaknesses, shift the responsibility away from yourself. Conspiracies are convenient ways of explaining the inexplicable. Otherness — difference — produces a primitive, instinctive reaction in the brain, but most people choose to override it."

"A tribal survival mechanism."

"Exactly. If there weren't any Jews, new scapegoats would soon be found. Negroes, Catholics, Armenians, homosexuals . . ."

"And yet Jews invented the concept."

"That's right." Adler raised his glass to him. "Which university did you attend?"

"I didn't. Couldn't afford it."

"Ah, well it stems from the Hebrew word *Azazel.* You can find it in Leviticus: *And Aaron shall place lots upon the two he-goats: one lot for the Lord, and the other lot for Azazel.*"

"So why would someone select you as a scapegoat?"

36

"I don't know. Perhaps the attack has nothing to do with my being Jewish."

"It must have. It's Saturday — the Jewish Sabbath. The blood must be a reference to historic blood libels."

"But I haven't crucified any Christian kids or drunk their blood. I haven't poisoned any wells."

Suddenly the expensive Bordeaux didn't taste as good.

"No, but you're about to become the figurehead of the financial centre of the world. Many people see bankers as bloodsuckers. In their blinkered eyes, the fact you're Jewish simply makes matters worse."

"I'm not a practising Jew though. As you see, I don't observe the Sabbath. I don't have ringlets. I don't dress entirely in black. I don't work for a Jewish bank. You could say I'm totally unorthodox."

"Why did you want to be Lord Mayor?"

"What financier wouldn't? It's an honour. Proof I've assimilated myself into a secretly hostile environment. Chairmanships and presidencies are all very well, but the mayoralty is a unique position. It's a chance to do an immense amount of good — for both the companies and charities I'm involved with. And, of course, I'll be able to help my friends . . ."

He topped up Johnny's glass.

"What d'you want me to do?"

"Find out who's behind this campaign. I don't have much faith in the police. Ironic, isn't it, that the top brass are based in Old Jewry? Did you know the Great Synagogue there was burned down before Edward I expelled the Jews . . ."

★ ★ ★

37

When Johnny, somewhat squiffy, re-emerged into daylight, the working week was over. The army of bank messengers, dispatch cases chained to their wrists, had marched off home, leaving the streets to the City's "submerged tenth": watchmen, sandwich-men, hawkers, beggars and bible-bangers. The lamps slung on wires above them swung in the strengthening wind. Plane trees shed their last few leaves.

Johnny hadn't finished work though. He decided to walk back to the office to clear his head.

He preferred being on foot — relying on his own resources — to being driven by someone else. London was a never-ending variety show, every pedestrian a character in an impromptu promenade performance. It was impossible not to cheer.

Even so, as he strode down Ludgate Hill, St Paul's standing proud behind him, his spirits sank. He'd two meaty stories to pursue, but what was the point if the country was waltzing towards war? His flat feet would keep him out of the army yet he was determined to make himself useful. Perhaps Adler could recommend him to the Ministry of Information when it was finally re-established.

He'd read too much to harbour any illusions about the reality of war. Chamberlain had declared there must be "no more Passchendaeles" — Johnny's father had been killed in the battle in 1917 — but, for all his good intentions, he was a politician not a magician. Peace couldn't be produced, like a rabbit, out of a hat. Before long, ignorant armies would once again clash by night. If Johnny couldn't report on it he could at least help pick up the pieces: carry a stretcher or drive an ambulance. Matt, Lizzie and Lila Mae were the only family he had. It wouldn't matter if he were blown to bits.

What bollocks! He shook his head to dispel the gloom. Evil had to be confronted wherever it lurked. He nodded to the commissionaire and headed for the lifts, noticing in passing that the sunburst ceiling, dazzlingly lit, made the doorman's shoes shine.

A pall of silver cigarette smoke drifted over the stalls. Johnny, sprawled on the front row, smirked at the portrayal of hard-drinking, hard-talking newspapermen in *I Cover the Waterfront*. He could see why the American tale of people-trafficking had taken five years to reach these shores.

The ABC in Islington High Street had been the Empire until a few months ago. Movies had replaced music-hall turns in 1932. When he was a child his mother had often treated him to a Saturday afternoon show. In those days the Victorian concert venue had been known as The Grand. The more things changed the more they remained the same.

There was no food at home so he'd hopped off the tram at the Angel and bought a couple of stale rolls — at a discount — from the French & Vienna Bread Co. next door and smuggled them into the picture house.

If he was with a girl he usually steered her to the back row where, inevitably, the film took second place to smooching. However, when alone, he liked to be as close to the screen as possible so that the characters were literally larger than life.

Claudette Colbert, especially in the brothel sequence, was captivating — although he preferred her darting eyes in *It Happened One Night* — but Ernest Torrence's evil sea-captain stole every scene. His best line came as one of the Chinamen he'd drowned was fished out of the Pacific: "Not more'n a day. Crabs ain't got 'im yet." The Scottish actor was dead now: gallstones.

As he cut through the crowd of couples dawdling in the foyer, reluctant to return to the real world, he regretted not asking Rebecca for a date. Once outside, all thoughts of her disappeared as torrential icy rain threatened to drown him.

His flat was not far away so he decided to make a run for it. Dead leaves made the pavements treacherous. Each time he skidded the gutters seemed to gurgle with laughter.

Key in hand, he turned into Cruden Street. There was someone huddled in the doorway.

"About fucking time," said Matt.

CHAPTER
FIVE

Monday, 31 October, 8.30a.m.

Despite reports to the contrary, the world was not coming to an end. Planet Earth had not been invaded by Martians. Johnny grinned at the gullibility of the public. *The War of the Worlds* was a radio play, not reality. Did no one read H. G. Wells across the Atlantic? All the same, he couldn't wait to hear the programme.

Orson Welles, the director, claimed the whole thing had been a prank to mark Halloween. If so, why had it been broadcast the day before? And why had it created so much hoo-ha?

There was nothing new about using fake news bulletins for dramatic effect on the radio: Ronald Knox had used them in *Broadcasting from the Barricades* on the BBC, during which rioters were supposed to have taken over the streets of London. Johnny suspected the American press, like its British counterpart, was suspicious of the relatively new medium, afraid of its ability to report news so much quicker, and was seizing the opportunity to bash the competition. However, with Germany and Japan banging the drums of war, it had been cynical of Welles to capitalize on fears of global invasion.

"The balloon won't go up for another year or so, if Wells is to be believed," said PDQ. "In *The Shape of*

Things to Come he predicts that a new world war will begin in January 1940."

"Let's hope he's wrong."

"Let's hope you haven't done anything wrong. Stone wants to see you."

The red light above the door to the editor's office went off and the green light came on. Johnny tapped on the polished wood and entered.

"Ah, Steadman. What have you been up to now?" Victor Stone peered at him over the top of his half-moon glasses.

"Sir?"

"I've had a call from our new Lord Mayor. Anything to tell me?"

"Wish I had."

Stone smiled. "Stand at ease. Must be getting old, Steadman — no one's complained about you recently. Quite the opposite, in fact. Leo said what a personable chap you were. I gather you met on Saturday."

So Adler and his boss were on first-name terms . . .

"He wants to know who attacked him. Doesn't trust the police."

"Quite. Yet they've already ascertained the attackers used pig's blood. Talk about adding insult to injury."

"Attackers? Adler said the man was alone."

"Indeed. But, according to the times established by the bluebottles, a single individual couldn't have attacked all five banks as well as Adler."

Where was Stone getting his information from? Why hadn't anyone told him this? It was supposed to be his story. Johnny knew better than to ask.

"Is Adler clean?"

"As far as I know. Go on . . ."

Conscious of the black eyes boring into him, Johnny obliged. "Well, pigs aren't kosher, are they? Jews consider them unclean. The blood could be a reference to some sort of dirty business. Insider dealing is even more common than people suspect."

"Adler has only got where he is today by being whiter than white. He is extremely conscious of his reputation."

"He that filches from me my good name . . ."

Johnny, not for the first time, had opened his mouth without thinking. Iago was a villain and, at this moment, quoting from *Othello* immediately raised the spectre of Shylock.

"Precisely. *Reputation, reputation, reputation!* Lose the immortal part of yourself and what remains is bestial. That's why you must help him. It's your number one priority."

"So the two murders are less important?"

Stone stood up and came round the corner of his enormous desk. The fitness fanatic did callisthenics every morning in his office. "Beauty hurts!" was his catchphrase. He had a good body and, as a member of the Open-Air Tourist Society, was not afraid of showing it.

"Anyone else been killed?"

Johnny could smell the carrot juice on Stone's breath. He stood his ground.

"No."

"Anyone been arrested?"

"No."

"Anything new to report at all?"

"Not at this point."

"Well, get going then. Who's to know what your snouts have unearthed? If they haven't heard anything about Adler's attackers they may have heard something about the dead men."

He strolled over to the window that — despite the janitor's best efforts — was still flecked with blackout paint.

"Adler isn't going to speak to anyone but us. It'll be an exclusive. One in the eye for the *Financial Times*. A successful outcome would benefit us all — especially you. Herr Patsel is an excellent news editor, but he can't stay here, cling on to power, much longer. A reshuffle is on the cards."

"I'm a newshound, sir, not a house cat. I belong on the streets not behind a desk."

"Think about it. Now go get me a story."

Most newspapers used City spies and featured City diaries — published under such pseudonyms as Midas and Autolycus ("a snapper-up of unconsidered trifles") — to prove it. The City had a tradition of secrecy and worked hard to cultivate its mystique. Attempts to cast light on its activities were viewed askance. Consequently, relations between Fleet Street and Threadneedle Street were often strained.

In the Square Mile it wasn't only the streets that followed mediaeval courses. The business of buying and selling remained the same. The exchanges didn't like change. Profit always came at someone's expense. It was all a game: beggar-my-neighbour or strip-Jack-naked.

Johnny shared Dickens's opinion of bankers. The crooked financier Mr Merdle — who was full of shit — lived down to his name. Was Adler a mutual friend?

Moneychangers — even before Jesus threw them out of the temple — had never been popular. In a time of hardship though — and when wasn't it? — Johnny deemed it obscene to be a fat cat while everyone else was tightening their belts. The poor, as Jesus said, were always with us, but that didn't mean they had to be grist for the City's satanic mills. Moneymen were routinely demonized in some sections of the press. To counter this, Sir Robert Kindersley, the head of Lazards — aka "The God of the City" — tried to establish a "Bankers' Bureau" to enhance the image of the Square Mile. However, when the clearing banks failed to cooperate, the talking shop failed.

The City could only do what it always did: put a brave face on it. The banks conducted their business in imposing buildings, the columns — whether Corinthian, Ionic or Doric — hinting at the figures being totted up by hand-operated machines inside. *Tap-tap-tap screw! Tap-tap-tap screw!* However, it was all a front. The white stone was hung on steel girders like so much sugar-icing. Inside, the banking halls had their own marbled facades. Behind the mahogany veneers, away from the public gaze, there lay a maze of dark and dingy cubbyholes where the real work was done. No matter how much money was donated to charity, bankers couldn't disguise the fact that, robbing from the poor to give to the rich, they were the opposite of Robin Hood.

Which of his informants should he call first? Johnny reached for the phone but then pushed it away. He would speak to them face to face. It would make it easier to tell if they were lying.

Hughes, no doubt, would be bothering corpses at Bart's: he wasn't going anywhere. Culver had switched bucket shops but wouldn't be free till the evening either. Quicky Quirk, on the other hand, had been released from Pentonville only last week. It was time they caught up.

Lila Mae would not stop screaming. It was astonishing that such a little thing could make so much noise. Lizzie had fed her, changed her, rocked her and sung to her without success before giving up hope and returning the baby to her cot in the boxroom that Matt had decorated. He had been so proud, and so pleased, when she'd told him she was pregnant. Rampant too.

Lila's brick-red face was scrunched up, her tiny fists clenched, her bootied feet kicking the air. Lizzie, sleep-starved and nipple-sore, stared at her daughter. How quickly a bundle of joy became a ball of fury.

If she cried much longer she would have a convulsion. What was the matter with her? What should she do? She picked Lila up and clutched to her breast. For a second there was silence then, lungs refilled, the caterwauling resumed.

Lizzie walked round the room, shushing her baby, whispering into one of her beautiful, neat ears.

"*Hush-a-bye baby, in the tree-top, when the wind blows the cradle will rock . . .*"

The rocking horses on the wallpaper seemed to mock her. Was she going off her rocker?

Who could she call? Not her mother. She'd offered to pay for a nanny, but Lizzie didn't want a stranger under the roof of their new home. When she'd said she could manage, her mother had said nothing but smiled as if to say she knew better. Maybe she did. Lizzie wasn't going to admit it now.

She couldn't stay within these four walls any longer. She'd never felt so alone or so frustrated. She had to get out. Perhaps a ride on a choo-choo train would do the trick.

The incessant rumble of traffic in Holborn Circus came through the ill-fitting window. A draught wafted the thin, striped curtains that shut out prying eyes. The occupant of the top floor room remained oblivious. All the person could hear was a man screaming for his life. Sheer, naked terror. When it came down to it, that's all there was.

The freshly sharpened, freshly polished knife reflected the killer's handsome face. The sealed vial stood to attention on the table. Mask, gloves: just one more thing. How little was needed to take a life!

If you were lucky, death was instantaneous, a flick of a switch producing eternal darkness. If you weren't, if the fates were unkind, your last moments could be filled with infinite agonies. Everyone was helpless in the face of death. No one could turn back the clock.

The past, if you let it, would imprison you. Each man was serving a life sentence. And yet one quick movement, a simple gesture, could change the world.

CHAPTER
SIX

The last time Johnny had seen Quirk he'd been in the dock at the Old Bailey. The boot clicker turned house-breaker had been given a five-year stretch and yet here he was, free as a bird instead of doing bird, after less than two years.

The snug of the Thistle and Crown in Billiter Square was empty except for Quirk and an old man nursing a pint at the bar. Johnny had ten minutes before the lunchtime crowd would pack out the pub.

Quirk's lantern-jaw was busy chewing a pickled egg. He scowled, swallowed and began to get up.

"What? Not pleased to see me? Stay where you are." Johnny pointed at his beer glass. "Another?"

"You said you'd put in a word with the judge."

Bits of yolk flew through the air. Johnny narrowly avoided getting egg on his face.

"I tried, but your record spoke for itself. Stop sulking. D'you want a drink or not?"

Quirk sniffed. "Bell's. A double."

Johnny, hiding a smile, went to the bar. What the hell? He'd have the same.

"So why the early release?"

"You know me. Made myself useful."

"If you were that useful I'm surprised they didn't keep you."

There was no shortage of snitches inside. It was a dangerous business: eyes and ears could be gouged out or lopped off with ease. Then, given Quirk's previous profession — cutting out shapes of leather for a shoemaker — he was a dab hand with a knife. He'd only got into trouble when he realized how quickly a blade could open a sash window.

Quirk sipped the Scotch and licked his lips.

"I see you've done all right for yourself. Read the *News* in Pentonville — before I wiped my arse with it. How d'you hear I was out?"

"You of all people should know how rumour spreads. What have you been up to since?"

"Not much. Sitting here. Enjoying the company — till now."

Quirk hailed from Seven Sisters but, having worked in nearby East India Street, the Crown had once been his local. It was strange how humans were such creatures of habit. Perhaps, surrounded by warehouses full of textiles, furs, dried fruit and furniture, he found comfort in the ceaseless commerce. Traders were not the only ones who thrived on word of mouth.

"Anything to tell me?"

"About what?"

"Pig's blood, for starters."

Quirk grimaced. "There's no blood on my hands."

"Any idea who's behind the attacks?"

"Take your pick. Bloody Jews. Cause grief wherever they are."

"What have they done to you?"

"Nothing, yet, but if they get their way we'll all be in the shit come Christmas. I've just got out of uniform. Don't want to put on another."

"Ever worn a black shirt?"

"Maybe. What's it to you? No harm in standing up for your own folk."

"I thought you only believed in money. If you believe in Mosley too, perhaps you should try growing a moustache."

"Not likely. Don't want a skidmark on my lip."

"Still in touch with any Biff Boys?"

"Might be."

"Ask around. It'll be worth your while."

Quirk drained his whisky glass and held it out. Johnny ignored it. "Anything on the grapevine about Chittleborough and Bromet?"

"Who?" He waggled the glass. "Oil my cogs — and I'll have another egg while you're at it."

Johnny, after his first drink of the day, was feeling benevolent. As he suspected, Quirk claimed to know nothing about the two murders but the squealer promised to keep his ear to the ground.

They left the pub together and, to avoid the endless stream of peckish secretaries, clerks and messengers, turned into the covered passageway that dog-legged between Billiter Square and Billiter Avenue.

The man at the bar followed.

Hughes, emerging from the mortuary at the rear of St Bartholomew's Hospital, spun on his heels and walked quickly in the opposite direction.

"Hey! Percy! Don't be like that." Johnny ran down the corridor. The green linoleum, rain-slick, was like an ice-rink. He had to grab Hughes to keep his balance.

"Gerroff me! I ain't done nuffink."

"Did I say you had? Where you off to in such a hurry?"

"Canteen."

"Good idea. Fear not, I'll pay."

They crossed the courtyard, piled high with sandbags, and entered the mess-room for non-medical staff. Janitors, porters and cleaners, all in brown dustcoats, sat elbow to elbow on benches either side of long trestle tables. No wonder the floors had not been mopped. A miasma of steam and cigarette smoke hung over the plates of mutton stew and sausages and mash.

Hughes, all arms and elbows, wolfed down his meal.

"How you can have an appetite after what you've been doing is beyond me."

Hughes shrugged. "A man can get used to anyfink."

The pathologist's unglamorous assistant refused to say another word until his belly was full.

Outside, the shower had passed so they paused by the central fountain. Its water music was the last sound Johnny's mother had heard.

"The lads weren't brung 'ere. Got taken straight to Bishopsgate — but Farrant did the PMs."

"And what did your boss say?"

"Never seen anyfink like 'em. Todgers sliced clean off." He winced. "No funny bottom business though."

"That's good to know." Johnny wasn't sure that would have been the case had Hughes been left alone with them. "And . . . ?"

The gannet held out a callused hand. Johnny produced a ten-shilling note but ensured it was out of reach.

"Speak!"

"The lads had something else in common. Stomach contents. Their last meal was boiled pork and pease pudding."

The "Hello Girls" had been busy in his absence. Several people had telephoned and left messages. Matt: *Call me.* Lizzie: *I need to see you.* Henry Simkins: *I've booked a table for 1p.m. at the London Tavern tomorrow. Be there!*

Matt was not at Snow Hill police station. Lizzie was not at home in Bexleyheath. Simkins, his long-time rival at the *Daily Chronicle*, was, of course, out to lunch. He liked nothing more than sweet-talking waiters at his club.

Johnny turned his attention to the second post. Press releases, book launches, exhibition openings and an invitation to a premature Guy Fawkes party hosted by the Grocers' Company at the Artillery Ground on Friday evening. There was a handwritten message on the back: "Do come! Rebecca."

How could he refuse?

CHAPTER
SEVEN

Alexander Vanneck didn't like Mondays. After a blessed day off, the drudgery of the London branch of the Guaranty Trust Co. of New York seemed even more depressing. *Modern Times* didn't show the half of it. Today, though, he'd reached rock bottom.

As a male typist it was his job to keep his manager happy — but Jock Wilderspin was not a happy man and made it his business to share his misery with as many of his subordinates as he could. He stood on ceremony even when seated on his throne-like chair. Woe betide a minion caught using the Partners' Entrance. As for sneaking into their marble lavatory, you could forget it. It wasn't enough that the nobs had their own dining room: Fullers in Gracechurch Street was off-limits too. Staff wishing to pop out for a sandwich were expected to restrict themselves to the nearby ABC or a Lyons tea-shop but — fuck it! — Wilderspin had seen him leaving Fullers at lunchtime.

The bastard took his revenge at four o'clock when he presented Alex with three pages of foolscap and told him to type it up immediately. He did so and — trying to please — corrected a few spelling mistakes. Twenty minutes after he'd taken the letter up to be signed the buzzer went. Wilderspin was in a right tizzy: he objected to being corrected and demanded the letter be typed exactly as it had been written. Alex had nearly bitten his tongue in half trying not to answer back.

His good intentions had led to him leaving the office thirty minutes late. Oh for a tommy-gun! He imagined the gutters of Lombard Street flowing with blood. Pinstriped bodies lying everywhere. Top hats rolling down the pavement . . .

His stomach rumbled angrily. He'd half a mind to return to Fullers — but he couldn't afford it twice in one week. He'd go to Lockharts in Fenchurch Street instead.

Johnny, unable to contact Matt all afternoon, took the liberty of using the police box in Eastcheap to have one last go.

"Working late?"

"Could say the same for you," sighed Matt. "A policeman's lot is not a happy one."

"Anything to report?"

"No. Spent most of the shift being passed from pillar to post by the army. It was suggested there might be some sort of a military connection between Bromet and Chittleborough — they were both fighting fit — but getting information from the War Office is a thankless task."

"The top brass have other things on their minds. What did you make of the post-mortem reports?"

"Not much."

"At least we know they weren't Jewish — unless they were force-fed."

"There's no evidence of that. What's religion got to do with it anyway?"

"No idea. Might be completely irrelevant. Our new Lord Mayor, on the other hand, was clearly attacked because he is Jewish. Any arrests so far?"

"Not for blood sports."

"Why did you want me to call then?"

Matt sighed again. "It's Lizzie. She thinks I'm seeing another woman."

Johnny was early. He couldn't help it: age had not diminished his eagerness, his keenness to follow a story wherever it led. He stamped his feet and blew into his cupped hands.

They had arranged to meet outside the Post Office on the corner of Eastcheap and Philpot Lane (named after a former Lord Mayor). On the opposite corner, high up on the front of the building, two mice nibbled a piece of cheese. The small sculpture commemorated a fight that had broken out on the roof of the building when one workman accused a colleague of eating one of his sandwiches. During the exchange of blows that followed, one of the men fell to his death. Only then was it discovered that the actual culprits were mice.

Talk about hard cheese. Johnny lit a cigarette. He should have made more of an effort to contact Lizzie. He could have put her mind at ease.

The bell of St Margaret Pattens in Rood Lane chimed seven times.

"Steadman! How the devil are you?" Culver shook his hand with enthusiasm. After the day he'd had it made a pleasant change to be greeted warmly.

"All the better for seeing you."

Johnny followed him through the doors of the General Wolfe Tavern. A blast of heat, noise and smoke engulfed them.

In his line of work Johnny was no stranger to the company of thieves but he'd yet to encounter a more plausible rogue. David Culver was the black sheep of a good Yorkshire family, privately educated, morally bankrupt. He made his money in one of the 180 or so bucket shops that tarnished the jealously protected image of the City. Their brokers, not bound by the rules of the Stock Exchange, were free to pursue share-plugging projects that were little better than systematic attempts to defraud the public. Nevertheless, Johnny — aware of the paradox — considered them more honest than their regulated, apparently respectable, rivals.

"Champagne?" Culver grinned, revealing surprisingly small, sharp teeth. Then again, he was known as the Shark. "It's been a good day."

"Don't tell me. I'm all out of righteous indignation. It's the sins of others that interest me today."

In fact Culver was the nearest thing the City had to a saint. He gave away a lot of his ill-gotten gains merely to prove a point. If people could afford to play the stock market, they could afford to lose. Or rather, they should be compelled to share their fortunes with those less fortunate.

"Your very good health!" Culver lifted his silver tankard. The landlord kept it behind the bar for him; Culver claimed the precious metal was the only thing that did not taint the Laurent-Perrier.

Johnny raised his glass.

"Typical socialist!" Culver sneered. "Always willing to share his thirst with your champagne."

The bottled sunshine tasted exquisite.

"I take it you've heard about the murders?"

"Who hasn't? I also heard the poor buggers lost more than their lives."

"Where'd you get that from? So far I've only written *mutilated*. The police haven't released any specific details."

"Officially."

As usual Culver was extraordinarily well informed. "Chittleborough worked round the corner. The rumour mills, naturally, have been spinning yarns."

"Did you know him?"

"No. He was small fry. Can't think why anyone would want to kill him. As you know, I only go after big fish. When I make a killing, it's strictly metaphorical."

"Why bother though? You could do anything you want."

"I'm doing precisely that." He waved his arm expansively. "It's all a game. I enjoy it. There are a lot of clever, rich people in the City. I want to prove I'm cleverer — and want to be richer — than all of them."

"And how are you going to do that?"

Culver swigged from his tankard. "Don't play the innocent. You're not as green as you're cabbage-looking. Knowledge is power."

58

"Indeed — but information is not a bar of Cadbury's. If you eat the chocolate, the bar is gone."

"And if you give it to a friend, he'll eat it, not you."

"So that's where shares, selective leaks, come in."

"Yes — but open secrets are worthless. The more people who know, the less powerful the knowledge, the less profit you'll make. And, of course, word travels fast. I knew about Chamberlain's little piece of paper before the ink on it was dry."

"Pease in our time."

"*Peace* in our time."

"Indeed — but the dead men had both eaten pork and pease pudding shortly before they died."

"Ha! Jack the Quipper strikes again."

Culver poured the last few drops into Johnny's glass. Some believed that meant he'd never have a child. So far the superstition had not been disproved.

"Let's have another. One is never enough."

The Shark disappeared into the sea of swaying backs and soon returned with a second bottle plus a plate of oysters. The landlord clearly knew where his best interests lay.

"So will there be another war?" Johnny helped himself to one of the creatures that, until recently, had — like him — survived by picking up tidbits.

"Indubitably. The City doesn't want military action — it interrupts revenue streams — but it will, of course, make the best of it. Arms manufacturers, textile makers and anyone else who lands a government contract will earn millions. Then there are the deals that will never see the light of day."

"Such as?"

Culver leaned closer. "Cheques can bounce but Hitler's proved Czechs can be double-crossed too."

Johnny's antennae quivered. Culver was a master bamboozler, a king of bluff, but he sensed that on this occasion he was on the verge of telling the truth.

"Montagu Norman is forever on the phone to Berlin."

The governor of the Bank of England — accurately nicknamed Mountebank — was anxious for business with the Third Reich to continue.

"Deutsche Bank, Kleinworts, Schröders — there are plenty of German banks in London and there are still plenty of people willing to arrange credit for the Fatherland."

"The City's bankrolling the Nazis?" Culver feigned astonishment.

"You might say that. I certainly didn't."

"Does Leo Adler know about this? He's Jewish!"

"Why don't you ask him?"

"Don't you worry, I will. Thank you, David."

A surge of adrenalin swept through him. This was the break he'd been searching for. His spirits soared.

"What can I do for you in return?"

"Nothing, Steadman." He watched a bead of condensation trickle down the side of his tankard. "Nothing yet. Consider it a gesture of goodwill. A big chocolate bar."

"Thanks for sharing it with me — whatever your motives."

60

"Remember to keep my name out of it. As a glorified salesman, my mouth is all I've got."

"Of course. Of course."

Johnny, somewhat unsteadily, got to his feet and shook Culver's hand. The moneyman didn't let go straightaway.

"While you're at it, you might ask about the gold deposited in the Bank of England by the Czechoslovak National Bank. It's worth at least six million . . ."

CHAPTER
EIGHT

Tuesday, 1 November, 6.20a.m.

Someone was hammering on the front door. The vibrations, travelling through the floorboards and up the frame, triggered the recurrent nightmare in which an unknown figure loomed over his bed, where he lay paralyzed with fear. However, before the incubus could crush his chest, reality intervened.

The room was pitch-black and freezing. He dragged himself out of bed, fragments of bad dreams — half-remembered lovers, pain and guilt — clogging his head. A hangover from Halloween? More like all the alcohol still in his blood. He must cut down. The hammering continued. Repercussions.

Johnny, clad only in pyjamas, stumbled down the narrow staircase and flung open the door. Had he forgotten to lock it? A young constable from the Met, fist still raised, stood on the step. Startled, he didn't bother to say good morning. He was chilled to the bone, dog-tired and at the end of a very long shift. He'd also been knocking for more than three minutes.

"Detective Turner sent me, sir. He's just around the corner in Packington Street."

"Why?"

"A man's been murdered."

★ ★ ★

A discarded pumpkin lantern lay in the gutter. One kick wiped the grin off its face. The flames of the gas-lamps flickered palely in the frigid air. Dawn was a pale smudge behind the spire of St James's. A milk-cart came rattling down the hill from Essex Road. Johnny tried to flag it down but the driver looked the other way.

There was no mistaking which house it was in the shabby Victorian terrace. Two police cars — one from the City and one from the Met — and an anonymous black van were parked in the empty street. Even at this hour a flock of early birds had gathered by the area railings. They stared enviously as Johnny was allowed to climb the six, awkwardly steep, steps and enter the lobby of the raised ground floor. Matt came clumping down the stairs.

"You could have brought me breakfast."

"I tried." Johnny yawned.

"Bad night?"

"Yes — and no."

"This way."

The stale air smelled of damp clothing, fried food and nappies. On the first floor Matt rapped then opened a door to reveal a harassed young couple being interviewed by DS Penterell, who scowled at Johnny but said nothing. A baby in the woman's arms started wailing. Matt pointed to the ceiling, where there was a heart-shaped stain. A drop of blood plinked into a metal bucket.

The room above was like thousands of others in the capital: little more than a box for living in. Cheap furniture: table, two chairs and a bed. Threadbare rug and thin curtains. A few books on a shelf, a few clothes on pegs. A cracked sink. Cobwebs.

The bare bulb cast a yellowish pallor over the corpse tied to the bed. It was that of a fat, middle-aged man with more hair on his body than his head. Once again there was a shocking absence in the groin — and the inevitable presence of far too much claret. Johnny pulled a handkerchief out of his pocket and held it to his nose. Blood wasn't the only thing that had leaked from the victim. He walked over to the open window.

"He who was living is now dead."

"What?"

"Eliot. *The Wasteland*."

"If you say so," said Matt. "He's Karl Broster. A tallyman."

Someone else who milked the misery of the poor.

"Is he German?"

"If he was, he didn't have an accent. Not very popular with the neighbours though. Too fond of beer."

"You can see that." Johnny pointed at the proud pot-belly.

Matt sniffed disparagingly. Smells never troubled him. "I think we can say that the motive wasn't sexual."

"Wrong! We can't all have a body like Tarzan." While Matt was no ringer for Johnny Weissmuller, his body attracted almost as many admirers. The only thing Johnny had in common with the actor was his Christian name. "Sex must have something to do with it. Mind you, he's nothing like the other two."

"Well, he's dead — and died slowly. It takes a while to bleed to death."

"Perhaps he was unconscious."

"Look at the wrists and ankles. The restraints have sunk into the flesh. He was awake all right — and he must have fought for as long as he could."

"Christ! Imagine having your cock chopped off."

"I'd rather not," said Matt drily.

"It must hurt like hell."

"Pray you never find out. If it's any consolation, it appears to have been a single slice. Quick and clean."

"What the fuck are you doing here?"

Commander Inskip blocked the doorway. They had been so engrossed in the horror of the scene they'd failed to hear the stealthy tread of the superior officer. Matt turned pale.

"Get out, Steadman, before I have you arrested."

"Get out of the road then. I was just passing by on my way to work. As you're no doubt aware, I happen to live around the corner."

Inskip didn't move. He was at least six feet four. His deep-set eyes glared at Matt.

"Turner, escort your friend off the premises."

The way he said it, you'd have thought *friend* was a dirty word. However, Inskip was the one rumoured to be dirty.

Johnny, once again, was glad of Matt's company. Had he not been there it would have come as no surprise if the Commander had clipped him round the ears or even cuffed him and given him a kicking. Their paths — and swords — had crossed several times.

They paused in the hall before opening the front door.

"Sorry for getting you into hot water."

"It's hardly the first time," said Matt. "Don't worry about me. I can handle Inskip."

"More trade secrets? Care to tell?"

Penterell, oozing smugness, appeared on the landing.

"Not now," said Matt. "Let's just say, if I go, he goes."

"So what else is new? One of these days his luck will run out."

"It will if you have anything to do with it."

The door swung open to admit two men with a stretcher. "Sorry, gents," said Matt. "The photographer's not here yet. You can leave that here, but you'll have to wait in the van."

The men rolled their eyes and — like Tweedledum and Tweedledumber — toddled off down the steps.

There was no sign of any other pressmen. Johnny needed to capitalize on his head start.

"Thanks for the wake-up call. Which reminds me — I must telephone Lizzie today. I'll do my best to put her mind at rest."

"Do that." Matt put a hand on his shoulder. "Careful what you say though."

The thousand words — more colour than content — were on PDQ's desk before 9 a.m. Johnny scanned the other newspapers. His competitors were as much in the dark as he was. There was nothing new about Adler's attackers or the double murders. The New York Stock

66

Exchange had introduced a fifteen-point plan intended to beef up protection for public investors. The Great Depression refused to lift.

"Excellent stuff!" Quarles was still wearing his coat. "Not many facts though. I'm sure Patsel, wherever he is, will splash on this, but see what else you can find out."

He went off in search of the tea-lady.

It was too early to contact Adler, and Matt would still be out making enquiries. To pass the time, Johnny picked up a copy of a new weekly magazine called *Picture Post*. The cover showed two women in polka-dot blouses leaping in the air.

"Colposinquanonia!"

Louis Dimeo, who wouldn't let anyone forget that Italy had won the World Cup again in June, was breathing down his neck.

"Sixteen letters," said Tanfield. "Estimating a woman's beauty based on her chest."

"How on earth d'you know a word like that?" said Johnny, looking at Dimeo in astonishment. "Anything over seven letters usually gives you a headache."

"That would be telling." The sports freak bestowed a dazzling smile upon his colleagues. "That said, breast-stroking is the national sport of La Bella Italia — after football, of course."

"A quid says no one can get the word in the paper," said Johnny.

"You're on," said Dimeo and, before nipping smartly back to his desk, took the risk of ruffling his red hair in a gesture of friendship. He was wasting his time; Johnny would never forgive him for sleeping with Stella, even though he knew how Johnny felt about her. Dimeo's behaviour was rarely sporting.

Johnny had only loved one other woman more than Stella — and Lizzie was married to Matt. He'd made up his mind to ask Stella to marry him but instead of meeting him at St Paul's so he could get down on one knee she had deliberately disappeared. It turned out that she'd been secretly seeing Dimeo as well. And that wasn't the only way she'd betrayed him.

"What was that about?" Bertram Blenkinsopp, a reporter before Johnny was even born, watched Dimeo chatting up a secretary from the seventh floor.

"Nothing. Ask Valentino. What are you working on?"

"Suburban neurosis."

"What's that when it's at home?"

"Very good. I'll use that." He chewed his lip. "Lord knows why they always land me with these stories. Anyone stuck inside the same four walls day after day would go out of their minds."

"Prisoners don't."

"Sure about that?"

"No — but many of them are mad before they go in."

"It's a sign of the times," said Blenkinsopp. "Freed from the necessity of foraging for food or seeking shelter, the pampered middle-classes have nothing to occupy their tiny minds. That's why they lose their marbles. Mark my words, it'll vanish once war breaks out."

★　★　★

68

The London Tavern on the corner of Fenchurch Street and Mark Lane was a temple devoted to pleasure. Within its walls there were snack bars, cocktail bars, oyster bars, grill rooms and restaurants. The original tavern in Bishopsgate — where, in *Nicholas·Nickleby*, a public meeting is held "to take into consideration the propriety of petitioning Parliament in favour of the United Metropolitan Improved Hot Muffin and Crumpet Baking and Punctual Delivery Company" — had been demolished half a century ago but the owners were determined to keep its spirit of service with a bow and scrape alive. Consequently, it was a popular venue for City banquets.

Simkins had reserved a table in the fish restaurant. A bottle, tilted at the angle of a Nazi salute, was chilling in an ice-bucket beside it.

"Johnny dearest!" Simkins leapt to his feet and kissed him on both cheeks.

A murmur of disapproval rippled round the dining room. Bloody Continentals!

Johnny, accustomed to his rival's flamboyant antics, merely smiled. Once upon a time he would have blushed.

"Hello, Henry. What do you want?"

"Don't be like that." Simkins, gratified by the stir he had caused, finally sat down. "It's All Souls Day. Don't you want to enter the kingdom of Heaven?"

"I'm not Catholic."

"Doesn't stop you being in purgatory though."

Simkins twiddled the stem of his empty glass between his thumb and forefinger. "Have a drink." He pulled the wine bottle out of the bucket. It was already half-empty.

"No, thank you. Just Perrier for me."

"Water? What the hell is wrong with you?"

"Nothing. I overdid it last night, that's all. What d'you want?"

"Let's order first. The turbot's supposed to be divine."

Johnny, in his days as a cub, had written too many stories about fatal fish bones for his liking so he restricted himself to Morecambe Bay shrimps and scallops from Whitstable.

Simkins, chitchatting away, filleted his food with admirable dexterity but Johnny could tell he was nervous. His trademark insouciance seemed put on.

"Come on then, Simkins. Spit it out."

"In the circumstances, not the best choice of words." Simkins winked at the waiter, who was ceremoniously pouring coffee from a silver pot.

"Henry, I won't ask again."

"Our old friend is back in town."

"Who?"

"Cecilia Zick."

There were times when Johnny wished he'd never saved Henry's life — and this was one of them.

"Don't hit me." Simkins tossed his chestnut curls — the envy of many a girl.

"I'll say this for you," said Johnny. "You've got balls."

"Not remotely funny. Not funny at all. Such a remark is unworthy of you, Steadman."

"Where is he?"

Johnny balked at referring to the transvestite as a woman.

"I don't know, I swear. He hardly trusts me any more than you."

"What brings him back here? Surely he knows he's playing with fire?"

"Blame Hitler. Berlin isn't what it used to be. Lots of rats are deserting the blinking ship."

"Better the devil you know? Well, he's very much mistaken."

"That's where I'm supposed to come in. Zick's all too aware that your bosom friend, Detective Constable Turner, has it in for him. He wants *me* to persuade *you* to persuade *him* to let bygones be bygones."

"Not a chance. No." The anger came from nowhere. "You must be fucking joking."

"I wish I were. I'm sorry, Johnny. I truly am — but I don't have a choice."

"You always have a choice. What makes you think you haven't?"

"You're not the only one he's got pictures of."

Johnny's heart sank. Each time he thought he'd recovered at last, finally come to terms with what had happened, something or someone brought it flooding back. Perhaps this was why he'd woken up with such a sense of foreboding.

"I need a drink."

Simkins nodded in sympathy. "Me too. Brandy?"

They moved on to the cigar bar. Leather armchairs, mahogany panelling, obsequious staff.

"You assured me everything had gone up in flames, like the bookshop. If Matt finds out those photographs —"

"He won't find out — unless you tell him. It seems Timney retained copies in case Zick returned to London. Call it leverage. He's no happier to see him again than I am."

Johnny still felt in some way responsible for the death of Timney's son two years earlier, even though he hadn't been the one who'd set the fire.

"So the photographs are of me?"

"And your friend."

Johnny, suddenly exhausted, sighed deeply. He'd been undercover, desperate to identify a killer. Instead, he and Matt had found themselves in the frame.

He glanced at Simkins's lap.

"Is life simpler without them?"

"By no means. The attraction remains, but my ability has gone."

"There must be other ways of achieving satisfaction."

"Yes, but the underlying frustration never goes away."

"Purgatory."

"Indeed. This is hell, nor am I out of it." Simkins stared into his glass.

The fact his rival hadn't broached the subject of the murders during the meal made Johnny suspicious.

"Why would anyone sexually mutilate a man?" he asked.

"Because they're mad. Why else? Think my injury gives me extra insight? It doesn't. The real interest lies in what has made them lose their mind. For example, desperately wanting something, and knowing that you'll never get it, is enough to drive anyone to distraction."

"So, assuming the killer's an invert, he takes the one thing he desires above all else . . ."

"Except that doesn't explain why he only takes the tally-whackers," said Simkins. "And, if the motive is sexual, why is there no evidence of hanky-panky?"

"It doesn't make sense." Johnny shook his head. "Crime stems from desire: for love, revenge or money. It must be one of them."

"Or all three," said Simkins.

Their eyes met.

"How's your love life?" asked Simkins.

"Non-existent — except in my head."

"See — we're more alike than you think."

"No we're not. We've different backgrounds and different futures."

"Futures? This isn't the Stock Exchange," said Simkins. "It's never been more vital to live for today. *Carpe diem!*"

"Perhaps," said Johnny. "But tomorrow certainly won't come if we don't deal with Zick once and for all. What can we do to change his mind?"

"There isn't anything."

"Everyone has their price."

"Not him. What about you and Turner though? What would encourage you two to turn a blind eye?"

"Nothing. Compromise is a dirty word."

Simkins leaned over and grabbed his wrist.

"Don't be so ridiculous, Johnny. You're in no position to be high-minded. Morals are a luxury you can't afford. Do you want to see your reputation destroyed for the sake of a mucky picture? Don't underestimate Zick. If blackmail fails, he'll only try something much, much worse."

CHAPTER
NINE

The brandy made him feel both better and worse. He crossed Fenchurch Street and went down the alley alongside Clothworkers' Hall. The Crown and Thistle was about to close for the afternoon. Quirk, as expected, was slouched in a corner of the snug. He perked up when he saw Johnny.

"Not here!"

Johnny followed him outside. The informant didn't stop or look back till they reached Lime Street Square. It was a blustery day. Dust devils sent refuse spinning.

"I were coming to see you. Should've saved your shoe leather."

"I was passing anyway. How d'you get that?"

Quirk's left eye — purple, yellow and black — was almost shut.

"How d'you bloody think? Some bastard punched me." He raised his prognathous chin. "It's nothing."

"What have you got for me?"

"A name."

He held out his hand. Johnny took out his wallet. Quirk licked his lips.

"This didn't come from me."

"Of course not," said Johnny. "Have I ever got you into trouble?"

"S'pose not."

Quirk checked that no one was pretending not to watch them.

"It ain't right, Mr Steadman. I'm no saint but I know true evil when I hear it. Rick Hollom. Works at Otarelli's in Saffron Hill. Drinks in the Mitre most days."

Johnny extracted a note but, before Quirk could take it, snatched the reward away.

"Is he expecting me?"

"No."

Quirk grabbed the money and ran.

Leo Adler luxuriated in the opulent surroundings of the Mansion House. Yes, he would be more than comfortable here — and once Harry, who was showing him round, had moved out, he would feel much less of a sightseer.

"And this," said Sir Harold Twyford, "is the one millionth telephone made in Britain. It's solid gold."

"Does it work?"

"Why don't you try it?"

The outgoing mayor — whose own substantial corporation seemed to symbolize the City he still represented — chuckled at Adler's surprise.

"Whatever you do, Leo, don't lose the Midas touch!"

They processed through to the equally plush domestic quarters where a maid was setting out afternoon tea.

"By the way," said Twyford, "that arrived today. Bit premature, don't you think?"

He pointed at a parcel on a piecrust table.

"Why would it be sent here?" said Adler. "It's no secret where I work."

"Search me. Open it and find out."

Adler, checking the handwritten label, pulled off the string and undid the brown paper. He sniffed the small box suspiciously.

Twyford, who'd joined him, huffed with impatience. "Go on, man. It's not a bomb."

Slowly, Adler lifted the lid.

Eager to follow up the lead Quirk had given him, Johnny dialled the number for Otarelli & Sanna, long-established makers of scientific instruments based in Charles Street. The telephonist informed him that Mr Hollom was unavailable. Johnny thought it prudent not to leave a message.

When he looked up, Tanfield was hovering by his desk. As instructed, he had spoken to Matt when he called the newsroom in Johnny's absence.

"Broster was separated from his wife. No love lost there, apparently. DC Turner said she's a real dragon." The junior reporter shuddered. "Glad I'm not married."

"How old was he?"

"Forty-two."

"He seemed older."

"That's what booze does to you."

"Meaning?" He was aware he still had a brandy bloom.

"Nothing, Johnny."

It was clear Tanfield couldn't work out whether he was being serious. Which was exactly how Johnny liked it.

"What did the neighbours say to the police?" he asked.

"Nothing worth reporting. Should I go and talk to them?"

"There's no point. Everyone else will have heard what they've got to say by now."

"I'm not everyone else." The cub was becoming a fox. "Bert's gone to a hold-up in Farringdon. He'll be back soon."

"OK. Take the mugshots with you. See if anyone recognizes Chittleborough or Bromet."

The telephone rang. It was the commissionaire.

"There's a Mrs Turner to see you, sir."

Johnny's heart skipped a beat. "Thank you. Tell her I'll be straight down."

He couldn't put it off any longer.

The ear lay on a piece of crumpled tissue paper. It was approximately three inches long, reddish-brown — with purplish veins — and covered in down.

"Wood Ear," said Twyford. "Splendid example."

"What?" Adler regarded the Lord Mayor with distaste. "It looks like calves' liver."

"Well, it's not. It's a fungus. Not poisonous. A staple of eastern cuisine. You should try hot-and-sour soup. Yum-yum!"

"You seem very well informed on the subject."

"Fret not, my good man. Mycology is one of my pet pursuits. I visit the Natural History Museum whenever

I can. Fungi are fascinating organisms. Feeding on detritus, they create the most astonishing of forms."

"Are they parasitic?"

"Ah, well, some species are. This one isn't."

"I suppose that's something. Why send it to me?"

"Must be the name." Seeing the blank expression on his guest's face, Twyford cleared his throat and continued: "It grows mainly on the elder — the tree from which Judas hanged himself. Hence the name, Judas Ear. *Auricularia auriculajudae*. However, others call it something else."

Adler braced himself. "Do tell."

His imminent predecessor winced.

"Hairy Jew's Ear."

She was gorgeous. He was lucky to know her. Johnny walked taller as he crossed the lobby, aware that both male and female passers-by were appraising his visitor. They shook hands.

"If Mohammed won't come to the mountain . . ."

"Sorry, you know how it is."

"No, I don't. That's why I'm here."

"Fancy a cuppa?" Lizzie hesitated then nodded. They headed for the doors. "Where's my darling god-daughter?"

"At her grandmother's."

The ABC Cafeteria was practically within earshot. The Lincrusta walls were covered with large spotted mirrors, which enabled single diners to watch each other surreptitiously. Johnny usually avoided the haunt of lowly clerks, office boys and secretaries. Aside from the lack of privacy, the screeching hot-water urns, clashing stainless-steel tea-pots and general gossip bouncing off the marble table-tops made it impossible to think, let alone read. Sweaty waitresses yelled their orders: "Two poached eggs and a Cornish pasty", "Two egg-and-veg and a Melton Mowbray, luv!" Women, though, tended to feel comfortable in the chain of cafés and it seemed more appropriate than taking Lizzie to a pub.

Fortunately, the place quietened down in the afternoon. They found a table in a corner and ordered tea for two.

"Aren't you going to take off your headscarf?"

It was decorated with battleships, marching soldiers, gas masks and bombs. The legend printed round the edge declared: *Peace in Our Time, 1938.*

Lizzie had beautiful hair. She'd grown out the bob in favour of a more up-to-date style, all curls and waves.

"No. I can't stay long. Matt bought it for me. Must have been feeling guilty. It's rayon, not silk."

Her bourgeois upbringing had made her prize quality over quantity. Her father, a doctor, had been appalled when, instead of accepting a position at Selfridges in Oxford Street, she'd chosen to join Gamages in Holborn Circus.

"It's good to see you," said Johnny.

She smiled tightly. The face powder didn't quite hide the dark semicircles under her eyes.

"What's wrong?"

"Everything! Nothing! It's the not knowing that's worst."

"What can I tell you to make you feel better?"

"The truth!"

Johnny wasn't sure about that. "The truth about what?"

"Is Matt seeing someone else?"

"Behind your back, you mean?"

"Well, he wouldn't do it under my nose! He wouldn't dare!"

"He hasn't said anything. Why would he? He adores you."

"He used to, that's for sure."

"What's changed then?"

"We're parents now. A little tyrant rules the house."

"Jealous of the competition?"

"Maybe I am."

She fell silent as the waitress appeared. Having plonked the tea things on the table, the woman leaned in conspiratorially. "How about a Chelsea bun? They've been half-price since a minute ago."

The tang of her perspiration did nothing for the taste buds.

"Not hungry, thanks," said Johnny.

They watched her waddle back to the counter.

"Before we got married," said Lizzie, "I had a job that I enjoyed and, if I wished, I could go out every night. Now my life's shrunk to a semi in Bexleyheath. It's stultifying."

Johnny thought this wasn't the time to mention suburban neurosis. Instead he ventured, "Lila must be some sort of company."

"You can say that again." She laughed ironically. "The word you're looking for is *limited*. I've been trying to wean her for weeks, but she's not interested in a bottle."

"Who can blame her?"

For a moment he thought she was going to slap his face, but suddenly she relaxed.

"You'll have to make do with the bottle."

"Story of my life."

She put her hand over his. He put his other hand over hers.

"How long have you been feeling like this?"

"Six months or so. I don't think it's the baby blues. It started when Matt became a detective. At first I was delighted for the both of us, but nowadays he's away from home more than ever. He's a doting father, but he might as well have a wet-nurse or a nanny instead of a wife. In fact, he'd probably prefer it. Some young slip of a thing with big bosoms."

"Don't say that. I know he loves you more than anyone else on the planet."

"You'd never guess that if you saw us. Try living with him!"

Although the final deadline of the day was looming, Johnny decided to escort Lizzie to Blackfriars Station. He didn't spot Tanfield on the other side of Fleet Street.

The sun had set but it was not yet dark. It was the violet hour. The office blocks resembled gigantic Advent calendars, their occupants dreaming of home or escape. Publicans and restaurateurs polished glasses and smoothed down tablecloths. Kitchen devils peeled the spuds. Musicians pressed their penguin suits.

Performers, gazing in Hollywood mirrors, applied their slap. It was time to face the music and dance.

Arm-in-arm, Johnny and Lizzie shouldered their way through the crush. They didn't talk. There was no need — each thought they knew what the other was thinking. They were both mistaken.

At the bottom of Water Street, behind Unilever House where Bridewell Palace once stood, Lizzie stopped to face him.

"You'd tell me if anything was going on, wouldn't you?"

"Of course I would, silly! I've always wanted both of you to be happy. If you're not, I'm not."

He was going to peck her on the cheek — a farewell kiss — but at the last moment she turned so that their lips met.

Her cool skin intensified the heat of her mouth. He should have pulled away, broken the embrace, but he did neither. He'd often dreamed of such a kiss, imagined what Matt nightly enjoyed, but the real thing was better. He didn't care they were in public — albeit in a quiet, unlit corner of the City. He cared about Lizzie. Pent-up frustration poured out of them both.

Someone was coming. They separated but, at the same time, joined hands. Johnny thought he could see joy in her eyes. Wrong again. It was regret.

"That will never — ever — happen again." She sounded breathless.

"It's my fault. I'm the one to blame."

"I believe I was involved too."

"I was trying to make things better, but I've just gone and made them worse."

"I'm not going to pretend I didn't enjoy it. I did — a lot. If it weren't for Matt, I'd do it again." Lizzie shivered. "Don't tell him."

"Why would I? He'd kill me."

"Yes, most likely he would." She patted his arm. "Look after him. If he lets anything slip, do let me know."

"I won't spy on him."

"Remember what you once said to me? *I'll do anything for you.*"

Johnny glanced up and down the street. Without meaning to, he raised his voice.

"You're placing me in an impossible position. You're forcing me to choose. I won't do it."

"Would you prefer I made your mind up for you?"

"Lizzie, Matt is not seeing anyone else. I promise."

"Why didn't you say so before then? I might be going round the bend but I can still tell you're hiding something."

"I can't win, can I?" He was already regretting their brief encounter.

Lizzie shrugged. Her eyes, flashing in the twilight, suggested she felt the same way.

"You want the truth? No."

CHAPTER
TEN

Friday, 4 November, 10a.m.

"It's not a bad view, is it?" The moderne chair creaked as Adler sat back in satisfaction.

They were on the top floor of the Albany Credit Trust on King William Street. On the left, the twin turrets of St Mary Woolnoth were dwarfed by the Bank of England's monolith. On the right, the golden pineapple atop the Monument sparkled in the sun. Pigeons practised dive-bombing above the glass canopies of Leadenhall Market. Each street ended in a blue mist.

"I thought the Bank of International Settlements was your main concern," said Johnny.

"At the moment it is," said Adler. "I'm a director of several companies though. I started here in 1920. Worked my way up from the bottom. I wasn't a daddy's boy who simply swanned into the City after three or four years of partying in Oxbridge."

"Wish you had been?"

"If you'd asked me when I was starting out, a carbuncular youth, I'd have said yes. Now I'm grateful for the experience. If you don't have family connections you soon learn to stand on someone's neck to get a bit higher."

Johnny nodded in agreement. For some reason Tanfield sprang to mind. His family had money; he'd been to university. Johnny was self-taught and yet he was the one who'd helped Tanfield learn the ropes, just as the late Bill Fox had helped him. Tim certainly had a lean and hungry look.

He picked up the box. "Doesn't smell much, does it? I presume it was meant to cause offence."

"Hairy Jew's Ear? It can hardly have been sent with kindly intent."

"The question is: why was it sent at all?"

"It's obviously a message — same as the bottles of blood."

"So someone doesn't like you. Why not?"

"I'm Jewish. I'm a banker. I'm about to become Lord Mayor. Take your pick."

"Whoever it is might be wrong in the head."

"Maybe. There's no shortage of meshugas round here."

Johnny walked over to the other window. It was business as usual in the hives of Abchurch Lane. Managers sat at lonely desks, secretaries carried papers, typists fluffed their hair. In one room two lads traded insults then blows.

"What exactly does the Bank of International Settlements do?"

"It was set up seven years ago to implement the reparations imposed on Germany by the Treaty of Versailles."

"So the Germans resent it."

"No doubt — but they're still members of it."

86

"Who are the other members?"

"Britain, America, France, Belgium, Italy, Switzerland and Japan."

"Are its headquarters in London?"

"No. Basel. The Swiss pride themselves on their neutrality."

"Not taking sides is the same as taking everyone's side — or at least taking everyone's money."

"Economics and ethics are like oil and water. They don't mix."

The boys had finished fighting. One offered the other a cigarette. It was easy to feel superior when you were this far off the ground. No wonder bankers felt they were above the law.

Johnny turned back to Adler, who was watching him with amusement.

"The fungus must have something to do with your work. If it's a message, it must symbolize something."

"Such as?"

"Fungus thrives on dead things." It was time to wipe the smile off his face. "What do you know about six million pounds' worth of Czechoslovakian gold?"

"I might ask you the same question. Who told you about it?"

"You know I can't answer that."

"Yes. So you'll appreciate that I can't answer your question either." Adler stood up. "I'm afraid the Old Lady calls."

"Threadneedle Street is seconds away. Look, the fungus is a warning. Whoever sent it wants to stop something happening. You could be in danger. It might be your ear next."

"I had thought of that, but I've every confidence in you. Rest assured, Czechoslovakia has nothing to do with this. The answer lies much closer to home."

The newsroom was buzzing. A Jersey Airways de Havilland had crashed soon after taking off for Southampton. Fourteen people — a dozen passengers, the pilot and a farmhand — had died. Johnny was shocked at the number of fatalities — it was the deadliest air accident in British history — but he felt the greatest sympathy for the bloke on the ground. Poor sod! There he was, innocently tilling the soil, when death fell from the sky.

"Your friend called with the post-mortem results on Broster . . ." Tanfield consulted his notebook. "There were traces of *Amanita Aureola* in his blood . . ." He paused dramatically. "It's a fungus — Gold Cap. It produces a mycotoxin which, in solution, has much the same effect as chloroform."

"In other words, he was drugged."

"It explains how the killer managed to tie him up without much resistance."

"Could have been deviant sex." Johnny was being mischievous. He didn't think so for a minute.

"Hardly," said Tanfield. "The neighbours would surely have mentioned it. Those places have thin walls."

"*Those places?* Not everyone can live in a Wimbledon villa."

His junior laughed. "I didn't mean anything by it. What's making you so chippy?"

"None of your business. Have any of the neighbours come back to you?"

"No."

"So you were wasting your time on Tuesday." Johnny was glad. The murders were his story, not Tim's.

"Not entirely."

Johnny didn't wait for an explanation. "Did DC Turner say anything about the stomach contents?"

"No."

Did that mean Broster had eaten pork or not? At least Matt hadn't spilled all the beans.

"If there's nothing else . . ."

Tanfield hesitated then took the plunge. "I've been thinking . . ."

"Oh, yes?" Johnny leaned back in the chair he'd inherited from Bill. So far it had only tipped over backwards once.

"You know how you say there's no such thing as a coincidence . . . ?"

". . . Only the moment when preparation meets opportunity."

"Yes. Well. Perhaps the fact Broster lived so close to you is not pure happenstance."

"Twelve letters!"

"I'm serious, Johnny. There has to be some method in this madness. Consider the approximate locations: Fenchurch Street, Aldgate and Essex Road. All of them have stations."

"So we're looking for a potty porter?"

The tip of Tanfield's nose went white. It was as if a fuse had been lit.

"Sorry, Tim. I'm annoyed with myself, not you. Go on — but remember Bromet died first."

"Indeed. Bromet, Chittleborough, Broster. Notice anything about the names?"

"BCB? It's not a telephone exchange, is it?"

"No."

"Pity. Let's hope the next victim — if there is one — is an Adams, then we'd have our own ABC murders."

"Mrs Christie would be proud of you. My point is, all three are right at the beginning of the alphabet."

"So the killer, like Koko, has a little list."

Tanfield, instead of throwing the notebook at him, forced a smile. It was almost convincing.

Johnny spent the afternoon on the telephone, chasing leads, but only succeeded in chasing his own tail. Those who'd worked with the three victims, if willing to speak at all, revealed nothing of interest. Family members were either tongue-tied with grief or mouthed platitudes. He needed someone to speak ill of the dead.

The mood in the newsroom darkened as the sun disappeared. Hitler was on manoeuvres again. Thanks to his so-called arbitration, it had been "agreed" that Hungary would annex southern parts of Slovakia and Ruthenia.

Cups of stewed tea went cold; ashtrays brimmed with dog-ends. Johnny slammed down the phone. He was wasting his time, asking but not receiving, while surrounded by people who were asking too much of him. Tanfield, Adler, Simkins, Zick, even Lizzie: all of them were encroaching on his territory. He still didn't know how to proceed . . .

Yes, he did. He'd go for a drink.

Mischief night. The expected knock on the cellar door came at the exact appointed time. He handed over the money.

"There's a lot more where that came from. Keep up the good work. You know what to do. I'll be back on Monday."

The two toughs laughed when they saw the crate. This time the bottles were full of petrol, not blood.

He didn't recognize her. At first glance he thought she was a man. It was only when she smiled — no lipstick this time — and waved that he realized the person in the trouser-suit and fedora was Rebecca. And yet, as he studied her, she didn't really look like a man at all. The way the tailored suit hugged the hips meant that it could only be a woman.

"Hello again." They shook hands. "What can I get you?"

She glanced around the Three Bucks; there were no other female customers. She shook her head and turned back to him. "Let's go. We don't want to miss anything."

They took a taxi to Chiswell Street. A huge bonfire, at least thirty feet high, had been constructed in the centre of the Artillery Ground. It was unnerving, being in such a vast, open space after the close confines of the

City. A Guy Fawkes, complete with wide-brimmed hat, was roped to a stake on top of the woodpile.

Rebecca slipped her arm into his and shivered.

"It won't be lit until after the fireworks display. Let's get something to warm us up."

"Here." He draped his old mackintosh over her shoulders. It wasn't as gallant a gesture as it appeared. Alcohol was already oozing out of his pores.

There were at least two hundred people milling around the hog-roasts and the beer tent. Overexcited children in masks ran through the crowd with sparklers, trying to write their names in the air. Johnny spotted Commander Inskip deep in conversation with a couple of aldermen decked out in their traditional finery. It was good to know that three dead men and a deranged killer — still at large — were not interfering with his social life.

"How's Mr Yaxley coping?" he asked.

Chittleborough's landlord refused to speak to him again until his invoice was paid. He'd have a long wait: Johnny had tossed it in the bin.

"Don't know, don't care. I moved out on Wednesday. He and Wally were two of a kind."

"What d'you mean by that?"

"I'll tell you later. Come on, the fireworks are starting."

Since Crystal Palace had burned down two years earlier, such public displays had become less common. This one must have cost a fortune. Tourbillions and Catherine wheels whirled whitely. Girandoles — red and green — spun. Roman candles spurted gold.

Fizgigs fizzled and jumping jacks cracked. Maroons exploded, rockets shrieked and magnesium chrysanthemums bloomed overhead.

So much money up in smoke! Before the drifting fumes cleared, before the oohs and ahs of the crowd died down, two men with torches lit the bonfire. Tongues of flame raced round the base. They must be using an accelerant.

The makeshift ziggurat glowed from within as the fire roared up through its core. Smoke snaked out from between the old planks and tea chests. Moments later the whole pyre was ablaze.

Johnny thought nothing of it when the woman screamed. However, others soon followed suit. They were pointing towards the top of the heap. He squinted through the shimmering heat-haze. Guy Fawkes was moving.

PART TWO

Ironmonger Row

CHAPTER
ELEVEN

Members of the Auxiliary Fire Service were on standby — they needed all the practice they could get — but there was little they could do. The hand-pumps produced such a feeble stream they might as well have been pissing on the inferno.

The flames continued to reach for the sky. Guy Fawkes didn't make a sound. The silence made his writhing all the more appalling. It only stopped when, wreathed in smoke, the flickering fire started to lick his feet.

Rebecca buried her face in Johnny's shoulder. At least she hadn't fainted like some spectators — female and male. He held her tightly and waited to see who would take charge of the incident.

A captain of the Honourable Artillery Company, barking orders, soon had his men passing buckets of water along a hastily formed line. A battered army ambulance came bouncing over the grass. Commander Inskip, surveying the scene, supped his beer but stayed put.

"I thought you liked getting your hands dirty."

The policeman didn't rise to the bait.

"Good evening, Mr Steadman. As you can see, my military colleagues have everything under control."

A huge cloud of sparks went up as the bonfire began to collapse. The crowd murmured in horror as the slumped figure, still at the stake, lurched then fell into the heart of the blaze.

"Now that's what I call a fall-guy," said Inskip.

"How can you be so heartless?" Rebecca's reddish-brown eyes glowed in the firelight.

The Commander stared at her. "Aren't you going to introduce us, Steadman?"

"Alan Inskip, Rebecca Taylor."

Inskip extended his hand, clasping her hand a second too long.

"I thought perhaps you'd already met," said Johnny. "Rebecca knew Walter Chittleborough."

"Haven't had the pleasure — till now." Inskip smiled. "Two murder scenes in one week, Miss Taylor. You're quite the femme fatale."

"Have you found Wally's killer yet?"

"No — but we're working round the clock."

"So I see." She turned to Johnny. "I'll be back shortly."

Inskip watched her walk over to one of the aldermen, who immediately put his arm round her.

"Has she told you anything useful?"

"Not so far." It was too good an opportunity to miss. "Anything more to say about the anti-Semitic attacks?"

"We continue to make inquiries. I hear you and Adler have become quite pally. When did you plan to

98

hand over the new evidence?" He glared at Johnny. "Don't look at me like that. I know about the fungus."

"We needed a photograph of the Gold Cap to accompany the story. It's much like any other clump of mould. You're welcome to it."

"I'll send someone round tomorrow morning. Now, if you'll excuse me . . ."

The fire was at long last dying down. Acrid steam rose from the blackened debris.

"Hang on! What are you going to do about the reappearance of Cecil Zick? I'm told he's up to his old tricks."

Inskip turned his back on him and set off across the Artillery Ground. Johnny, ducking under the rope that encircled the smouldering pyre, followed him.

"Sure that's the way you want to play it? *When asked to comment on the return of a suspected blackmailer and whoremonger, Commander Inskip of the City of London Police turned his back on the* Daily News . . ."

There were too many witnesses for Inskip to knock his block off. Instead he gripped Johnny's bicep as hard as he could.

"You mightn't give a damn about your own well-being, but consider that of Detective Constable Turner. He's an excellent copper — and a good man — but when it comes to his wife — and anyone else laying hands on her — he can't help seeing red. It would be a crying shame if such a promising career were to be destroyed because his runt of a friend can't keep his trap shut."

Inskip was right. If he told Matt that Zick was back in London, he would certainly go after the bastard. Alternatively, if he kept silent, Matt would — sooner or later — find out that Zick was back in business. Either way, he'd go after him with a vengeance. And that was exactly what they didn't want. The consequences could be fatal.

Johnny would have to solve this particular problem on his own.

Rubbing his arm, he watched the Commander take charge. The excited soldiers retreated when they saw the gold braid on his epaulettes. Here, as elsewhere, rank was everything.

The charred corpse was placed, still smoking, on to a stretcher. A sweet smell, not unlike that of the hog-roasts, seeped through the air. However, this one made Johnny lose his appetite.

"At least he's still got his teeth," said Inskip, poking what was left of the face with a pencil. "It's the only way we're going to get an identification."

He was wrong. Johnny would have known that projecting jaw anywhere. He kept his trap shut.

Lizzie was at home. Where else would she be? It was Friday night and yet here she was, a prisoner of the hearth. Yes, she was warm and dry. Yes, she had eaten. Even Lila Mae was slumbering soundly for once. But was Lizzie content? Absolutely not.

Felix Aylmer, dignified and donnish, was reading one of Leslie Halward's short stories on the wireless. *The Money's All Right* was a typical morality tale in which the values of working-class life were tested and, depending on your point of view, found wanting or rewarding. Did she really need to be reminded that something that did not make a profit could still be of value?

Love, loyalty, discretion — all three were priceless. She couldn't get Johnny out of her head. She replayed the events of the previous evening once again. It was her fault. If she hadn't turned her head, if she'd kept her resolve, she wouldn't be in this pickle. How could she live with the memory of her awful daring? A moment's surrender had put all her relationships — with Matt, with Johnny, and with her family — in jeopardy.

The front door closed with a click. He was always careful not to disturb them. She heard the oven door open and then a curse as he dropped the hot plate on the table. He never learned. She crept into the hall.

His blond, close-cropped head was bent over his food. His right arm guarded his plate as if he were afraid someone would try to take it away from him. He shovelled the stew into his mouth as fast as he could. Lizzie sighed. He ate like a convict.

Matt glanced up and grinned at his wife. In spite of herself, she felt a rush of tenderness. No man — especially a boxer — should have such beautiful cheekbones. His face was flushed.

"You're drunk. Again."

"No I'm not. Only had a couple."

"Of what? Bottles? Barrels?"

"Pints. It's been a long day."

"I couldn't agree more."

Matt pushed his plate away and belched.

"How's Lila?"

"Fine. She missed you at bathtime. So did I."

"Don't start."

Lizzie knew if he said anything else she would lose her temper. Without a word she returned to the parlour. Matt went upstairs to check on the baby. He didn't come down again.

Rebecca insisted on staying at the Artillery Ground in case she was needed.

"This reflects badly on the Grocers' Company. We'll have to issue a press release."

Johnny didn't see why the livery company should be so concerned — unless it was one of its men who'd burned the informant.

It was after 8.30p.m. when, entering the newsroom, he cried: "Hold the front page!"

The hoots of derision turned to howls of glee once he'd explained that he'd landed an exclusive.

"Shame you don't know why Quirk was killed," said Patsel.

"It must be because he talked to me," said Johnny.

"You can't confirm that," said PDQ. "Nor can you reveal the information he gave you. You should have made contact with Hollom as soon as you had his name."

"I tried — more than once. He's not been at work. I don't have a home address."

102

"Let's hope he still needs one," said Patsel. "The flamboyant manner of Quirk's death suggests it was intended as a warning to anyone else who was thinking of talking to you."

"It may have been flamboyant but it was also cruel," said Johnny. "How about *The Flaming Boy* as a headline?"

"Too flip," said PDQ. "We need to know why he was released early from Pentonville. Tanfield, see if you can get a quote from the governor."

"He's probably at the lodge, sir."

"If so, we'll say he refused to comment."

The final copy deadline was 9p.m. but, in exceptional circumstances, it could be extended by up to an hour. Johnny filed his five hundred words in thirty minutes.

The absence of any official police report did not prevent him naming Quirk nor claiming his death was murder. However, Patsel blue-pencilled his implication that it could be connected to the recent murders of three other men.

"Save it for the follow-up tomorrow," said PDQ. "Keep your gunpowder dry."

Johnny was on the point of complaining that his mouth was dry when the telephone rang: a summons to the seventh floor.

"Bad news travels fast," smirked Tanfield.

The red light went off and the green light came on. Several dark suits and grey heads were sitting round the conference table with copies of the early edition spread out before them.

"Ah, Steadman. Come with me."

Johnny followed the editor along his private corridor, past a kitchen, bedroom and bathroom, and out through the fire exit. Rather than descending the fire escape, they went up to the roof.

A hard frost now gripped the capital. However, it wasn't only the cold that took his breath away. London always seemed more beautiful by night. The sky, way above the ever-present pall of smoke, was clear. Its stars gazed down on those of the West End. Fiat lux. Gas-lamps in Mayfair, floodlights in Trafalgar Square, strip lights in Soho. Beyond the Strand, the sweet Thames flowed like black silk. Big Ben bonged ten.

"I've a good mind to fire you."

At first Johnny thought Stone was joking. He'd been expecting congratulations, not recriminations.

"What were you thinking, man? You might as well have called Adler a Nazi. Were you trying to be offensive?"

"No. Would you rather I pretended I hadn't heard about a theft of six million? All I did was ask him about a deposit of Czech gold. I didn't accuse him of taking it."

"That's not what he said."

"Well, he's a liar."

"Why would he lie? I told you to help him, not hinder him."

"I have been helping him. Instead of collecting mushrooms I could have been chasing the man whose name got my informant killed tonight."

The more Johnny thought about it, the angrier he became.

"What's Adler got on you? I appreciate you're Jewish, but there has to be more to it than that. Is it mere coincidence, Herr Stein, that the Gestapo's bank is J.H. Stein? I thought the Nazis were more interested in burning books than balancing them."

If he were going to get fired it would be right now. He wasn't that worried. With his track record, he could walk into another job tomorrow. War was coming: what did it matter whether he wrote for the *Daily Brute* or the *Daily Beast*?

His editor, or ex-editor, burst into laughter. He gripped the handrail and stared down the grand canyon of Fleet Street.

"That's my boy!" His words hung, then slowly evaporated, in the thin air. He turned to face him. "Why take everything so personally?"

"I might ask you the same question."

"Leo is married to Honoria's sister."

Stone's wife had taken a maternal interest in Johnny since his earliest days on the paper. Furthermore, Captain Vic, as he mentored him, had become a father figure. That was why it had hurt when he seemed to doubt him.

"Why didn't you say so before?"

"You've just answered your own question. I didn't want any ugly rumours to start about another Jewish conspiracy. I should have borne in mind your over-active imagination. I've been waiting for someone to point out the coincidence regarding J. H. Stein. I assure you, there's no familial connection."

"I'm glad to hear it. I apologise for calling you Herr Stein."

"Apology accepted. This is a time of heightened sensibilities all round. We need to tread carefully. Our impartiality is our greatest selling point. We can't be seen to be in cahoots with anyone."

He came back from the edge and patted Johnny on the shoulder.

"I'll speak to Leo and say something about wires getting crossed. Concentrate on the murders now. Your top priority is to track down Quirk's contact."

CHAPTER
TWELVE

Saturday, 5 November, 8.50a.m.

A board between the two sash-windows of the establishment informed passers-by that Otarelli & Sanna sold barometers, thermometers and hydrometers. Johnny, standing in a doorway on the opposite side of Charles Street, stamped his feet. He'd been in position for only twenty minutes, yet already he was frozen.

Quirk had told him Rick Hollom drank in the Mitre but he didn't want to wait till lunchtime nor ask the staff for him by name. Hollom was in enough potential danger as it was. Had news of his acquaintance's death made him disappear?

Workers continued to enter the premises but Johnny failed to spot anyone who looked likely to have been an associate of his informant. Then again, Quirk had known a lot of people; his livelihood had depended on it.

How did you put a face to a name though? There was no correlation between the two: everyone's name was a combination of inclination and inheritance. His own parents had liked the name John. However, that didn't make him look like a John Steadman. Or did it? How strange that one's spoken identity was so arbitrary . . .

A school photograph would do the trick — if you knew where your target was educated. A criminal record would have a mugshot — if you knew the right person to retrieve it. He hadn't spoken to Matt since he'd seen Lizzie. More than twenty-four hours had passed, but he could still feel her lips meeting his. He must call him. There was a police box in Hatton Garden.

The long, wide street — the centre of the diamond trade — was a world unto itself. Clusters of Jewish men — Orthodox and otherwise — stood on the pavements, swapping information and gossip. Three Is dominated their working lives: Integrity, Intelligence and Industry. A merchant's reputation was everything; trust had to be earned. Strangers — those outside the faith — found it a tough market to enter. Most of the businesses that bought and sold gold, silver, jewellery and objets d'art were family affairs.

For once he was put through straightaway.

"Why didn't you tell Inskip it was Quirk?"

"He was being his usual obnoxious self. Bet his face was a picture when he saw the *News* this morning."

"He hardly needs another reason to hate your guts," said Matt. "What was so important that Quirk had to die?"

"I don't know. All he gave me was a name . . ." He paused. Was it time to share his chocolate bar?

"What are you waiting for? D'you want me to beg?"

"Course not. It's just . . ." He reminded himself that Matt couldn't help him unless he shared the information. "You'll keep it to yourself, won't you? At least until I've had a chance to speak with him?"

"If you're quick about it — and he doesn't turn out to be wanted for anything else."

"He's called Rick Hollom. Works at Otarelli & Sanna in Charles Street. I'm round the corner from the shop now. Quirk said he drinks in the Mitre."

"I'll meet you there at two o'clock."

The day had started like all the others that week. Lizzie, up half the night with Lila who was teething again, had been out for the count when he'd got up at six. Even if she had been awake, she was unlikely to have said much. How had the stony silences begun? What had he done wrong? Something or someone had disappointed her. He hoped it wasn't him.

Lila, exhausted after her nocturnal caterwauling, was fast asleep. Matt stroked her fair hair — his hair — and kissed her on the forehead. She was his reason for living — the proof of his love for Lizzie. His family was his greatest asset. Only Johnny meant as much to him. And he was almost family . . .

He bought a copy of the *Daily News* at the station and, as usual, immediately scanned it for Johnny's byline. He didn't have to search for long. It appeared at the top of a single column headed EXCLUSIVE which ran alongside the lead story, a plane crash in Jersey.

As soon as he read it he knew what kind of welcome awaited him at Snow Hill. Inskip and his cohorts would take it personally. The fact that he'd been in the dark as much as them would be no defence. They relied on him to keep Johnny under control.

He watched the suburbs of South London scroll by, willing the train to slow down. They should know by now that Johnny was a law unto himself.

Perhaps there was little demand for scientific instruments at the weekend. The window-shoppers seemed far more interested in diamonds. Girls with glowing cheeks, arm in arm with their catches, pointed to racks of rocks encased in rings. They believed they had a future together — or were they simply taking refuge while they could? Matrimony provided a degree of security in an uncertain age. Link arms or take up arms? What was he going to do? One failed marriage proposal was enough for him. There was safety in singledom. No love to lose.

A gang of street Arabs, bare feet blue with cold, propped up their dummy in the porch of a pub on Greville Street. "Penny for the Guy! Penny for the Guy!"

Two minutes later the attic windows of a workshop juddered open and a shower of coppers rained down. The kids scrambled to collect them but — with yells of outrage — dropped them immediately. The watching apprentices — who had heated the coins with their welding torches — cackled and returned to their benches.

Johnny stood his ground till ten o'clock. If Hollom were working today then he had to be in the building. The time for discretion was over.

The shop was an Aladdin's cave of glittering devices. He remembered gyroscopes, theodolites and anemometers from his school days, but he could only guess what the others were designed to measure.

"Good morning, sir. How may I be of assistance?" The handsome young man had a slight foreign accent.

"I'm here to see Rick Hollom."

"Who should I say is calling?"

"A friend."

"One moment please."

He disappeared into the back room. A conversation in rapid Italian ensued. The only word Johnny could make out was *Tesoro*.

"I beg your pardon, sir." His teeth were dazzling. "Mr Hollom is not available."

"Sure you weren't speaking to him?"

"Quite certain."

"What does he do here?"

"Why do you ask? Who are you?"

"I'm a newspaper reporter. A friend of his suggested I talk to him. Do you have an address for him?"

"No. I'm sorry. If you leave your details I'll see that he gets them."

"Thank you." He gave the counter-jumper his card. "Tell him it's urgent. Tell him if he needs help, he now knows who to call."

Jock Wilderspin flung the document at him.

"You're a bloody fool, if you don't mind my saying so."

Alex did mind — very much so. You'd have thought the old bastard would have known how to spell embarrassment by now. After Monday's performance he'd refrained from correcting any errors in his manager's prose.

"A thousand apologies, sir. How could anyone forget it's not *as* but *ass*?"

He deserved a medal for keeping a straight face.

Vanneck re-typed the document and, at ten to one, hauled himself up the dilapidated hydraulic lift, to get it signed again. Thank God it was Saturday. The game didn't start till three. He'd have lunch at Lockharts. With any luck that bobby-dazzler of a waitress would be on duty.

Ye Olde Mitre was impossible to find unless you knew it existed. Hidden down a snicket called Mitre Court that ran between Hatton Garden and Ely Place, the ancient hostelry, with its low ceilings and oak-panelled walls, was the perfect place for secret assignations. Elizabeth I — no stranger to discreet trysts — was said to have danced round the trunk of the cherry tree that, now preserved, graced a corner of the bar.

Johnny, having tipped the landlord generously, asked him to let him know if Hollom made an appearance. The pub was packed. It required careful timing to lift a glass to your lips without spilling any beer.

Matt might as well have been Moses the way the sea of bodies parted to let him through. He was too big to argue with — and he was a man who invariably attracted second looks. Johnny was proud to be his friend.

"Any luck?"

"No," sighed Johnny. "He must have gone into hiding. What are you having?"

"Pint of Hammerson's, please."

"Not fighting tonight?"

Matt shook his head. "Not in the ring, anyway."

Once they'd been served, they elbowed their way into an anteroom called Ye Olde Closet where a table had just become free.

"Find anything on Hollom?"

"Not a sausage."

"Ah, well. We tried. I gather you spoke to Tim Tanfield on Tuesday."

"What of it?" The bitter had given Matt a froth moustache. He wiped it away with the back of his hand.

"Did you mention Broster's last supper?"

"No. He was only interested in the traces of Gold Cap."

"Was there any pork in the stomach?"

Matt shook his head. "No. He appears to have had a liquid dinner."

"So he was drunk and drugged."

"Hmm. Perhaps he moved in different circles to Bromet and Chittleborough."

"Perhaps he was Jewish."

"He was definitely a juice-hound. His liver was cirrhotic."

Johnny sighed. "We're going round in circles — different or not. Anything else to tell me?"

"I wish there was. Inskip's on the warpath. Four murders and a spate of anti-Semitic attacks. Adler's demanding the culprits be found before the Lord Mayor's Show on Wednesday."

"Shame he won't lose his job if he fails."

Johnny stared through the bottle-glass window.

"All of us need a break," said Matt. "What's the matter? Seen a ghost? This place is said to be haunted."

Johnny took a slug of beer to give himself time to think. He hadn't seen a ghost. He'd seen Henry Simkins leaving the pub, followed by Cecil Zick.

What should he do?

He knew Matt would have received a lot of flak because of what he'd written. He owed him more than a couple of pints. There was no good reason to withhold the information any longer: Zick and Simkins were clearly not bluffing.

"They were ghosts, of a kind. Henry Simkins has just left — with Cecil Zick. Wait!"

It was no good. Matt steamed out of the pub leaving overturned tables and slopped beer in his wake. Johnny, apologizing profusely, righted the furniture and offered refills to the disgruntled drinkers.

"Don't worry," he told the landlord. "He's a copper."

"They're the worst of the lot! Is he coming back?"

"I hope so. Do you know Henry Simkins from the *Chronicle*?"

"The geezer with a taste for champagne?"

"That's him. Where was he? I didn't see him when I came in."

"Closeted with an older chap who can't be short of a bob or two. He hired the Bishop's Room. Always does."

"He's been here before?"

"Twice a week for the past month."

"Why? What's so special about this place?" Before the host could answer Matt appeared at Johnny's side.

"There was no sign of them. Must have flagged down a taxi."

Johnny bought another round and returned to the snug. "What would you have done if you'd caught Zick?"

"Beaten the shit out of him. Slowly."

"Wouldn't you rather get him sent down for a long time?"

"We both know how difficult — and how improbable — that would be."

"Friends in high places."

"Don't I know it? That's why it'll be so satisfying when my fist meets his face. He deserves it for what he did to Lizzie — and he's hardly likely to go crying to the cops."

Johnny wasn't going to waste his breath saying violence was a tacit admission of defeat. Matt had taught him how to fight but he still considered his tongue his best weapon.

"Why d'you think Zick's come back? He knows you'll be after him."

"You asking questions that you know the answers to again?" Matt wasn't stupid.

"Simkins told me a couple of days ago. This is the first time I've seen you since."

"Go on." Matt's blue eyes deepened — a sure sign of emotion.

"He's intending to set up shop again."

"You mean a knocking-shop."

"Yes — and he wants me to persuade you to back off."

"Why would you do that?"

Johnny leaned closer. "He's still got the photographs."

Matt put his head in his hands and groaned. "Fucking hell. Will this never end?"

The sordid business had awoken forbidden feelings in both men. He, unlike Johnny, refused to acknowledge them. He'd long suspected that Johnny harboured strange ideas about their friendship but he would not discuss them with him. What was the point of talking about something that could never become a reality? He had no desire to live with another man. He preferred the company of women. And yet the disturbing dreams — not exactly nightmares, not always — persisted.

"The photographer kept copies," said Johnny. "Simkins is desperate for us to come to an arrangement."

"What's he got to do with this? Hasn't he learned his lesson?"

"Knowing Zick, he's probably blackmailing him too. Simkins is acting as his go-between."

"After you saved his life. There's gratitude for you."

"He's as trapped as I am. We have to find a way of putting Zick out of business once and for all."

"If we'd known Quirk was going to die, we could have pinned Zick's murder on him."

Was he joking? Once upon a time Johnny would have had no hesitation in saying yes. However, Matt's

116

youthful idealism — his unwavering faith in the rule of law — had been challenged and found wanting as he'd gained experience on the streets of the City and in the offices of his superiors. Day by day his black-and-white world had blurred into one giant grey area.

Zick's death would be the simplest solution to the problem. What did the life of one villain matter when so many innocent people were under the threat of war? Johnny had killed a man before — but not in cold blood. Besides, it had been to save the life of another as well as his own.

Johnny drained his glass.

"We have to get Zick arrested outside the City of London so that his protectors can't intervene."

"The brothel is bound to be within the Square Mile though. Crooks are like dogs — they always return to their vomit. His previous places have been in the City so it's a fair bet his new one will be too."

"Simkins swears he doesn't know where it is."

"He might do now. Why's he met Zick today?"

"I'll find out."

"What are your plans for tonight?"

"I'm taking Rebecca Taylor to the pictures."

"Business or pleasure?"

"Both — but I'd settle for the latter."

"Good luck. I'm working tomorrow, so call me," said Matt, getting up and ruffling Johnny's hair on his way out.

Johnny remained sitting at the table even though a brace of bankers was casting covetous glances at it. How different his life would have been had he and Matt not been placed in the same class at Essex Road. He'd known him longer than anyone else on the planet. It was his only lasting relationship. No one — not even Lizzie — should be allowed to come between them. She'd threatened to do so once before but somehow he'd managed to do the right thing, or rather to do nothing while she chose Matt over him. She must have had her reasons. So what was she up to now?

His reverie was broken by the landlord.

"Hollom's at the counter. The eyetie's drinking red wine. Always does."

Johnny followed him into the main room. He appeared to be chatting to one of his countrymen. White teeth flashed. Rick Hollom was the shop assistant he'd spoken to earlier that morning.

CHAPTER
THIRTEEN

Johnny's first impulse was to interrupt the animated conversation by introducing himself — loudly. He didn't like being taken for a fool. Discretion, discretion, discretion. Once again doing nothing, saying nothing, was the equivalent of doing the right thing. Johnny remained at the end of the bar and stared at the man.

It wasn't long before Hollom's primeval instinct kicked in. Humans, whether hunting or gathering, quickly sense when they're being watched. His eyes widened and his mouth closed when he spotted Johnny. What would be his reaction? Fight or flight? Neither — they were no longer roaming prehistoric plains. He nodded towards the door and, saying farewell to his friend, who did not look round, walked out of the tavern.

Instead of turning left towards Hatton Garden, Hollom turned right and headed for Ely Place. His shoulders were so broad they brushed the sides of the narrow passage.

They emerged opposite a terrace of stately Georgian houses. The autumnal sunlight made them squint. A watchman was polishing the window in the door of his lodge. Hollom, though, turned away from Charterhouse

Street and, walking past St Etheldreda's, made for the high brick wall that formed the end of the cul-de-sac.

However, if you were a pedestrian, Ely Place was not a dead end. A rickety wicker gate led into Bleeding Heart Yard. The name of the cobbled courtyard fascinated Johnny almost as much as Dickens, who discussed its origins at length in *Little Dorrit*. Heraldic imagery? Tragic romance? Cabbies would have none of it: the place was "bleedin' 'ard to find".

Hollom stopped outside a garage that had already closed for the weekend. Oil and grease had left iridescent stains on the stones. Johnny prepared to grease the palm of his only lead.

"Put that away." Hollom nodded at the wallet. "I don't take bribes."

"Why couldn't you speak to me in the shop?"

"Would you like your employers knowing your private business?"

"Quirk gave me your name. You know he's dead?"

"Yes. That's why we're here."

He glanced round to check that the yard was deserted.

"Are you in danger too?"

"Don't think so. I'm not a snitch. Also I can take care of myself."

Johnny didn't doubt it.

"How did you meet him?"

"He was a member of England For Fascism — as am I."

If he was trying to shock Johnny, he'd failed.

"Are you British?"

120

"My mother is Italian. She married beneath her so I was brought up in Clerkenwell. I was christened Ricardo but, as far as Londoners are concerned, I'm Richard. My cousins are supporters of Mussolini. Quirk admired him too. We fought together in Cable Street."

"Is that why he was killed?"

"I do not think so. He was hardly alone in his views. Why would our enemies choose him? There are plenty of more prominent members to target if the murder was supposed to make a political point."

"He was sent down for burglary soon after Cable Street, so he can't have been active since then."

"That's true. He was busy trying to look up old friends, but his early release from prison made them suspicious."

"Did he tell you how it came about?"

"It was a reward — for keeping his mouth shut."

"You're pulling my leg."

"No." The Italian was serious. "He'd learned something that, in his words, was pure gold. He said it was more than his life was worth to reveal it. His vow of silence earned him remission."

"So," said Johnny. "He must have broken his word."

"He didn't tell you?"

"No, he bloody didn't, and now it seems he should have."

Hollom appeared to share his disappointment.

"He died for nothing then. A great shame. I've got your card now. If I hear anything, I'll let you know. Quirk may have been a petty criminal, but his heart was in the right place. If I were you, I'd search for his killers elsewhere — they deserve to be punished."

"Are you warning me off?"

Hollom smiled. It was unusual for an EFF boy to have all his teeth.

"Giving you friendly advice, that's all. I'd hate for you to waste your time — or get hurt."

He crossed the yard and turned into Charles Street. They had come full circle. And Johnny still didn't know why Quirk had given him Hollom's name.

Fleet Street was due south. Johnny, deep in thought, strode down Shoe Lane, determined to confront Simkins. The marble foyer of the *Chronicle* was a dance floor on which telegram boys, reporters and visitors waltzed round each other with only the occasional collision.

"After a job, Steadman?" The managing editor, who had evidently enjoyed a splendid lunch, slapped him on the back. "Where's your portfolio?"

"I'm happy where I am, thanks."

"Well, if you change your mind . . ." He sauntered over to one of the lifts. Its door slid open and Louis Dimeo stepped out.

"What are you doing here?"

"I might ask you the same question."

"Shouldn't you be at a football match?"

"Not this weekend. I'm covering the boxing at Olympia tonight."

The receptionist informed Johnny that Simkins was not in the building but was expected shortly. He didn't leave a message.

122

Dimeo accompanied him back to the office.

"Don't tell anyone you saw me. They'd only get the wrong end of the stick."

"So let me guess," said Johnny. "If you're not jumping ship, you're sniffing round a girl."

"With a body like mine it would be selfish not to share it."

"Are all Italian men arrogant?"

"Not arrogant. Self-confident."

"If you say so — but it's your brain that interests me. What does *Tesoro* mean?"

"Are you actually asking me for help?"

"If you don't know, I can easily look it up in the library . . ."

"Of course I know. It means *treasure*."

The Blue Hall on Upper Street was said to be the oldest cinema in Britain. Films had been shown there since 1900. Part of the Agricultural Hall complex, the space had originally been designed to show pigs. Tonight it was showing *The Lady Vanishes*. Although set in the fictitious Central European country of Bandrika (Yugoslavia? Czechoslovakia?), Hitchcock had shot some sequences just up the road at Islington Studios.

The comedy thriller had been released four weeks ago, yet the magnificent red-and-gold auditorium, which seated more than thirteen hundred, was full. Johnny and Rebecca were not alone in gasping at the fireworks on the screen. A collective sigh of satisfaction could be heard when the credits rolled and the lights went up.

"Yes," said Johnny. "But who killed the folk singer at the start? We're never told."

"He must have been a British agent as well," said Rebecca, slipping her arm through his. "Hitch likes to leave you guessing."

"Did you spot him?"

"He's hard to miss. He was at Victoria Station."

"His first-ever appearance was as a newspaper editor in *The Lodger*."

"So that's why you're such a fan." She looked at her watch. "It's time I caught a train too."

"Sure?"

He could see himself reflected in her fathomless eyes. Rejected too. He had planned to invite her back but it was probably for the best. When she'd kissed him on arrival, an image of Lizzie had popped into his head.

"I'm sure."

He walked her to the Angel tube station on City Road. It was a direct journey to Tooting Bec.

"Why haven't you mentioned last night?"

"I'm trying to forget it — although I did, of course, read what you wrote."

"That's not why I asked. The victim, Quirk, was a Mosleyite."

"No loss there then." She raised her chin as if expecting contradiction.

"Was Wally a fascist?"

"Yes. I was shocked — no, revolted — when he told me."

124

"Is that why you stopped seeing him?"

"It would have been — but, as I said, he spurned me before I could spurn him. Fascism is only another name for bigotry."

So why had Wally stopped seeing her? Was she too clever for him? Didn't he like women with brains? Was he so lacking in self-confidence he became angry if a girl dared to challenge or contradict him? Poor sap. Mental attributes could be just as arousing as physical ones.

"Let's have dinner next week."

"That would be lovely." She kissed him on the lips. "Thanks for the picture show."

He waved to her as she entered the brightly lit station. Hereafter he would always think of her as Tooting Becky.

There was a whiff of gunpowder in the air. Pigeons wheeled in panic as rockets whooshed past their roosts. Homeward bound, he could hear the distant detonations of the display in Highbury Fields. A taste of things to come.

The Bevis Marks Synagogue, the oldest in Britain, was unoccupied. Its seven brass chandeliers from Amsterdam were unlit. Moonbeams made the fake-marble ark gleam. It was actually made of oak. The clock above the entrance showed it was five minutes to midnight.

The first firebomb broke one of the lower arched windows. The second smashed against the double doors. Others hit the bare brick walls. The sweaty thugs were enjoying themselves so much they ignored the first policeman's whistle but when it was answered by that of a colleague, and the sound of running feet, they darted down the alley leading to Mitre Square where an accomplice, fag dangling from his mouth, was already gunning the engine of a truck.

Lights off, rattling loudly, the rusty crate and its exultant crew swung into Mitre Street and careered towards Aldgate. The bus came from nowhere. It struck the getaway vehicle head-on. Female passengers screamed, male passengers cursed, but none of them were seriously injured. The same could not be said of the arsonists. Legs crushed, yelling in panic, the trapped men soon had more than their fingers burned.

CHAPTER
FOURTEEN

Sunday, 6 November, 2.45p.m.

A man stood on his head in the middle of Club Row. Another, dressed in reach-me-downs, tore sheets of newspaper into doilies and silhouettes. Most of the strolling crowd ignored the beggars — they were more interested in the competition: caged animals. Some of them, dreaming of new homes, also knew how to sit up and beg. It was a dog-eat-dog world.

Johnny sympathized with the desperate performers. He earned his living by entertaining the masses too. There were always more hoops to jump through.

Perhaps he should get a pet. A dog, not a moggy — cats were too selfish. It would be good to be met by someone glad to see him, no matter what time he came home; to have a warm body to share his bed. Love without strings — if you didn't count the lead. It would be unkind to keep a canine cooped up all day though. Dogs needed constant exercise — even small ones like Jack Russells. Short, determined, fiercely loyal: he saw himself as the human equivalent of a terrier.

He'd certainly like to get Zick by the neck and shake the life out of him — but not until he'd told him where the photographs were stashed. What was Zick's real motivation? Increased revenue, or naked revenge? The only way to find out was to ask him. The sooner he had an address for Zick the better. Perhaps he — or someone else — could trail Simkins to his lair. The *Chronicle* man was a liar. He must know where Zick was hiding.

He'd have to keep the location a secret though. Matt might resemble a Golden Retriever, but he could also be highly disobedient.

No, another time perhaps. He had enough on his plate without having to care for a dumb animal. Besides, you never knew when man's best friend might turn on you. Even police dogs were known to bite the hand that fed them. Humans had to take precedence. He turned his back on the captives' big, wet eyes and cut through Arnold Circus to Shoreditch High Street, in search of a number 6 bus to take him back to Hereflete House.

Sunday afternoon was the most difficult time of the week. It was when their lives had changed for ever. Nothing had been the same since. Work kept the mind occupied. Concentrating on minor details blurred the bigger picture.

The sun was already sinking behind the Royal Courts of Justice. The pale parallelogram slid across the dusty floorboards. Fear in a handful of dust. What was there to fear when everything you'd had was lost? Fear weakened you; fury gave you strength.

Coughing chimneys expelled more coal-dust into the air. A brown haze hovered over the roofscape. What pleasures were being enjoyed, what atrocities being

128

endured, beneath the lichened tiles? It was time to prepare for the next bout of bloodletting.

Cecil Zick regarded himself in one of the new two-way mirrors that had cost him a fortune to install. Secrecy didn't come cheap. He looked every inch the prosperous businessman — and there were a lot of inches. His portly frame was encased in a Turnbull & Asser shirt and a three-piece suit from Anderson & Sheppard. His tiny feet — which had helped Cecilia win several ankle competitions — were shod in John Lobb's finest brogues. You would never guess they'd been fitted with steel toecaps — until they cracked your shins.

Simkins would explode — with anger or glee? Probably both — when he learned the address. Hanging Sword Alley, off Fleet Street, was the perfect location. It wasn't only a matter of cocking a snook at the Fourth Estate — which pretended to be appalled by his activities while purveying every last (publishable) detail to titillate its readers — the bordello had to be convenient for his clients, some of whom worked in the inky trade, and within the boundary of the City.

The house could be approached from three directions: north, west and south. The Fleet Street entrance to the alley looked like an empty doorway and, if you didn't know it was there, could be easily missed. A cut-through from Whitefriars Street was the shortest route, while the longest and most discreet access was from Tudor Street via a winding, uphill passage.

It was coming, he could feel it. The air, even the very stones of London, seemed heavier. He'd been twenty years old the last time. The Zeppelins had brought out the hedonist in him. It was better to die fucking than fucking die — and he'd done a great deal of fucking behind the front line. Deemed unfit for combat, he'd found his place in the catering corps and did his best to cater for all tastes. Terrified men were grateful for any kind of affection — if the circumstances were right. He remembered them all: the ones who, overcome with shame, lashed out; the grateful ones who wouldn't let go; the ones who cried when they came.

He had a pornographic memory and yet tears still sprang to his eyes when he recalled one particular boy. Curly hair, hazel eyes, so strong and yet so tender. Delirium in a derelict barn. Soft lips, hot skin, pressing so hard as two became one. A single star glimpsed through the shell-damaged roof. He never saw him again.

If the Great War — the war to end all wars — taught him anything it was that conflict created wealth. Capitalism was war by other means: safeguarding supplies, devising tactics, crushing the opposition. This time he was ready. Property prices would plunge as soon as the bombs started falling. Every cloud had a golden lining.

Meanwhile, there were appetites to be piqued and quenched. Not all young men were keen to get to grips with Jerry. Some would rather stay at home for as long as they could — and he generously rewarded loyalty. There was nothing more satisfying than when the naked self-interest of several parties coincided for the greater good.

And, regardless of what Inskip said, no junior detective was going to spoil this party. If he'd had his way, Turner would be dead already. Steadman, too, if he hadn't been so potentially useful. Accidents happened every day . . .

He licked his lips. Four thirty. The perfect time for afternoon tea. Scheming invariably gave him an appetite. He'd give Simkins one more day to straighten things out then, if the eunuch failed, he'd take matters into his own hands. He winked at himself in the mirror. No one was going to queer his pitch.

Only a skeleton staff worked on Sunday afternoon. It was the deadest time of the week. Most of Monday's first edition was put to bed on Saturday. The night shift didn't turn up till six. Martial music was playing on the BBC.

"Mr Steadman. What are you doing here?" Gustav Patsel roused himself from his slumbers. "You are not required until tomorrow morning."

"Nothing better to do. I'm meeting a source later on. Thought I'd catch up on some secondary reading."

"Most conscientious." He couldn't have sounded more sceptical. "How's your new friend, Mr Adler?"

"I wouldn't know. Haven't heard from him since Friday."

Why did he want to know?

"The synagogue in Bevis Marks was set on fire last night."

"Don't sound so pleased about it. Why wasn't I told?"

"The Fire Brigade, considering the date, was commendably prompt. Then again, its officers only had to come from Bishopsgate. Perhaps they were half-expecting such a call. Certainly, the damage was not extensive. A broken window, a few charred pews. Mr Tanfield can take care of it when he arrives shortly."

"There's no need. I'll chase it up now."

"As you wish." Patsel slumped back in his chair. "Please keep your voice down."

Johnny didn't bother to take off his coat before making the phone call.

"Why didn't you tip me off about the arson attack?"

"I was about to," said Matt. "Keep your hair on. Another hour or so won't make any difference. As far as I know, none of your competitors have been in touch."

"Won't make any difference to what?"

"Your story. The culprits have been caught. The twerps crashed on their way home. They're in Bart's now. Two in the emergency ward. One in the mortuary."

"Congratulations. Let's meet in the Coach & Horses. It's closest."

"The first round's on you."

Death never took a day off. Its scythe never needed whetting. There was no end to human stupidity.

Percy Hughes was removing other, rather smaller, cutting tools from the autoclave when Johnny burst

132

through the rubber doors. A couple of the ghastly instruments slipped off the metal tray and clattered on to the antiseptic ceramic tiles.

"Now look what you bleedin' made me do!"

"What's it matter? A corpse can't catch anything."

"No — but I can." Hughes sniffed in disgust. "What you want this time?"

"A body was brought in late last night or some time today. Vehicle smash."

"Harold Ensom. Broke his neck going through the windscreen. Sherman fished a fag out of his gullet."

"Where's he now?"

"Who?"

"Sherman, you idiot. Ensom's hardly likely to have walked out."

"He's finished for the day. Think I'd be talking to you otherwise?"

"What else can you tell me?"

"How much you willing to pay?"

"Five bob."

"Not enough."

"Ten — if it's worth it."

"See what you think."

Hughes walked over to one of the humming refrigerators and slid out the lowest shelf. With a heartless lack of ceremony he whipped off the sheet.

A black-and-white still from a horror movie. Everything below the waist was carbonized. It was as if two bodies had been joined together by a latter-day Frankenstein. The forked incision down the torso had been sewn up with garden twine but did not obscure the large tattoo on his chest.

"Pretty, ain't it? Black and red go well together."

"If you say so." The design didn't seem to concern Hughes at all.

"Satisfied?" He rubbed his fingers together. "Come on, Steadman. I'm on the ribs."

"So's the swastika." Gallows humour was a necessary sidekick on the crime beat. Johnny handed over a ten-shilling note.

"I'll say this for you — even though you're a pain in the arm. You've never tried to twice me." He sniffed again as though he'd finally made up his mind. "PC Watkiss said his cronies have the same tattoo."

CHAPTER
FIFTEEN

Monday, 7 November, 8.35a.m.

"Celebrating, were we?" Tanfield failed to disguise his pleasure in Johnny's evident discomfort. He held up the front page. "I don't blame you. This was quite the scoop."

"If it bleeds, it leads." Johnny couldn't stop coughing.

"I don't suppose you'd . . ."

"You suppose correctly." Johnny shuffled off to the canteen. He must be coming down with something.

The seventh floor, prompted by PDQ if not Patsel, had decided to lead on his story of an anti-Jewish conspiracy. Having sweet-talked a nurse at Bart's, he'd seen for himself the swastikas inked on the chests of the two survivors who remained in no condition to talk to him. Even so, he'd had no hesitation in naming them and their dead accomplice, or implicating all three men in the assault of the Lord Mayor-in-waiting as well as the arson attack on the synagogue. Ensom, Leask and Ormesher were mere foot soldiers though. Who was the general?

It had been as well they'd changed the venue. By the time Johnny had filed his thousand words and returned to Smithfield the previous evening it was after 9.30 and Matt had been three sheets to the wind. The Coach and Horses in Bartholomew Close, hidden down a passage between two banks, made for a discreet watering-hole.

"Glad you could make it." Matt, sprawled in a corner like a punch-drunk pugilist, looked as if he'd got through several rounds. "It's almost closing time — and it's your shout."

Johnny knew better than to argue. He ordered them each a double whisky. Matt downed his in one. He'd absorbed too much alcohol to take in the news about the tattoos. An old couple, the only other drinkers, said goodnight to the landlord and left. Seeing the state Matt was in, he called last orders. Johnny refilled their glasses. He was exhausted.

"Saved by the Bell's!" Matt staggered to his feet. "All right if I stay at yours tonight?"

When Johnny had woken that morning Matt had already left. He'd tried to get Matt to tell him what was wrong but, since he'd kissed Lizzie, his friends' marriage had become even more of a minefield. "If you want to help, get hold of Simkins," said Matt. After that he hadn't said a word.

Johnny was sweating yet shivering. Overnight a great heaviness had settled on him. His blood felt like molten lead. He was racked by a hacking cough. There was so much he had to get off his chest.

It took a superhuman effort to shave, wash and dress. He didn't even make the bed before he set off for the office.

136

Matt stared at the figure bound — like Saint Andrew on the cross — to the double bed. He tried not to heave. It wasn't the blood — it was what was in his own veins that was making him nauseous. He never used to get such vicious hangovers. He must be getting old.

That was one problem Francis Felshie would never have to face. His gymnast's body wouldn't thicken round the middle, nor would hair start to spring from the unlikeliest of places. His ears wouldn't grow larger, nor would his balls — which were, it had to be said, like hen's eggs — hang lower year by year.

"Poor bastard. Wonder what he did to deserve this?"

Penterell strolled round the sodden mattress. "Perhaps he was a turd-packer."

"Meaning?"

"No loss to humanity."

"Humanity? What would you know about that?" Matt resisted the impulse to grab one of the Indian clubs that stood in the corner. Braining his colleague would make him no better than the killer.

The mournful horns of tugs and barges drifted through the open window. Ducksfoot Lane was an odd, dog-legged thoroughfare that climbed from Upper Thames Street to Cannon Street. Shrieks and hisses, slams and whistles, came from the Stygian terminus that was less than two hundred yards away.

The photographer, encumbered with paraphernalia, arrived at the scene of the crime. Matt left him in the dubious company of Penterell. Death didn't trouble him — well, no more so than anyone else — but there was something creepy about gazing at a corpse when it couldn't gaze back. Dead people didn't need privacy — their bodies were merely cast-off garments — but you wouldn't stare at live folk's discarded underwear either — unless you were sick in the head. And he wasn't, he really wasn't.

However, the killer patently was insane. And sooner or later they'd make a mistake. The more confident they became, the more likely they were to blunder. Matt hoped that blunder came soon. He needed to shine on this case, get Inskip off his back. The Commander had made it abundantly clear that both their careers depended on keeping silent, maintaining the status quo. Matt couldn't go on like this, though, knowing the sword of Damocles could fall at any moment.

His life would be immeasurably simpler if it weren't for other people. But Lizzie, Lila Mae and — damn him! — Johnny were his whole world. Without them, he was nothing. They all wanted so much from him. Could he give them what they wanted? What about what he wanted?

A locked room, no witnesses, a single man unmanned. Johnny would love this.

The telephone, as if to spite him, would not shut up. Each trill drilled into his aching head. The Hello Girls downstairs had no sympathy; they kept putting the calls through.

Stone: "Bravo! Find out who paid the goons. They can't be acting alone. We need another splash tomorrow."

Adler: "I owe you, Steadman. Keep up the good work. Your editor's proud of you. Let me know if there's anything I can do for you."

Simkins: "I need to speak with you. Not on the telephone — at my club. One o'clock." Before Johnny could reply the line went dead.

Rebecca: "I feel honoured to know you! There's an exhibition of new work by the Euston Road School opening tomorrow night. Thelma Hulbert's invited me. Fancy coming along? It promises to be a super evening. We could catch a bite afterwards . . ."

Culver: "Tally ho! The hunt is on. Don't stop now." Johnny sneezed. "Someone getting up your nose?"

"You could say that . . ."

Johnny looked up, sensing eyes on him.

Tanfield, annoyingly healthy, smirked from the next desk. "Acute nasopharyngitis."

"What?"

"You've got a cold."

"Tell you what you need," said Culver. "A Turkish bath. Have you been to the ones in Ironmonger Row? Let's meet there at noon tomorrow." He lowered his voice. "Something else to tell you."

And, finally, there was a call from Turner: "You sound how I feel."

"I hope for your sake that's not true. Simkins has proposed lunch. Three-line whip."

"Shift your arse, then — I need to see you first. Number four's turned up."

Johnny grabbed his hat and coat.

Tanfield, trying to find a fresh angle on the weekend's litany of drunken mishaps and mayhem, stopped typing. "Bet the name begins with D!"

The London Stone, next door to the Chamber of Commerce's Court of Arbitration, was one of the most popular pubs in Cannon Street. It served Truman, Hanbury and Buxton ales and hot food in a grill room on the first floor and a dining room on the second. Tall, narrow and sloping westwards, it resembled one of its customers propping up the bar.

"Why couldn't we meet at the scene?"

"Inskip's on the warpath. He's told everyone not to cooperate with you."

"That's not very nice."

"Well, he isn't, is he? What're you having?" Matt's glass was almost empty.

"I'll get them." Johnny ordered another pint plus a whisky and hot water for himself. "I feel as though I'm dying."

"There's a lot of it about."

"So where is this crime scene?"

They moved away from the counter.

"Round the corner in Ducksfoot Lane. It's a flat above the showroom of Price's Candles. No other tenants."

"Name?"

"Felshie. Francis Felshie."

Ha! Tanfield was wrong. Right end of the alphabet though.

"Can't tell you much more than that at present."

"Time of death?"

"The manager saw him go out at midday on Saturday."

"So he could have died at any time over the weekend."

"We should have narrowed it down by the end of the day."

"Who found him?"

"We did. A suspicious neighbour reported an open window. She'd seen pigeons flying in and out, clustering round something. The beat constable got the shock of his life when he kicked the door in."

"Same as the others?"

"Afraid so."

"Any tattoos?"

"None that I could see. You're not suggesting this is connected to Adler's fan club?"

"Just a thought. Which reminds me. Speaking of plain bogeys, Watkiss asked me to put in a word for him. Here's one: nitwit."

"He's all right when you get to know him."

"How can you say that? I know you were at Peel House together, but he's hardly covered himself in glory since."

"True, but you and he got off on the wrong foot."

"He was jealous."

Matt scratched the side of his head. "No, he wasn't. Anyway, we haven't spoken in ages."

"Which is presumably why he sent me as an emissary."

"Perhaps. Most likely he wants to raise his profile — and his salary. Probably wants to start a family."

"Bad timing."

"Why? He doesn't have to fear conscription."

"A bomber — like blind justice — does not discriminate."

"Don't talk to me about justice," said Matt. "Inskip is bound to want more men on this case now we've got another victim. I'll tell Watkiss to volunteer, if he hasn't done so already."

"And what am I to tell Simkins? I'd rather not get beaten up by Zick's henchmen again."

"Tell him whatever you want. We might as well play their game for now — even if we're only playing for time. Give him my word that I won't seek revenge. Necks aren't the only things that can be broken."

"Don't forget the photographs."

Matt stared into his eyes.

"How could I?" He finished the beer and wiped his mouth. "I've got to get back. Give me a two-minute start."

"OK. Thanks, Matt."

"If you see Penterell when you get there, ask him about the two tumblers we found in the flat. One of them has lipstick on it."

Before Johnny could ask any further questions, Matt was back on the street.

The bells of St Swithin's struck noon. Deep in thought, Johnny didn't notice the man at the end of the crowded bar. If he had, he'd have recognized him.

142

CHAPTER
SIXTEEN

Fog everywhere. Fog up Cannon Street, where it mixed with exhaust fumes and smoke from coal fires; fog down Cannon Street, where it merged with the black steam of trains and the belches of tug-boats. The sun was a pale disc seen through grey gauze. Johnny's eyes stung as he stood on the pavement and, befuddled, tried to get his bearings. Grim-faced workers jostled him, adding their foul fag-breath to the general fug.

On the corner of Abchurch Lane a brazier cast a rosy glow on the chestnut-seller's face. The looming copper, instead of moving him on, accepted a paper cone. The temperature was dropping, yet Johnny felt as though he were burning up. He had to get his own nuts out of the fire.

He crossed the road and entered Candlewick Ward. The location of Price's Patent Candle Company was not a coincidence. Halfway down Ducksfoot Lane, where it opened out into an unexpected crescent, there was a pillar box.

"Nasty cough, you've got there. Should get it seen to."

"What're you doing here?"

Simkins, swathed in cashmere, teal silk scarf round his neck, snorted at the stupid question.

"Same as you, of course."

"Not posting a letter then?"

"Only a lit match." He stepped closer. A cloud of sandalwood enveloped Johnny. "Come on, there's nothing to see."

"Forgive me if I don't take your word for it. I won't be long."

"As you please. You know where to find me." He stalked off into the murk.

Head down so he wouldn't be recognized, Johnny merged with the huddle of ghouls loitering outside the showroom. Its electric candles — for display purposes only — tinged the scene with sepia. The covered corpse was being loaded into a van. A horrified murmur greeted the glimpse of a bare arm as it fell off the stretcher. It had been worth the wait.

You couldn't get a quote from a corpse though. Johnny lifted his gaze. It was a four-storey building with a single entrance leading to the accommodation above the shop. The place was a fire-trap. If the killer hadn't used the front door he must have got in through the window. How though? It didn't seem possible.

The bedroom window was still open. Johnny could see a figure standing beside it: Penterell? He'd be only too pleased to keep his trap shut.

A black Wolseley, headlights raking the gloom, pulled up at the kerb. The driver nipped out smartly and opened the right-hand passenger door. Commander

144

Inskip stepped out and, smoothing down his braided uniform, studied the crowd.

"Four dead men and a gang of Jew-haters on the rampage, isn't it about time you considered your position, Commander?" Johnny emerged from the shadows. "What d'you think the Home Secretary will say?"

"Why don't you ask him?"

Inskip flashed his crocodile grin and, nodding to the PC on the door, entered the house.

The spectators, disappointed by the lack of confrontation, drifted off. Johnny, however, was satisfied. A refusal to talk, a reluctance to share information, were signs of weakness. Suddenly his appetite was back.

Lila Mae suckled greedily. Her blue eyes — her father's eyes — gazed up at her mother. Lizzie winced as an erupting tooth caught her nipple.

"Ouch! Stop that! You can't eat Mummy. Little girls shouldn't bite."

The baby's sole response was a slow blink. It was almost as if she'd done it on purpose. Lizzie scolded herself. Where had that evil thought come from? Lila might be the cause of her exhaustion and depression, but she was still an innocent.

She buttoned up her blouse and, resting Lila's head on her shoulder, gently patted her on the back. She was soon rewarded with a shockingly deep burp. Round the kitchen, through the hall, up the stairs: they wandered through the house that was as quiet as the grave.

Mist, the colour of cobwebs, drifted down Izane Road and mingled with the smoke from heaps of damp, smouldering leaves. All the new homes were occupied now. The windows were curtained; the gardens laid out and tended. Apart from delivery vans, few vehicles sped over the recently metalled surface, but — wait a minute — there was one approaching.

She lay Lila down in the cot and stroked her hair. Tummy full, she was already blissfully asleep. If only it could always be like this. Lizzie watched her daughter in rapture, once again ambushed by love.

She was brought back to earth by a knock on the door.

The Walbrook Club, in the street of the same name, was a home-from-home for former public school boys whose alma mater still loomed large in their privileged lives. Consequently the menu rarely changed and was designed to remind the diners of the meals they should have left behind. Stagnant soups, pies of dubious content, dry roasts and overcooked vegetables. The lumpy gravy covered a multitude of skins. But then that was what the City was all about: gravy, gravy, gravy!

Simkins had his nose in a glass of claret. He rolled his eyes in pleasure.

"Just what the doctor ordered. Nothing better on a day like this. You can taste the warm south."

"If you say so." Johnny, bunged up, had lost his sense of smell, but the alcohol would help him get through the day. He was running on empty.

146

"I took the liberty of ordering for us both. Asparagus soup — although it won't be fresh — steak and dumplings and apricot crumble. We both have rather a lot on our plates. Ha!"

"Thank you. The stodge will stand me in good stead." He took a sip of wine. "Why the ultimatum?"

"Zick wants an answer this afternoon. Is your pet policeman going to behave? Or is the world going to see you in a whole new light?"

There was no point in prolonging the inevitable.

"OK. You win." The painful confession made his head ache all the more. "Turner will turn a blind eye — unless another body turns up."

"I'm so pleased. That is good news! Now we can all be friends."

"Fuck off!"

"Shhh!"

Simkins glanced round the dining room. There was — praise be! — no sign of his father, the honourable member for Grafton. As someone who made it his business to épater la bourgeoisie, Simkins could be surprisingly prudish. None of the bankers raised their heads from the trough.

"What's Zick got on you?"

"You're the last person I'd tell."

"I was very nearly the last person you ever saw."

"I know. I know. How could I forget? I wouldn't have put you in such an invidious position were it not for the fact I'm in a similar one myself. Zick's made a fortune out of giving people what they want — but he's good at getting what he wants too."

"Call it leverage," said Johnny. "Applying force, exerting influence. In other words, blackmail."

Simkins winced. "*Sotto voce, per favore.*"

The first course arrived on a trolley. Condensation had already formed on the silver tureen. The Italian waiter lifted the lid with a flourish. Johnny half-expected a frog to leap out.

"One must speculate to accumulate," said Simkins. There was irony in his soul. "As far as business or affairs of the heart are concerned, there is no reward without risk." He sniffed the green liquid tentatively. "Hmmm. Scrummy!"

The soup was reassuringly hot and wet. Simkins made a show of cleaning his bowl with a hunk of bread — the only time he demonstrated his solidarity with the common man.

"Why has Zick survived so long?"

"You know why," said Simkins. "Friends in high places. You've met at least one of them."

"Inskip." Johnny sneered then — involuntarily — coughed. "He's a useless ass."

"Not to Zick he's not. He considers every penny Inskip pockets to be money well spent. All of us need a protector."

The claret was having the prescribed effect. Simkins began to sing "Someone to Watch over Me". The Gershwin brothers would not have approved. The fortunate arrival of the main course ended the performance.

Johnny was happy to let Henry rattle on as he concentrated on filling his belly.

"What you have to remember about Inskip is that he's a mere figurehead, a puppet. If he resigned or was sacked, he'd simply be replaced with someone else equally compliant. Have you ever wondered why the City has its own police force, quite separate from the Met? It sees itself as a mini-state and as such capable of passing its own laws, even if most of them don't reach the statute book. If they can't always change the laws of the land they can certainly influence the way they are enforced within the Square Mile. It's no coincidence that the Lord Mayor is the Chief Magistrate. Throughout history the privileged few have done their utmost to preserve their special status. The main role of the City force is to maintain the status quo. Anything that is bad for business — unwanted publicity, unwelcome attention — must be quashed —"

"Or, in the case of the little man, squashed." Johnny wiped his mouth with a napkin. His upper lip was beaded with sweat.

"Indeed," said Simkins, stabbing the air with his knife. "And in this case, that means you. Johnny, I'm trying to protect you. Believe me, you can't win this battle."

"We'll see."

"Yes, we will. Don't say I didn't warn you."

The pudding was an unpleasant mix of cement and slime. Johnny ate it regardless. He refused an offer of a glass of brandy — he was feeling dehydrated — but accepted a cup of coffee.

"Why are you so jumpy, Henry? I've given you what you want."

"I'm expecting a telephone call."

"From Zick?"

"How did you guess?" He ordered another brandy. "We're due to meet this afternoon — hence our lovely lunch."

"Where?"

"That's what I'm waiting to find out."

"Well, good luck." Did he mean that? No. "I wish I could keep you company, but I must get back to the office."

"I understand." Simkins winked. "One of my underlings will have filed a report on Mr Felshie's murder by now."

"I expected nothing less. Thanks for lunch — and the advice. Next time I'll bring a longer spoon."

He took a cab to Fleet Street even though it would have been almost as quick to walk. The traffic could only creep through the fog. The driver had to wake Johnny when they finally arrived at Hereflete House.

The newsroom — which felt hotter, brighter and noisier than usual — seemed to be under naval attack. Sea scouts scurried up and down the aisles selling perfumed sachets that they had made themselves. Tanfield couldn't stop sneezing.

"Bless you!" said Johnny. "Now you know how I feel."

"I'm allergic to lavender."

"Aren't we all?"

Dimeo grinned at his own wit. Johnny ignored him.

The foreign bureau that now comprised six desks instead of the traditional four — a sure sign that events abroad were finally being taken as seriously as those at home — was buzzing with the news that a German diplomat had been shot in Paris. A Jewish youth, protesting at the Gestapo's deportation of his family back to Poland, had gained access to the German embassy in the Rue de Lille and fired five bullets into the belly of one Ernst vom Rath.

Patsel, reeking of indignation, was jabbering in his native tongue into alternate telephones.

"Such a harsh language," said PDQ. "Harsh sounds for a harsh people. Still, in the circumstances, it's useful to have our own fuhrer. What's the latest?"

"The police found traces of lipstick on a glass in Felshie's flat. It's the first time they've found evidence of anyone other than the victim. It might be significant. It might not . . ."

"Do they know how the killer got in?"

"Don't think so. I'm about to call for an update."

"Let's hope they still haven't a clue. Give me a thousand words on the series of locked rooms. Hate laughs at locksmiths etc . . . Play up the deepening mystery — and the misery the boys must have endured."

"What if they turn out to be Jewish? We'll look damned silly — not to say hypocritical — if the killer's carrying out his own pogrom."

"We'll worry about that if and when it turns out to be true. I'd say it was unlikely though. Why remove evidence of circumcision if you're intent on killing Jewish men? It doesn't make sense."

"Removing the foreskin is an act of faith. Removing the whole todger removes the badge of that faith, thus making the man not only un-Jewish but unlike any male on earth. The fact the victim is alive when it happens makes the insult more grievous. Even if, by some miracle, they were to be saved, they'd have to live without a vital part of their identity."

"Why d'you think the Jews were forced to wear red hats in Venice?" Tanfield, never shy to show off, stuck his oar in. "It was an offensive symbol of what the mohel had removed."

"They made little purses out of the offcuts," said Dimeo. "If you rubbed them, they turned into sacks."

"I'll sack the lot of you if don't get back to work!"

Patsel shooed the idlers away and patted his forehead with a freshly ironed handkerchief. He turned to PDQ.

"It seems the shooting in Paris was nothing more than a sordid homosexual tiff — nothing to do with politics."

"I find that hard to believe." PDQ twirled the pencil that could usually be found behind his right ear. "A jilted lover — even if he's an invert — doesn't go to all the trouble of getting inside an embassy unless he has a point to prove. It smacks of calculation, not desperation. Still, it makes a change for German territory to be invaded, doesn't it?"

Johnny's laughter provoked another fit of coughing.

"Haven't you got enough to do?" Patsel, as usual, failed to see the funny side. "Do you want that I should send you to Wapping? A woman threw herself off Tower

152

Bridge but landed on a coal-barge. Broke her neck instead of drowning."

"That sounds like a job for Blenkinsopp."

The general reporter, who had been observing the stand-up conference from the comfort of his swivel-chair, gave Johnny the finger.

"The poor woman can't be arrested, so it's not really a crime story. Only someone with Soppy's peculiar skills will be able to bring her back to life."

Patsel couldn't tell if Johnny was joking. "Have you found out any more about the arsonists?"

"I have," said Tanfield, springing to his feet. "Mr Steadman asked me to do some digging."

"I was at the fourth murder scene," explained Johnny, before turning to Tanfield. "So what did you discover?"

"Ensom and Leask were at school together in Camden. And all three arsonists worked in Brick Lane." Tanfield was a human sunflower: his head lifted as he basked in the attention. "Ensom was a cabinet-maker at Swinchatt's, and Leask and Ormesher were machinists at Roitman's."

"So their employers were Jewish," said Patsel. "Probably underpaid them. Maybe this is also not political but personal."

"Then why not burn down their workplaces?" Johnny was not convinced.

"Too obvious," said Tanfield. "The synagogue made a better target for their hatred — and preserved their jobs."

"Excellent, Timmy. Keep up the good work." Having bestowed his approval, Patsel headed back to the foreign desk.

"Well done, *Timmy*." Johnny nodded his head in the direction of the departing news editor. "Perhaps he'll take you with him when he goes."

"Would you like that?"

"No. I like working with you — most of the time. You keep me on my toes. But it would be wrong of me to stand in your way as you climb the monkey puzzle tree."

"The Chilean pine. Latin name, *Araucaria*."

"Button it."

"In a minute. What was the dead man's name?"

"Felshie. Even you can't be right all the time."

"He was found close to a station, though, wasn't he?"

"Yes. Yes, he was."

Tanfield smiled in triumph. "Perhaps Mr D and Mr E have yet to be found."

Johnny, having spoken to Matt once again, decided to make the most of the lipstick as he reported the latest death and rehashed the details of the previous three. Was there a femme fatale haunting the streets of London? A female Ripper, seducing men only to unsex them, a walking *vagina dentata?* Probably not. However, it made good copy. As every cub learned early on: sex sold, but sex and death sold more.

He handed the pages to the runner who would wait for PDQ or Patsel to read them before taking it to the subs. His head and chest felt ready to explode. For

154

once he was looking forward to an early departure. He grabbed his hat and coat.

The telephone rang. Tanfield glanced up. "Want me to get it?"

Johnny almost said yes, but stopped himself.

"It's OK. Concentrate on finishing your story."

"I've only got two hundred words!"

"Johnny?" The Hello Girl sounded excited. "I've got the Lord Mayor's office on the line."

"Thank you. Put them through."

"Steadman? Adler here. I've received another present."

"What is it?"

"A book. *Der Giftpilz*."

"So what's that? The gift book?"

"Not at all. *The Toadstool*."

CHAPTER
SEVENTEEN

The fog, like his hopes of a hot bath and bed, had vanished. An icy wind rushed between the high buildings, trying — like a preacher in Hyde Park — to scour the filthy gutters of Fleet Street. Pedestrians, buffeted in the back, were forced to perform a quick-quick-slow as they made their way home.

The buses, nose to tail like a parade of circus elephants, were packed yet going nowhere. Johnny shivered. He pulled up his collar — it was high time he got himself a new coat — and set off walking.

Head down, he passed the entrance to Hanging Sword Alley and began to climb Ludgate Hill. The full moon, a new-minted shilling, created a crisp silhouette of St Paul's.

Seconds later Simkins emerged, sated yet frustrated, from the alley. Zick had let him take his pick. The fellow certainly had a nerve. If the location was under their nose, the name of the establishment was in their face: Cockaigne Corner.

The experience, although intensely pleasurable, underlined once again that there was something lacking in his life. Not his balls — a lover. Work no longer kept the loneliness at bay. A culture of deadlines didn't encourage you to take the long view. Should he, like many of Zick's clients, take a wife and hide his true self?

He suspected that only a woman would accept him in his current physical state. He was, even if he said it himself, handsome and well heeled. He came from a "good" family, although his mother was a lush and his father a cunt who couldn't keep his hands off other men's money or wives. They would be delighted if he were to get hitched. He could give a woman everything — except a child. Too bad; he liked children.

Johnny and he would make a good team, but that was never going to happen. Since the incident, Johnny — although he would never admit it — had become his hero. It wasn't merely gratitude for being rescued: he had come to appreciate that his rival was a force of nature. He might be socially inferior (and all too aware of it), and impulsive, but he was also intelligent, loyal and kind. And, even on the makeshift operating table, he couldn't help noticing his slim yet muscular body. The milky whiteness of his skin made his copper-coloured hair and green eyes blaze all the more.

Johnny's attraction — and attractiveness — to women presented Simkins with a challenge that he couldn't ignore. He enjoyed flirting with Johnny: his anger and embarrassment only heightened the fun. Johnny was a man of the world, usually contemptuous of conventional morality, but the one time he'd lost his temper was when he'd teased him about Turner. Clearly, there was something beyond friendship between them — but what? The thought of them in bed together was arousing, but you only had to look at Turner to see how unlikely it was to happen in real life.

Zick's cameras — hidden behind two-way mirrors — had enriched the brothel-keeper and his cronies for years. Silence was golden. Tomorrow their lenses would start to capture the action again. Different place, same practice. The suckers kept on coming. The photographs of Turner had protected Zick back in 1936 and 1937, and now those of Johnny appeared to be working their magic too.

"Appeared" because Johnny's acquiescence, albeit reluctant, had come too quickly. How had he managed to persuade Turner to come to heel? Johnny was a stubborn and resourceful so-and-so, therefore it would be no surprise if, regardless of the risk, he tried to double-cross Zick. It was Simkins's responsibility to ensure that didn't happen — no matter how much he liked him. He had no wish to be disinherited.

Zick, although pleased with the good news, shared his reservations. After the guided tour, and the free sample of the product, Cecil had cracked open a bottle of champagne.

"Fear not, dear boy. It had crossed my mind. Trust a gentleman of the press? Me? Never." He sipped The Drink That Is Never Wrong. "I've taken out extra insurance."

The bell of St Mary Woolnoth tolled seven o'clock as Johnny, sweating heavily, turned into King William Street. A newsboy, desperate to flog his last few copies of the day, struggled to make himself heard. He had to hold on to his cap in the wind. It seemed the Polish gunman was only seventeen.

Adler was alone. His suit jacket hung over the back of his chair. The flames of a generous fire were reflected in the black glass of the windows and the beeswaxed wainscoting. He stopped checking on the Old Lady and turned to face Johnny.

"You need a stiffener. Brandy do the trick?"

"Please."

"Take a look." He pointed at the desk.

The book lay in a pool of light from a single anglepoise lamp. The soupy green cover showed a red-spotted toadstool with the face of a stereotypical Jewish man staring from the stalk. There was a red ruff round his neck and a Star of David on his chest. Four other men, with equally large noses, peeped out from behind him. The author was Julius Streicher.

Adler handed him a glass. The tawny spirit was liquid fire. Johnny closed his eyes as he felt its heat spread through him.

"I can't read German."

"Let me give you a taste of the poison — that's what 'gift' means."

They sat down in the wingback chairs that flanked the hearth.

"It's a collection of short stories with titles such as 'How to Recognize a Jew', 'How Jewish Traders Cheat', 'How Two Women Were Tricked by Jewish Lawyers' and 'How Jews Torment Animals'. What makes it so sickening is it's meant for children. It's on the shelves of many school libraries in Germany. Streicher's the real poisoner — injecting young minds with such filth. He blames the Jews for everything: communism, unemployment, inflation and, of course, the killing of Christ."

"How original. Streicher owns a newspaper, doesn't he?"

"If you can call it that — *Der Stürmer. The Attacker*. It's equally anti-Semitic: *We will be slaves of the Jew. Therefore he must go*."

"The people who sent you this must want you to go."

"Go where though?"

"Anywhere but the Mansion House."

"Why don't they shoot me then? Nazis aren't squeamish."

"It's always easier to make someone walk to their execution, to dig their own grave."

"That's as maybe, but I'm going nowhere."

"Have you told the cops about the new arrival?"

"What's the point? One of their lot might have sent it."

"I doubt many of them can read German. When did it arrive?"

"I'm not sure. It wasn't delivered with the afternoon post, so it didn't pass through the mailroom. My secretary opened it. She said it had been left in reception."

"Any description of who left it?"

"The old soldier didn't see anyone. One minute the parcel wasn't there, the next it was."

"Now you see him, now you don't." Johnny consulted his notebook. "This morning you said you'd never heard of Ensom, Leask and Ormesher — they sound like a firm of solicitors — but have you been shown photographs of them?"

"Not yet. I'm due to visit Bart's tomorrow. As you can imagine, I'm rather busy this week."

"I'd have thought getting to the bottom of this would be a top priority. If these people aren't caught, who knows what they might do on Wednesday. The cops might postpone the procession if they deem public safety to be at risk."

"That won't happen." Adler stared into the flames. "It's taken me years to get where I am today. A bunch of ragtag bigots isn't going to stop me now. Cancelling the ceremony would be giving them what they want."

His confidence was impressive. Johnny caught a glimpse of the determination and ruthlessness Adler must have had to rise so high in the City. Inner resources.

"You must have made enemies on your way up. I'm told business is war by other means. There must be casualties — those who have lost money, lost control of their companies, or simply lost face. Can't you think of anyone who might resent your success?"

"Hundreds!" Adler laughed. He was actually rejoicing. "As Rochefoucauld or someone like him said: *It is not enough that I succeed. Others must fail* . . . However, the position of Lord Mayor is so powerful it's in everyone's interests to be on the same side as him. He can help his friends and frustrate his enemies. As long as the market keeps rising, nobody cares about the losers."

Johnny, for once, said nothing. There was no point in arguing about the Russian Revolution, declaring his solidarity with the workers. He was exhausted. He wanted to go home. The latest development would keep. Besides, there was something suspect about Adler's complacency.

Matt stared out of the window of the 8.20p.m. from Blackfriars. The tenements and terraces of Southwark slid past, offering fleeting images of other people's lives: a human zoetrope. What would they think if they could peep into his life?

A loving husband, a devoted father or a dedicated cop? He was all of these things — and more. Then why did he feel like a hollow man?

He no longer had a uniform to hide behind. Forced to compromise for the sake of his career, the heavy black cloth and brass buttons had become a disguise. Wearing his own clothes at work had made him take a good look at himself.

He liked what he saw, but not how he felt. He was angry with Lizzie. It was ridiculous — he knew it was — but he felt usurped by his daughter. Lizzie seemed to love her more than him and he was jealous. He was no longer the most important person in her life. He adored Lila Mae. He would do anything for her, but he adored Lizzie too. He would sacrifice his life to save either of them. He loved both of them equally. Why couldn't his wife do the same?

162

He had spent the afternoon searching the files for unsolved robberies. The killer, who seemed able to break into any premises, might be acting out of greed as well as bloodlust. It had been Johnny's suggestion. When he'd pointed out that the victims had hardly been well-to-do, Johnny had replied that not everything was about money. "Look at us: our friendship isn't about money."

The idea that it might therefore be, in some way, about sex made him squirm.

Why *were* they friends? Geography had a lot to do with it. There'd been plenty of other lads growing up in Islington though. There'd been a connection between them right from the start.

Physically they were poles apart — but opposites were supposed to attract. He'd felt sorry for the fatherless kid, but pity had no place in friendship. He'd admired Johnny's refusal to be bullied, his bravery in standing up to those who picked on him for the colour of his hair. He'd taught him how to fight and had always been aware that Johnny looked up to him. It had taken Johnny a long time to believe that Matt looked up to him too. He admired his quick wit, his honesty and sensitivity — even if he did sometimes make him feel a bit of a clod.

His search had been interrupted by the news that Ormesher had died of his injuries. Burns were hellishly difficult to treat. However, it was thought that Leask would survive.

When he'd called Johnny to tell him, Tanfield, his pushy sidekick, had picked up the phone. Johnny had just left, apparently. He promised to pass on the details then took the opportunity to ask him if he thought there was any significance in the fact that all four murders had taken place in the vicinity of a station: "Terminal territory".

His reply had not pleased the young pretender:

"Not much. The Square Mile is surrounded by stations."

Matt exited Bexleyheath station. Cauliflower clouds of steam evaporated in the frosty air. Should he go via Robin Hood Lane? A swift pint would hit the mark. Better not . . .

He could see the siren lights of the Robin Hood as he turned into Izane Road. The sight of their new home still filled him with pride. The process of buying a house — even if the bloody bank owned it — had made him feel grown up. He remained a kid at heart though.

He closed the front door, gently. Why was it so cold?

The parlour was in darkness. Only a few embers glowed in the grate. The kitchen light was on though. The wireless was off. No appetizing aromas either. Surely Lizzie, perpetually worn out, hadn't gone to bed already?

He tiptoed up the stairs and peered round the door of the nursery. Lila's cot was unoccupied. So were the other beds — and the bathroom.

The house was empty.

CHAPTER
EIGHTEEN

Tuesday, 8 November, 12.10p.m.

Ironmonger Row, between City Road and Old Street, had opened as a public washhouse in 1931 but the Turkish baths in the basement had only been open for three weeks. Everything seemed refreshingly — and reassuringly — new.

Johnny pulled back the cubicle curtain — which matched his blue chequered loincloth — and padded barefoot through the cooling-off area, where a couple of beached whales were deep in conversation, to the Tepidarium. Christ, if this was tepid, he wouldn't last long in the other rooms.

A bench wide enough to lie on ran round the gloomy, empty chamber. He sat down and immediately stood up again. The warmth, like that of a just-vacated lavatory seat, was shockingly intimate. He twisted the loincloth round so it covered his backside and sat down again.

The heat, which at first had made his skin shrink, soon began to soothe him. His hacking cough bounced off the tiled walls. They retained no impression of previous occupants. Was it their newness or non-absorbency? He usually got a sense of the history of a place, an inkling of what had happened there, an echo of the past. He had never told anyone that he believed humans left traces of themselves wherever they went, traces that the material world absorbed. As a writer he felt it was his duty to read these sermons in stones.

Some locations were more resonant than others. Smithfield screamed, St Paul's whispered (too much marble) and Hatton Garden babbled. It was the same with people. Some, like him, felt things keenly, whereas the nerve endings of others seemed to be coated in acrylic. Sometimes, he envied them.

His reverie was broken by an inrush of cooler air.

"So there you are! What're you doing in here? Nesh or something?"

Culver, stark-naked, filled the doorway.

"Follow me."

Johnny, determined to be unabashed, left behind his loincloth.

They entered the Caldarium. As an inner circle of Hell it was well populated. Culver nodded to his fellow men and strolled over to a corner. When Johnny sat down his buttocks stung.

"Nudity encourages honesty, don't you think?" Culver gazed round the room, openly sizing up the competition. "No hidden weapons. The naked truth."

"What about bare-faced liars?"

"Precisely. No one talks about bare-arsed liars."

The pipes groaned and hissed. Despite Culver's bravado, the protocol appeared to be lowered eyes and lowered voices.

"Why meet here?" Johnny was missing his notebook.

166

"Why not mix business with pleasure? You'd be surprised how much gets done here. These walls don't have ears."

"People do, though."

"Relax, Johnny. Concentrate on getting rid of your cold. I called you, remember. You won't have to sweat it out of me. What did our Jewish friend have to say when you brought up the subject of Czechoslovakia?"

"He denied all knowledge."

Culver gave an evil chuckle. "He won't be able to deny this one." He put a finger to his lips to forestall Johnny's next question.

Thwarted, Johnny asked him a different one. "Are you Jewish?"

The Shark smiled. "Been examining my assets, have you? Never judge a book by its lack of cover. It's tradition in my family, that's all. Some doctors swear by it."

"Only because they get paid for doing it."

The heat was becoming unbearable. Salt stung Johnny's eyes. His lungs seemed to have shrunk.

"It can be tough if you're not used to it," said Culver. "Come on, let's get a drink."

The lunchtime crush had arrived. Even here, class distinctions remained. Lawyers and bankers wandered round nonchalantly as though back at public school. The workers — clerks and cabbies — flaunted their nakedness as if it were an act of aggression. Only the middle class — managers and clergy — clung to their loincloths. The flimsy squares merely emphasized their vulnerability.

Several drinking fountains were available but Culver retreated to the Frigidarium where canvas chairs surrounded a cold plunge pool. An attendant, dressed in white, brought them beakers of soda water. Alcohol was not permitted. Even so, it tasted like champagne.

"All we need now are some of Tiberias's minnows to nibble our toes."

"They nibbled other bits as well."

"Indeed," said Culver. "Rather kids than piranhas."

Johnny no longer feared he would faint.

"Feeling better?"

"Yes, thanks."

"The City's beginning to panic," said Culver. "In times of crisis the price of gold soars. Bonds are all very well, but folk like to have something solid to hold on to. Gold symbolizes stability; paper fluidity. If need be, in times of chaos, governments can print as much money as they want. Look what happened in the Weimar Republic: hyperinflation soon made the mark not worth the paper it was written on. Gold is the only global currency." He checked that no one was lurking behind them. "And Adler is an expert in foreign exchange."

"He revels in the fact that everyone wants a piece of him," said Johnny. "I thought the definition of a banker was a man who wanted a piece of everyone else."

"A piece of every pie, certainly. And what's the biggest pie of all?"

"The Bank of England."

"Spot on. And there's a lot more than six million in its vaults. Imagine if it were to fall into the wrong hands. German hands . . ."

"The government must be taking precautions."

"Of course — but they don't want the public to know about them. It would seem as if they were preparing for defeat. Very bad for public morale."

"Well, we've all got gas masks now."

"The decision to distribute them might have suggested war is inevitable, but it's a sign of defiance. They're supposed to indicate we're determined to resist the Hun and prevent any invasion. Whereas shipping off our gold reserves to Canada could be seen as a tacit — and premature — admission of defeat."

"That's what they're doing?"

"Planning to. Can you imagine the risks? If a U-boat torpedoes a single ship, we'll all pay for it."

"How much are we talking about?"

Culver leaned over and put his mouth to his ear.

"Five hundred million pounds."

Lockharts was packed. The miasma of steam, sweat, cigarettes and cooked meat threatened to overpower him. He'd waited ages, even letting people go ahead, to ensure he got a table in her zone.

"Here again?"

Alex risked a look into her eyes. Black with flecks of gold. They regarded him with amusement.

"What's it today then? The usual?"

She held her pad immediately below her bosom. The thought of what lay behind the starched pinafore made him hard. He seemed to spend his whole life in perpetual hunger — for food, for sex and . . . for what exactly? Something else.

A lock of her lovely hair had escaped from her white cap. She pushed it back and grimaced as a careless customer jostled her. For a waitress she was quite impatient.

He smiled in sympathy. "I fancy . . . I fancy . . ." No, he couldn't say it. "A change. Pork and pease pudding, please."

Matt had waited up for as long as he could. He'd woken, cold and stiff, in an armchair shortly before two and then, to his dismay, crawled into the empty bed and slept like a baby.

On the way to Snow Hill he'd reasoned with himself that there'd been nothing else he could do. There was no sign of forced entry. No sign of burglary. No message on the kitchen table.

If Lizzie was trying to punish him, it was working.

He was only too pleased to let Penterell accompany Adler to the mortuary. No doubt the ambitious clown would take every opportunity to butter up the bigwig.

He wanted to stay by the telephone.

He'd called Lizzie's parents as soon as he arrived at the station but her father, in his usual tone of gentle reproach, said they hadn't seen her. He'd never approved of his daughter's choice of husband. Matt, not wishing to give him further ammunition — could he not control his wife? — had cut short the conversation. Where else could Lizzie be?

Inskip had decided to bring in a new DI to "oversee" the murder investigations. What he meant was "overhaul". Moxham clearly hadn't been up to it.

That's what happened when you promoted a man too soon. Tyser was different though — even if he was popular at the lodge.

Matt had been pleasantly surprised when Tyser congratulated him on his initiative: *Finding out how the murders are committed will bring us one step closer to finding out why they are committed.* He owed Johnny a drink.

The morning dragged on. For once the telephone, as if to mock him, remained silent.

He continued searching for similar break-ins. The only interruption came in the form of Watkiss.

"Hello, Herbie. I've been meaning to catch up with you."

"Really?"

"Yes. How are things?"

"Mustn't grumble — but I will. I'm tired of being a bogey, dealing with tosspots and tramps, nabbing petty thieves, helping confused old biddies. I need a chance to prove I can do more than that."

"Steadman said as much."

"He did?" That took the wind out of his sails. "He said he would, only I reckoned . . ."

"I know what you reckoned. Stop right there. We've got a new man in charge — Dennis Tyser. Tell him I said you may be of use."

"Thanks, Matt. You're a brick. I didn't mean anything about Steadman. Do give him my regards."

Ten minutes later Matt found it. A second-floor office had been broken into a month ago. Although it had been ransacked, the manager claimed nothing had

171

been stolen. The culprit was judged to have somehow got in through the open window.

He grinned when he read the address. The office was in Rose Alley, right behind Bishopsgate police station. If the break-in turned into a breakthrough, C Division would never live it down.

At last the telephone rang. It wasn't a female on the line though. It was Tanfield.

A corpulent man, unsexed by his sagging breasts and belly, calves bulging with varicose veins, waddled past and sploshed into the pool.

"You can use Canada to expose the Czech deal," muttered Culver, angrily wiping off the spray. "Adler's a pragmatist. There's no way he could survive the suggestion that he leaked government secrets, so he'll most likely settle for your exposure of German greed and his role in the appropriation of the gold. There'll still be one hell of a kerfuffle though, regardless of the fact that no crime has been committed. The transfer wasn't technically illegal, but it was most certainly immoral."

"Blackmail's both. Why are you telling me this? What's in it for you?" Johnny, astonished at the scale of the scoop, suspected a trap.

"Let's just say I'm no fan of Adler."

"Do you stand to make a profit if the story is published?"

"I damn well hope so. The Nazi appropriations have left me out of pocket. I want payback." He stood up,

172

forcing Johnny to do the same. He didn't want another eyeful of Culver's crown jewels.

"I've booked a massage," said Culver. They had passed the row of marble slabs on the way in to the Frigidarium.

"I'll meet you in the changing room in thirty minutes. A rubdown always gives me an appetite." He hesitated. "Why not try the steam room? It'll do you a power of good. Careful where you sit, mind. Some buggers don't care where they splash." He wasn't referring to water.

Laughing at Johnny's disgust, he sauntered off.

Surely it was too busy for that sort of thing, thought Johnny. Unless the exhibitionist had a death wish.

Three men emerged in a cloud of steam and headed for the showers. He ventured into the murk.

It was difficult to see further than his outstretched hand. The single bulb only deepened the darkness. Assuming — correctly — that the layout of the room would be the same as the others, he groped his way towards the back and, with only one slight mishap — "I do beg your pardon" — made it to the bench.

The enveloping warmth, the dimness and dampness, were soothingly womblike. Every so often the silence gave way to clanking and gurgling as more steam poured from the vent. An occasional cough told him he was not alone.

When he was sure there was no one near him he lay down on the bench and covered himself with his hands. There was no point in asking for trouble. He closed his eyes and imagined the germs flooding from his pores.

He was in a boat with Lizzie and Lila Mae. The sun was shining. Cherry blossom drifted down on to the surface of the water. Lila, making nonsense sounds, waggled her hands at the ducks.

He was rowing, smiling at Lizzie — and she was smiling back. Then he saw Matt on the riverbank.

He opened his eyes. He must have dozed off. The atmosphere in the steam room had changed. A naked man, with impressive abdominals, loomed over him.

There was a swastika on his chest.

CHAPTER
NINETEEN

The Bishopsgate lot were proud of their spanking new station house. Matt didn't think much of the Art Deco building. Travellers leaving Liverpool Street station across the road stopped to admire the gleaming limestone façade that was already streaked with soot. Its streamlined windows squinted back.

The massive grey entrance recalled that of a medieval gatehouse. Instead of a portcullis, letters spelling POLICE hung overhead. The City's banner — the same as the flag of St George except for the sword of St Paul in the upper-left quadrant — snapped in the stiff breeze. Its halyard twanged against the metal pole.

Matt turned his back on the twin blue lamps that were burning brightly and headed for New Street. He wanted to see what lay behind this bastion of dubious respectability.

The cul-de-sac ran along the south side of the block before dog-legging behind it. The Catherine Wheel, C Division's local, stood on the corner. Matt kept going. Warehouses, not content with their cargoes of furs and exotic textiles, also did their best to hoard the precious sunlight.

Rose Alley was now on his left. However, before he explored it, Matt walked through the filthy passageway that provided the only exit. It twisted between high, shuttered buildings to emerge beside a branch of Birkbeck Bank. Across Middlesex Street a line of broken men stood outside a Salvation Army shelter. Hunger made you swallow anything — even religion.

From the air Rose Alley, with its odd nooks and crannies, would have resembled a piece of a jigsaw puzzle. The police station lay at the end, its drainpipes and fire escapes forming an image worthy of Escher.

A row of garages faced a terrace of Victorian houses that had been converted into dingy offices and workshops. Most of them appeared to be occupied by drapers, clothiers and dressmakers, but the second floor of number 4, which had been broken into, was in darkness.

The windows were out of reach of conventional ladders. And how many burglars lugged ladders round with them anyway? They didn't clean windows, they broke them. There was no rear entrance: the terrace backed directly on to the buildings in New Street. The front door, according to the report, had been untouched. The intruder must have come over the roof.

He was still digesting what Tanfield had told him. The snide hound had seen Johnny and Lizzie kissing in public. He wasn't sure if he even believed him. If you couldn't trust what was in the papers, why trust those who wrote for them? It was Tanfield's job to cause mischief, make mountains out of molehills. Everything nowadays was calculated to produce a reaction.

Johnny was different though. He'd always trusted him. Had he been wrong to do so? A surge of anger coursed through him. The idea that he may have been betrayed by his best mate — his best man! — made him clench his fists. He was nobody's fool. He would find out the truth.

And where was Lizzie? He'd left strict instructions that any message from her was to be relayed directly. It wasn't like her to play games.

He couldn't reach either of them at present. A sudden feeling of loneliness, of vulnerability, swept over him.

He shook his head and, glancing up at the dirty windows of number 4, climbed the sloping steps. If there was no one in he'd talk to the neighbours instead.

There were four bells beside the door. He pressed the one marked EFF.

Lizzie was alone. She inspected the room.

A dressing-table set of pink glass sat on embroidered linen doilies. Matching candlesticks stood on either side of the mirror. The woman staring back at her had dark circles round her eyes. It wasn't make-up.

A pair of pottery rabbits on the mantelpiece, one dark purple, the other light brown — huge ears erect — listened to the silence. The grate was empty.

The scent of lavender leaked from the large satinwood wardrobe. Generic scenes of country life, genteel representations of grinding poverty — cowherds and shepherds, harvesters and ploughmen, all head down — clashed with the wallpaper on which rambling roses embraced and intertwined.

Lizzie folded back the creaking shutters and peered down into a large, well-tended garden. There was no shortage of odd-job men in London. The cityscape beyond was visible through bare branches like crooked fingers clutching at the sky.

She sat on the edge of the single bed and sighed. She had been angry with Matt for a long time but the prospect of losing him for good filled her with terror.

She should have told Johnny. Now it was too late.

Lost in thought, deep within herself, she was brought back to reality by a noise.

Footsteps were coming up the stairs. She began to cry.

The muscular youth, before he could react, grabbed him round the throat with one hand.

"On your feet, Steadman. I need a word in your shell-like."

He hauled Johnny upright. He tried to yell out but could do little more than croak.

"I'm not Steadman."

The grip tightened. He wanted to cough but couldn't. Black spots danced before his eyes. He flailed his arms. Another hand grabbed his balls. Hard.

"Don't lie to me again."

Before either of them could say another word the door to the steam room opened. His assailant flung him down on the bench and sat beside him. Two men, discussing a colleague, came in and perched opposite. Sensing tension in the air, their conversation dried up.

178

Johnny, rubbing his neck, prayed the fraught silence would not be misinterpreted.

One of the newcomers cleared his throat.

"I say, chaps. Not interrupting anything, are we? Can't see a damn thing in here. Thank God."

"Not at all, sir," said the tattooed thug. "We're just leaving."

"Not that we're running away," said Johnny. "Pity we can't stay longer." An elbow in his ribs shut him up.

One of the meaty paws seized his upper arm and escorted him out of the steam bath — but not to freedom.

"Don't say a word," muttered his captor. "I wasn't stupid enough to come here by myself."

At the end of the corridor was another room. The mosaic above the door read: RADIATUS. It was unoccupied — and no wonder.

As soon as they entered the blast furnace Johnny had to get out. The sweat that slicked their bodies immediately evaporated. The floor, too hot to stand on, forced him to hop from one foot to the other.

"Let me out of here. Please." The brute, who remained by the door, only laughed. He was wearing mules.

It was like being back in the fire at Amen Corner. This heat felt even drier though. It seared the inside of his lungs. It was already difficult to blink.

The man, who could still have been in his late teens, watched him with malign amusement. Johnny had a vision of him frying insects with a magnifying glass in the playground.

"You're only supposed to stay in here for a minute at a time. Any longer and your lips split and your skin cracks. Stay too long and you'll start sweating blood."

"What d'you want?"

Johnny's vision began to blur. It was hard to keep your balance when it was impossible to stand still.

"You've been bothering my friends. They want you to stop."

"Who?"

The brute traced the cross on his chest with a forefinger. There was something lascivious about the gesture.

"You know who."

"Ensom and Ormesher are dead. Fucking arsonists. Serves them right."

"Who's burning now?" He took a step towards him.

"I haven't spoken to Leask." His heart was bounding like a rabbit in a bag.

"And if you know what's good for you, you won't."

With the same forefinger he jabbed Johnny in the chest. That's all it took. His legs collapsed and before he knew it he was sprawling on the scalding floor. He cried out in pain. St Lawrence on the griddle popped into his brain.

The pale skin on his back and buttocks was thinner than that on the soles of his feet. He had to get up. If he stayed down here he would die.

Before he could do so a hairy foot stamped on his stomach, forcing him against the scorching tiles. Johnny screamed.

Everything went black.

180

CHAPTER
TWENTY

Matt had visited the offices of English & Scottish Co-operative Wholesale Societies, William Alma & Co. (Russian tongue importers) and Suggars & Sturrock (packing case makers). He had spoken to secretaries, clerks and counter-jumpers. No one had seen or heard anything suspicious on the night of the break-in. The only information he'd gleaned was that EFF stood for England For Fascists.

He'd heard of the British Union of Fascists, Mosley's mob — it was impossible to avoid them — but not the EFF. The splinter group was, of course, relevant to the investigation into the anti-Semitic attacks, but did it pertain in any way to the murders? Hardly. The victims — Bromet, Broster, Chittleborough and Felshie — weren't Jewish.

Tanfield's dulcet tones echoed in his ear: *All four murders have taken place in the vicinity of a station.* Aldgate, Essex Road, Fenchurch Street, Cannon Street. Liverpool Street was round the corner — but no one, as far as he knew, had been killed here. The fact that Bishopsgate fire station was also round the corner — literally — was surely of greater significance. One of its crews — or rather watches — had attended the blaze at Bevis Marks.

He needed to interview the effing geezer who represented the group. He hadn't given anything away the first time. By rights, he should have been hauled in straight after the fire. The swastika tattoos pointed to EFF's involvement. Intolerance was the badge of all their tribe.

Matt's rumbling stomach reminded him that he hadn't eaten for twenty-four hours. With a bit of luck there'd be a friendly face in the canteen — someone with whom he could chew the cud.

He headed for the grim back yard where those arrested — demonstrators, deviants, down-and-outs — were brought in by van for questioning. A uniformed PC guarded the tall black gates that were open like outstretched arms. What was he waiting for?

The answer was immediately forthcoming. A black Wolseley cruised past. He recognized the chauffeur opening the passenger door. Inskip got out.

When he spotted Matt approaching, the Commander smiled.

"Ah, Turner. This is a happy coincidence. What are you doing round here? It's not your patch."

He held up his gloved hand to forestall any reply.

"I need a word — but first I have a luncheon appointment in this splendid building. Wait for me."

Simkins refilled his fellow diner's glass.

"Thank you. I've only had the 1924 vintage once before. It's top-notch."

182

"I'm so glad you like it." Henry studied the face smiling at him. It really was quite handsome. Then youth had attractions all of its own. "It gives me pleasure to see others having pleasure."

"Selfishness and selflessness. The two rarely become one." The wineglass sang as the finger travelled round its rim. "What is it that you want exactly?"

Henry pursed his lips. "If only I knew."

The Colonial Restaurant, deep in the labyrinth between Fenchurch Street and Mincing Lane, was an ideal location for clandestine dining. Its tables were unusually wide apart. Patterned glass shielded diners from prying eyes. Deals of all kinds were conducted within its crooked walls. There were not many occasions when Simkins, a determined exhibitionist, did not wish to be seen, but this was one of them.

Tanfield took another swig of claret.

"You said that you had some information."

"Indeed. The devil of it is that I can't use it. Or rather, I can't be seen to be using it. That's where you come in."

"I'm not a puppet. If I do agree to help I'll use the dope in whatever way I think best."

"Bravo! Independence of mind is an admirable quality. However, when I spill the beans I think we'll see things the same way."

A charming blush warmed his guest's cheeks. "That's as maybe — but I'm not like you. Not at all."

"If you say so." Henry produced a tight little smile. "You might not like what you see now, but once upon a time I was ambitious too. Success often depends on doing things you'd rather not — and I'm not talking about sitting through endless speeches or standing in the rain for hours."

"I know what you mean." His proxy finished the wine and held out the glass. "This better be good."

Henry waved the waitress away. He picked up the bottle of Saint-Émilion.

"It is."

An agonizing screech went up as a dozen men pushed back their chairs and stood to attention as Inskip entered the canteen. He ignored them.

"There you are, Turner. Follow me."

Matt thanked his two messmates for their time and — feeling like the naughty schoolboy he had once been, all eyes upon him — trailed after the Commander.

They didn't speak until they reached the yard.

"May I offer you a lift?"

"No thank you, sir. I'm chasing a lead on the murders."

"So I heard. Good lunch?"

"Not especially."

"Pity. Mine was excellent."

He glanced over his shoulder. The chauffeur, some distance away, quickly snuffed out his roll-up.

"I trust you'll make the right decision, Turner. I'm counting on you. You're a good lad, just like your father."

Matt hoped not. His father was still wearing a sergeant's uniform when he retired.

"Thank you, sir."

"It's important to remember which side you're on. Who your real friends are. Check your locker when you get back to Snow Hill. You'll find something to help you pick the right team."

Inskip strolled over to the car. When the driver had closed the passenger door he wound down the window.

"Everything OK at home?"

"Yes, sir. Why shouldn't it be?"

"No reason."

Matt, with a growing sense of unease, watched the black car sweep out of the yard.

The light was dazzling. He heard a shout of surprise, a series of punches and a groan. It hadn't come from him.

Johnny groped blindly for the wall. He scrabbled around, trying to get to his feet, but his legs wouldn't work. He hadn't known such pain existed. He was a rapidly melting human candle. He didn't know whether he was going to be sick or soil himself.

Before he could do either he was picked up and slung over someone's shoulder. He was in a fireman's lift.

If the corridor felt shockingly cold, the plunge pool stopped his heart. Hydrocution. Blackout — again.

The person who had thrown Johnny in the water jumped in after him and, to a round of ironic applause, fished him out. He laid him on the floor and slapped his face. Twice.

Johnny's eyelids fluttered. A fit of coughing and spluttering ensued. His rescuer rolled him over and patted him roughly on the back.

"That fucking hurts. Stop it!"

He turned to see who had saved his life.

PART THREE

Robin Hood Yard

CHAPTER
TWENTY-ONE

A freak hailstorm had struck Tunbridge Wells. Witnesses claimed the town looked as if it had been covered in rice pudding. Matt shuddered and flicked through the pages of the *Evening News* for a third time. His fingers were smudged with ink. It wasn't his prints he was after.

He was in a pie and mash shop in Finsbury Market where Steven Hext was said to run a fruit-and-veg stall. The lunch-time rush was over; trade was slackening off.

None of the stallholders matched the description provided by the Bishopsgate boys. The Prince of Wales, on the corner of Vandy Street, had closed for the afternoon so he'd had to seek shelter elsewhere.

He wiped the condensation off the window in time to see a stocky young man take a pinstriped apron from the greengrocer. He was still tying its strings round his waist when Matt appeared in front of him.

"What can I do you for, guv? Sprouts is on sale."

"Cut the Cockney act, Mr Hext. You're from Burnley."

"How d'you know that?" His eyes, too small for his moonface, narrowed. There was alcohol on his breath.

"Where've you been?"

"What's it to you?"

"I'm a detective."

"Pardon me if I don't kiss your ring. What d'you want?"

"Information. That's all. I believe you're Secretary of an organization called England For Fascists."

"So what? It ain't banned."

"Not yet. You had a break-in last month. Is that correct?"

"A fuss about nothing. They didn't get away with anything."

"They?"

"Rats are rarely alone."

"You think the damage was done by some of your members?"

"Dunno. Mebbe."

"Why? They wouldn't need to break into the office, would they? They could stroll straight in — unless they wanted something they weren't supposed to have." He leaned across the crates of produce. "What was it?"

Before the barrowboy could think of a reply, an old woman, grey hair still in curlers beneath her headscarf, butted in.

"How much are them bananas? Ain't got me specs."

"'Ello, darlin'. For you, threepence each or five for a shilling."

"Give us five." She rummaged in her purse. "Fuck it — I'm a penny short."

Matt expected the street trader to wave her away with an air of munificence but he snatched up the brown paper bag and proceeded to snap a finger off the hand.

"You can have four, not five. You're still saving a penny."

"Don't be like that. The nippers are coming to see me after school. All five of them. What are you? A bleeding Yiddisher?"

Hext flushed. "You cow. You want a bunch of five, I'll give you one!"

"That won't be necessary." Matt fished out the change in his pocket and handed over a penny. "Give the lady her fruit."

"Thank you. Thanks ever so much." The granny, baring gappy teeth in gratitude, patted his arm and, with a scowl at Hext, dropped the bag in her reticule and toddled off.

"You mug," said the wide boy. "She tries it on every time."

"Learned it from you, did she? Look, if you won't come clean about the break-in I'll have no choice but to take you in for questioning. Have we got your prints on file? I'm after a killer. I'm not interested in sad little men like you."

"Which station? Upper Street?"

"What's it matter? Snow Hill."

"This ain't the City. You can't arrest me. We're in Islington."

Matt had had enough. Lizzie was missing — something that his best friend might be able to cast light on — and, to cap it all, he was being told to turn a blind eye to corruption. He hated what he'd become: complacent, suspicious, craven. Someone had to pay.

He grabbed the fascist round the throat. He could feel the man's Adam's apple in the palm of his hand.

"I can do whatever I want." If only that were true. He didn't care who was watching. "Tell me what was taken or it won't be only your fruit that gets bruised."

Hot tears leaked from the stallholder's eyes. He closed them slowly to signal his agreement. Matt relinquished his grip.

"No need for that." Hext spat viciously, as though the pavement were the copper's face. "Bishopsgate told me to keep it dark. I don't know you. I didn't know what to do."

"Well, you do now. Tell me."

The fascist, biting his cheek, checked no one was within earshot.

"They took our list of members."

Rick Hollom waited for him to stop coughing.

"You put me in mind of a king-size prawn — in ginger sauce." He threw a towel at him. "Cover yourself up."

"And you," said Johnny. Stretched out as if he were a fish on a slab, he was at enough of a disadvantage. The Italian was hung like a donkey. "Where's Culver?"

"Your friend? Let's say he had to leave. Here."

Johnny took the proffered hand and was pulled to his feet with embarrassing ease.

"Thank you — and thanks for intervening. I presume your being here is not a coincidence."

192

"Correct. Sit yourself down. I'll be back in a minute."

He was only too glad to do so. His body was shivering outside and quivering inside. He lowered himself into one of the canvas chairs. The attendant brought him two more towels and made him drink a whole jug of water. His skin was singing the "Hallelujah Chorus", tingling as though he'd been struck by lightning. It must be the shock.

The next thing he knew, Hollom was shaking his shoulder. For a moment he hadn't a clue where he was. The smell of chlorine acted like a madeleine, but it instantly transported him back to the present instead of the past.

Hollom had got dressed.

"You've no idea how much trouble you're in," he said.

The ground shook as trains thundered in and out of Broad Street station overhead. Matt was angry. He'd been given the runaround at Bishopsgate — and he was pretty sure he wasn't the only one being kept in the dark. He was on his way back there now.

He re-emerged into daylight on Pindar Street and immediately turned right down Sun Street Passage that squeezed between Broad Street and Liverpool Street stations. The cut-through was so long and narrow the air seemed to thicken as the brick precipices threatened to meet far above him. The sky had shrunk to little more than a silver thread.

He was breathing heavily when he reached the police box on the corner of New Broad Street.

The operator connected him to Snow Hill. Tyser was conducting an interview and only to be disturbed in the event of an emergency. However, there was a message for him. There had been an incident at the wash-house in Ironmonger Row. A man from the *Daily News* had been attacked.

So that's where Johnny was hiding.

The Turkish Baths would soon be closing. Only women were admitted between 3 and 6p.m. on Tuesday.

"Get your clothes on," said Hollom. "You're coming with me."

"No I'm not," said Johnny. He had no intention of jumping out of the fire into a frying pan. "Where's the gorilla who attacked me?"

"Don't worry about him. He's with me."

"Ah . . ."

He should have guessed. He'd not been thinking straight. The Good Samaritan was actually a bad penny.

"So what are you going to do with me? Why intervene if he was doing your dirty work for you?"

"He was supposed to scare you, not scald you."

"What's stopping me making a scene? Demanding that I be let out of here?"

"Go ahead. See how far you get. What d'you think would happen to a semi-naked man running and screaming down the street? You'd be arrested within minutes."

Hollom had a point. He was trapped.

194

★ ★ ★

Matt got off the tram outside Moorfields Hospital. In Lever Street he spotted Johnny getting into the passenger seat of a black Austin Seven. He didn't recognize the other man.

He opened his mouth to call out Johnny's name but quickly thought better of it. He didn't seem to be injured or under duress. Where were the cops? He kept walking.

The car drove off towards Clerkenwell — but not before he'd noted down the registration number.

CHAPTER
TWENTY-TWO

Hollom turned left into Goswell Road and headed south.

"Where are you taking me?" said Johnny.

"That depends on you."

He put his foot down to beat the new traffic lights at the junction with Old Street. A chance to leap out of the car vanished.

"It's very good of you to give me a lift," said Johnny. "Anywhere in Fleet Street will be fine."

"That's the problem. I need to know what you're going to write — if you get there."

"Wait and see."

"No time," said Hollom. "No need. Refuse to cooperate and I'll arrest you."

"You're a cop? Why didn't you say so?"

Hollom checked the rear-view mirror.

"The fewer people who know, the better. I tried to put you off the scent but you're a persistent blighter. I'm undercover. It's taken weeks for me to infiltrate the organization, to gain the trust of its leaders, now you come along and threaten to sink the whole operation. I can't — I won't — let that happen. There's a lot more at stake than the death of a snitch."

"So, one way or another, you're going to shut me up."

"You can count on it. My superiors need to know if they can count on you."

"Care to name names?"

The Italian, although half English, still believed in some form of omertà.

"No. Though you'd certainly recognize them if I did."

Johnny stared out of the window, not at the fleeting slide show that London always provided but into the uncertain future. He was on to something big here, a story of national importance, every instinct told him so. Whenever the powers-that-be told him to keep silent, he felt an urge to shout from the rooftops. On the other hand, he couldn't ignore his instinct for survival. What could he do if he were banged up? Nothing. He had been locked up before and he didn't like it. The mere thought of being immured in a police cell was enough to trigger his latent claustrophobia, which seemed to be getting worse as he got older.

The Austin swept round West Smithfield. Hollom parked outside Bart's.

"Decided which side you're on?" He pulled out a pack of Three Nuns and offered Johnny one.

"Thanks."

The nicotine worked its magic. Johnny felt calmer; his mind clearer.

"You can't win," said Hollom. "Either I drop you here so you can get something for your skin — you do want to save your hide, don't you? — or I take you round the corner to Snow Hill. And DC Turner won't be able to help you."

Johnny failed to mask his surprise.

"Yes, we know about your friendship. We know everything there is to know about you and him."

Johnny doubted that very much.

"He's showing real promise, apparently," said Hollom, following the progress of two nurses. They had to hold on to their caps in the wind. "You wouldn't want to do anything that might jeopardize his chances, would you?"

"No, I wouldn't."

"So if you don't care about yourself, consider what might happen to him."

"Can't you give me a clue what's at stake? Quirk was murdered. We all know that. Doesn't his death mean anything?"

"That's not the point. Even if I were to tell you who was responsible, you couldn't do or say anything about it. Silence really is the best option."

Johnny said nothing.

As soon as he got back to the station house Matt climbed the narrow staircase to the third floor. There was no one in the Detective Squad's locker-room.

His door had not been jemmied. He got out the key.

There was a white envelope on the top shelf. Someone evidently had a skeleton key. There was a lot of cash. Twenty crisp pound notes. Hush money. A typed note read: *Think of your wife and kid.*

198

His first thought was to tear up the note and flush it down the lavatory — but it was evidence of something.

He slipped the note into his jacket's inside pocket, stuffed the bribe into one of the boxing gloves that dangled from a peg, and relocked the door. It was unbearably hot in the locker-room. He couldn't breathe. He needed to get out.

He went up to the roof where a small terrace afforded panoramic views of the City. Bart's, St Paul's, the Old Bailey — where, so many times, he had sworn to tell the truth, the whole truth and nothing but the truth.

Twenty pounds? Was that all his soul was worth? He was sure the pay-offs would keep on coming as long as Zick was allowed to remain in business, but the first kickback was the one that counted. Once he accepted it, there would be no turning back.

It was against everything he stood for: he was supposed to fight corruption, not share in it. He would be damned if he did take it — but he would also be damned if he didn't.

Was it coincidence that he had received the note a day after Lizzie and Lila's disappearance or was history repeating itself? Had Zick (with Inskip's blessing) abducted his wife again? He'd rather she'd fled into Johnny's arms!

Zick was ruthless, not witless. Lizzie and Lila might be hostages but harming them would produce the exact opposite of what he wanted — Matt's silence. The detective gripped the rusty railing with both hands and tried to calm down. He needed to talk to Johnny.

There was a driving range on top of an office block in Giltspur Street. A lone golfer, practising his swing, sent ball after ball into the nets. It was all a game. Targets and goals were either hit or missed. When it came down to it, life was all about getting into and out of holes.

The fire-exit door banged shut.

"Don't jump! Don't jump!" Tyser joined him. He took a moment to admire the view. "I jest. At least, I think I do. What're you doing up here?"

"Considering my options. How did you know I was here?"

"Not much gets past me. You know what this place is like."

"Gossip Central."

"Indeed. But where would we be without it?" Twin streams of cigarette smoke shot from his nose. "What did you find at Bishopsgate?"

"A cover-up."

"Excellent! We must be getting somewhere."

"The break-in was at the office of the EFF. Their membership list was stolen. Someone in C Division told the Secretary, one Steven Hext, to keep quite about the theft."

"We need to find out if Bromet, Broster, Chittleborough and Felshie were on it. Leask is refusing to talk — and there's not much we can do about that while he's still in Bart's — but it's as sure as eggs are eggs that he and his tattooed dead comrades are on it."

"So someone is going round fixing fascists. Why should we give a toss?"

200

"We don't yet know if that is the motive," said Tyser. "But if we find whoever took the list, we'll be able to ask them."

"Why doesn't C Division want us to do that?"

"Good question. It's no secret that some cops, craving order, lean too far to the right. Such sympathies may be clouding their judgment."

"What are we going to do then?"

"Ask them, of course." He flicked his fag end towards St Sepulchre's. "Well, don't just stand there. Let's make some calls."

Matt hesitated. The golfer was still teeing off. The glove money could stay where it was.

It was after three when Johnny, covered in zinc oxide, arrived back at his desk. The doctor had assured him there would be no permanent damage. He'd assured the doctor that the *Daily News* would cover the bill.

Tanfield, receiver to his ear, was scribbling on a yellow notepad. "That's smashing. Thank you. Tinkerty-tonk."

He watched Johnny sit down gingerly.

"Good lunch?"

"I haven't eaten." He hadn't realized till that moment. "Been too busy. Got a lead on your ABC murders."

"Bravo!" Tanfield's expression suggested disappointment rather than delight. "Do tell."

"All in good time, Timmy. I need a word with PDQ or Patsel. They'd be put out if I discussed tactics with you first. Understandably."

"Fourteen letters," said Tanfield.

He was on his way back from the canteen when PDQ intercepted him.

"What have you done now? Captain Vic wants to see you."

They took the lift to the seventh floor. The red light was on, but the door to Stone's office was open. Patsel, gesticulating wildly, was arguing with the editor.

"He's refusing to accept that Vom Rath may have been Grynszpan's lover," whispered PDQ.

"*Naturlich*," said Johnny. "Everyone knows there are no homosexual Germans."

Patsel swivelled on his heels. His eyes glittered behind their twin portholes.

"Steadman! Whitehall is furious. You pose a threat to national security. You!"

"I thought you'd be pleased."

PDQ placed a warning hand on Johnny's forearm. "That's why we're here, Gustav."

Stone, behind his desk and behind the news editor's back, rolled his eyes. "Enough already! Let's thrash this out in a civilized manner." He pointed to the pair of chesterfields either side of the hearth.

The three subordinates sat on the sofas. Stone stood with his back to the fire.

"You'll get a headache," said Johnny. "My mother always said —"

"We don't care what your mother —"

"Shut up, Patsel." Stone looked at Johnny. "I've already got a headache." He removed his spectacles and

202

rubbed the bridge of his nose. "I gather you got into hot water."

"Cold, actually. I was meeting a source at the Turkish Baths in Ironmonger Row. A member of the EFF attacked me. He was supposed to warn me off but went too far — I could have died if Hollom hadn't intervened."

"Great stuff!" said PDQ.

"Indeed," said Stone. "Pity our intrepid reporter agreed to keep schtum — just as the government wishes."

"You yellow dog," said Patsel.

"I'm not the one hiding from a fight," said Johnny. "It was made abundantly clear that I could either cooperate or be arrested."

"So? Mr Tanfield would have been only too happy to make the most of your incarceration."

"Too right," said Johnny. "Except I wouldn't be able to follow up *my* story if I were in gaol — and believe me I still have a great story to tell."

"Go on," said Stone. "We're all ears."

Johnny picked up the plate he had taken from the canteen.

"May I? It's my first food of the day."

"If you must," said Stone, trying not to smile as Patsel turned puce.

Johnny took a bite of the sandwich and gave every impression of chewing over what he had to say. In fact he'd already prepared his script.

"Spit it out!" PDQ had an admirable poker face.

"Hollom's name was given to me by Quirk, who was subsequently murdered. He must have known something that the EFF did not want made public. Three of its members were probably responsible for the arson attack on Bevis Marks. Hollom is a government agent working undercover. Why would the government wish to protect a bunch of ragtag fascists? It doesn't make sense."

"No, it does not," said Patsel.

"It would make sense if they were after a multiple murderer, though, wouldn't it? Someone is killing Englishmen in their beds. If that someone were German, imagine the upsurge in anti-Nazi sentiment. The hackles of the Great British bulldog would rise. The prospects for peace are dwindling fast, but they would disappear altogether if news of the killer leaked out."

"We don't know that the victims were Jewish," said Stone. "The killer's made sure of that."

"It doesn't matter," said Johnny. "The fact is, they're dead. They could have been converts to Judaism and thus, in the eyes of some, traitors. They could have been converts to Christianity and thus, in the eyes of others, traitors."

"Or they might simply have been fascists," said PDQ. "Or members of the EFF who quit when they saw the direction the organization was taking."

"Yes and yes again," said Johnny. "The point is if we link my attack to my investigation into their murders — making no mention of the EFF or Hollom — we've still got a story."

204

"So the government will have nothing to complain about," said PDQ.

"And if they do, they can always arrest me and Tanfield can pursue the story."

Stone listened to his newsmen discussing the pros and cons of the ploy. He rocked back and forth on his heels — a sure sign the cogs were whirring. Was he convinced?

Johnny wolfed down the remainder of his sandwich.

The editor came to a conclusion.

"It's risky but it might work, Steadman. It would certainly buy you time to investigate further. And I've no doubt it would make gripping reading. Another exclusive. First, though, I need to make a couple of calls. Thank you, gentlemen. I'll let you know forthwith."

Johnny and PDQ, mindful of the liftboy, continued the conversation. Patsel maintained a prickly silence.

Johnny, now burning inside as well as out, this time with excitement, returned to his desk with a spring in his step. At least the ordeal had killed his cold.

Tanfield, twirling a pencil in his fingers, seemed to share his excitement.

"DC Turner is here to see you," he announced.

CHAPTER
TWENTY-THREE

Hext stopped and made a show of gazing in the window of a bookshop in Abchurch Lane. *Recollections from My Business Life* by S. Japhet, *Issuing House Yearbook and Financial A.B.C.*, *The Drama of Money Making* by Hubert A. Meredith: none of the titles on display appealed to him. His interests lay elsewhere.

He studied the view reflected in the plate glass. It wasn't easy in the twilight — especially when passers-by kept jostling him on the narrow pavement. He didn't like being touched.

He wasn't being followed. He was sure of it. The Snow Hill cop had rattled him though. Where'd he got his information from? Hollom? It wouldn't surprise him. That damned wop was forever asking questions.

A maid had lit the fire an hour ago. Lizzie watched shadow-flames flicker on the ceiling.

She was standing by the window. A single star glittered in the darkening blueness. The wind had dropped. It would be a frosty night.

A dozy winter fly blundered into a web that filled one of the small square panes. A spider, half the size of the insect, shot out from a corner, bit it, and — legs splayed like a pianist's fingers — proceeded to enshroud its victim in gossamer. Then, to her amazed disgust, the spider hauled its prey up, across the web, and out of sight. Such strength seemed impossible in one so miniscule. Hunger, though, was a powerful emotion.

Lila began to cry. It was time for another feed. Lizzie braced herself.

She wanted to go home. See that Matt was all right. She replaced the photograph in the brown envelope. It had been intended to persuade her to do as they asked. Prove to her that he was at their mercy. They didn't know she had seen it before.

Captain Vic, page proofs spread out before him, was thinking of something else entirely.

All the phones on his desk were trilling: a mad dusk chorus. Someone rapped on the door.

"What now? I said I wasn't to be disturbed."

A tremulous secretary — not his usual one who had bronchitis — ventured into the lion's den. "Lord Vivis wishes to speak with you, sir."

"Ah. Thank you, er . . ."

"Gracie, sir. My —"

"Thank you, Gracie. That will be all."

She closed the door behind her — not as quietly as she might have done. What was the bloody point in having four phones if you didn't answer any of them?

Stone braced himself. He hadn't expected the call to come so soon.

"Charles. How are you? I thought you were off hunting in the wilds of Canada. Not that there's much else there."

As proprietors went, LV was one of the more humane. He rarely concerned himself with the day-to-day running of individual papers, no matter which country they were published in. He preferred firing guns to staff. As long as the *Daily News* purveyed his views, and continued to print money, he was generally happy — which meant the call was serious.

"I was — I am — but you know I can't brook much beaver."

"Indeed." Max Aitken's appetite for appeasement made Charles Stogdale's blood boil. The barons were arch-rivals — something that Stone was hoping to play on.

"I'm told one of our reporters has blundered into a major undercover operation."

"It wasn't a mistake. He's investigating a series of murders. Possibly anti-Semitic murders."

"Excellent. Why does the government want him stopped then?"

"The EFF is involved."

"Really? Well, the fascists do have friends in Downing Street . . ."

The line crackled. Stone calculated it was about 11a.m. in Winnipeg.

"How can we get round this blatant act of censorship? I can't have the *News* shut down."

"Steadman — remember him? — has come up with a ploy to expose the culprits without jeopardizing the

208

operation. If he's arrested — which may well happen — it would still make great copy. We can portray his efforts as a patriotic attempt to preserve British decency in the face of lily-livered vested interests. Fascists don't like British blood being shed to protect the lives of foreigners."

The line crackled again. Was LV still there?

"It could put Beaverbrook, and Mosley's Biff Boys, on the back foot."

"Precisely."

"Do I need to know the details?"

"I see no reason why you should be troubled with them at this stage, sir."

"Good man. What's the latest advice? Keep acting like a clam and carry on. I'll do that."

The connection was broken. The editor grabbed one of the other phones.

"Mr Stone's office."

"Gracie. Mine is the only voice you'll hear on this line."

"Sorry, sir."

"Inform the news desk that Steadman may light the touchpaper."

He knew immediately that something was up. Matt stood in the foyer: a still, silent pillar in a swirling sea of small fry. He seemed oblivious to the glances of envy and admiration.

"What's happened?"

"Not here." Then, noting Johnny's hesitation, he added: "Don't worry. This won't take long. You won't miss your deadline."

He headed for the swing doors. Johnny had no choice but to follow.

Matt ignored the warm glow emanating from the Tipperary, where most newsmen drank and fought.

"Are we going to the King and Keys?"

"Wait and see."

Johnny stopped. Had Matt sensed his guilty conscience? "Matt, what's wrong?"

"Nothing, I hope." He turned to face Johnny. Commuters, anxious to get home, eddied round them. "Come on. I need a word, that's all."

Seconds later Matt disappeared down Hind Court, one of several alleyways leading to Gough Square. At the darkest point he stopped.

"There's every chance I'm being followed."

"Why?"

"Inskip doesn't trust me — although he now thinks I'm one of the gang."

He wasn't going to let on about the bribe. "Someone broke into the office of the EFF last month and stole the membership roll."

"I know who did it. Rick Hollom."

"The guy whose car you got into this afternoon?"

"How the hell d'you know that?"

"I was in Ironmonger Row."

"You were following me?"

"No. Don't blow a gasket. I heard you'd been attacked."

Johnny should have known better. Matt was always there for him when it counted.

"How?"

"An anonymous call."

Culver? Johnny had several questions for him.

"You traced Hollom's number plate?" Matt nodded. "So you know he's one of yours."

"Indeed. Interesting, don't you think?"

"He warned me off. Told me there's a lot more at stake than finding Quirk's killer. He threatened to arrest me if I didn't keep quiet."

"And are you going to keep quiet?"

"What d'you think?"

They laughed. Whatever tension there had been between them vanished.

Matt scratched the side of his head. "Someone at C Division wanted the break-in kept quiet too."

"Where's the office?"

"Rose Alley."

"In Bishopsgate? That's behind the police station."

Matt smiled. He'd known it wouldn't take long for Johnny to make the connection. "Quite a coincidence, isn't it?"

"It's only a coincidence when you've missed something."

"So what have we missed?"

"I don't know. Hollom must have staged the break-in to prevent suspicion falling on him. It would have been easy enough for him to get hold of a key."

"It was the locked-room aspect of the theft that drew my attention in the first place. Why didn't he get someone in C Division to confiscate the list?"

"He's undercover. They don't know about him."

"So why are they keen to keep the break-in quiet?"

Someone entered the alley. They waited in silence for the man to pass. As he brushed by he gave them an odd look. Their eyes met. His footsteps faded into the general hum of the City.

"Perhaps he thought we were canoodling."

"Hardly."

Matt stepped even closer. There was beer on his breath. Johnny's lips began to tingle as much as his singed skin.

It was the perfect moment for Matt to bestow a Glasgow kiss on his unfaithful friend. But had he been unfaithful? And even if he had, Johnny reassured himself there was no way Matt could know.

"What were you doing with Lizzie last Tuesday?"

Johnny couldn't have been more shocked if Matt had hit him. He stood back instinctively. A wordless admission of guilt.

"She told you, then?"

"No. Tanfield saw you."

"Saw what? Nothing happened."

"He saw you walking down Fleet Street arm-in-arm."

Relief flooded through him though he tried not to show it.

"There's nothing unusual in that. We do that in your company sometimes."

"Then why'd you look like a naughty schoolboy when I asked you?"

"Lizzie asked me not to mention our meeting. She turned up on the doorstep — same way you did. What's

212

the matter? You know neither of us would ever do anything to hurt you. We love you."

The four-letter word made Matt wince. He often used the word in his head but rarely enunciated it. The term was a sign of weakness.

"Why did she come to see you?"

"She's afraid you're seeing someone else."

Matt, as if he'd been holding his breath, gave a huge sigh of relief. His suspicions were unfounded. He pulled Johnny to him.

"So where is she?" Matt, whispering the words in his ear, held him tight.

It hurt. Johnny wriggled out of the embrace. "She's not at home?"

"No. The house was empty when I got back last night. There's not been a peep out of her since."

"And Lila Mae?"

"I presume she's taken her with her."

"Of course she has. Why wouldn't she? It's a good sign. If she'd been abducted, Lila Mae would have been left behind. There's no more telltale sound than a crying baby."

"I suppose so. I can't see Zick changing nappies. A little stranger would be bad for business."

"We've given our word — why would he spoil things now?"

"He has every reason to distrust us."

Fleet Street, at the end of the alley, was a vivid, moving picture postcard. It might as well have been on the other side of a looking glass. Most folk simply wanted to get on with their lives, uninterrupted and untouched by world affairs. Why couldn't he and Matt be more like them?

Johnny lit a cigarette and made no comment when Matt took one too.

"Have you called her parents?"

"Of course. Her father said he hadn't seen her or Lila . . . Why did she think I was being unfaithful?"

"I don't know. She's really down in the dumps though. Sitting at home all day, she's plenty of time to brood. You're working all hours while she misses going out to work."

"She's got Lila to look after."

"And you as well! But it's not enough. You know how she is. She's a woman of ambition."

"I'm working to give them what they want. That's why I do so much overtime. She thinks I'm neglecting her, does she? I wouldn't mind, but I'd be more than happy to laze around at home all day."

"You know that's not the case. We both want to get on, make a name for ourselves. There's more to life than getting and spending."

"Who said that? Coleridge?"

"Wordsworth: 'The World Is Too Much with Us'. Told you some of my reading would eventually rub off on you."

Matt smiled, unconvinced. "We need to read the names on Hollom's list. Ensom, Leask and Ormesher are bound to be on it, but we don't know if any of the murder victims are."

"Well, Hollom won't tell us. Surely the EFF must have kept a copy?"

214

"That's what I intend to find out. I'm going back to Bishopsgate now."

"And Lizzie?"

"Perhaps she's been in Blackheath all along. Nursing her resentment as well as Lila. I wouldn't put it past her father to lie to me. There's no doubt which side he'd be on if Lizzie was involved in a domestic dispute."

"Why would he lie though?"

"Probably doesn't want me breaking the door down if she is hiding there."

"Well, keep me posted."

"Likewise. And if you do hear from her, call Snow Hill straightaway."

"I will."

They embraced in the dark. This time Johnny put up with the pain. Matt wasn't usually given to such demonstrativeness. He must be overwrought.

"Sorry for doubting you." Matt ruffled his hair.

"Think no more about it. I'd have thought the same in your place."

They re-emerged into Fleet Street. Matt went one way, Johnny the other.

He almost ran back to the office. He wanted to know what Tanfield had to say for himself.

CHAPTER
TWENTY-FOUR

Hext was lurking in the foyer. He walked straight past him, nodded to the commissionaire, and entered the icy night. A moment later, Hext followed.

They didn't speak until he turned into Sherbourne Lane. He often called into St Mary's — for some reason the church reminded him of Amsterdam. It was an oasis of calm amid the hurly-burly of business. He liked to lose himself in the sublime complexity of Grinling Gibbons's golden altar screen. He left the praying to others. There was a lot of guilt in the City.

The younger man could hardly contain himself.

"A pig came sniffing round today. You promised there'd be no comeback."

"Nothing to do with me."

"But it is though, isn't it? Two dead men and a human torch in constant pain."

"I believe you hand-picked them. I trust their successors will be more careful."

"You want to go ahead then?"

"Of course — and if I ever see your face again, you'll be more than sorry. You were under strict orders never to approach me. Why didn't you telephone?"

"A little bird told me it wasn't safe."

"Well, dear boy, you're not safe here on the street either."

"Are you threatening me?" Hext squared up to the larger man and immediately crumpled as a gloved fist struck his stomach.

"Yes, I am. You were paid to do a job — paid handsomely, if you don't mind my saying so — and I expect you to carry it out to the letter."

"You don't scare me." The bullyboy, clutching his midriff, stepped back. "You forget we know where you live."

His employer smiled. Ignorance and violence were so often to be found in the same tiny mind.

"Let me tell you something. In the fourteenth century this quiet street was known as Shiteburne Lane. I believe you knew an unfortunate gentleman called Quirk. His conscience got the better of him. Before you do anything foolish, consider what happened to him."

Johnny was breathing heavily when he got back to his desk. He'd been so het up he'd ignored the lifts and taken the stairs at a lick. He regretted it now. The soothing ointment had glued his shirt to his back. This had done nothing to cool his temper.

"What's PC Watkiss's first name?"

Tanfield's question was so unexpected it stopped Johnny launching into his planned tirade. "Why?"

"It's not Albert or Alfred or Algernon, by any chance? Do say yes."

"He's a Herbert."

"Pity — A. Watkiss is an anagram of *swastika*. Has he got any tattoos?"

"I haven't the faintest." He hung his jacket on the back of his chair. "Not got anything better to do than play around with letters?"

The former public school boy pouted. "Thought you liked word games."

"I do . . ." Johnny was scribbling on a pad. "Oh, look! What a coincidence! T. Tanfield makes *defiant Lt*."

"You don't believe in coincidences."

Johnny smiled in victory. "I don't. Been speaking to Watkiss, have you? Not the only cop you've been blabbing to, is he?"

Tanfield reddened. "I thought he had a right to know."

"Know what?"

"That you're stepping out with his wife."

"You buffoon! We were only arm-in-arm. That's not adultery."

"Just good friends? Don't pull an act. I know what I saw."

"Nothing. That's what you saw." Johnny wiped his forehead. "Next time, remember there are no secrets between Turner and me."

"If you say so."

"I do. Watkiss say anything of interest?"

"He likes you. Said he was mistaken about you."

"Good to hear. It's so easy to form the wrong impression." He sat down. His anger had evaporated as quickly as it had flared up. "Anything else?"

218

"Chittleborough was poisoned. Broster too. Bromet's been buried though."

"That was quick. His murderer's still at large."

"The cops don't see any need to exhume him at present. He clearly died at the hands of the same killer."

"Saving the pennies again." Johnny scratched the side of his head. *"I'm half-inclined to believe there's some rational explanation to all this . . ."*

"Who said that?"

"I can't remember. Someone in *The Lady Vanishes.*"

"Oh really?" Tanfield twirled his pencil. "Isn't that movie set on a train?"

There she was: collar up, hat pulled down against the cold. Even so you could tell there was firm, lithe flesh beneath the tweed. He imagined putting his arm round the cinched waist; undoing the buttons, one by one.

He knew it was wrong to follow a woman — but he wasn't sick in the head. There was no use in making a fool of himself, risking rejection — public humiliation — if she already had a sweetheart. And why would a dish like her be alone? She didn't wear a wedding ring though . . . It would be typical of him to fall for someone else's fiancée.

Row by row, the lights in the café went out. The manager — who was by no means immune to her charms himself; he'd seen him watching her — locked the door behind him. They said goodnight and went in opposite directions. He towards Aldgate; she towards Gracechurch Street.

Alex crushed the dog-end beneath his foot and left his vantage point in the darkened doorway of the Trujillo Railway (Peru) Company.

She walked fast for a woman. Perhaps she had a date this evening . . . The besotted typist followed, determined not to lose sight of her as she forced her way against the tide of grey-faced office workers heading towards the station.

At the end of Fenchurch Street she stopped and glanced back. He dodged behind a police box. Surely he hadn't been spotted?

The ruins of All Hallows sparkled in the moonlight. Wren's church — deemed, like so many others, redundant — was being demolished to make way for the new headquarters of a clearing bank. Another triumph of Mammon.

She crossed the road and entered Lombard Street. Moneylenders poured out of the terraced temples. There was nothing like cooking the books to give one an appetite.

Past Clement's Lane, Birchin Lane, Nicholas Lane. The Mansion House and the Bank of England lay straight ahead. What business did she have in this part of the City?

None, most likely. However, she didn't disappear into the underground station. The woman who haunted his dreams turned sharply into Change Alley.

She didn't look back.

Clues, Jews and tattoos. Johnny's head was full of them — and yet he'd not been able to mention any of them in his article. He'd described the encounter in the Turkish baths as vividly as he could but, as agreed, linked it to the series of murders rather than the anti-Semitic attacks. Implicitly, not explicitly. Sometimes what was not said was as important as what was.

Hollom's name would not appear in print. The in-house lawyers had cleared every word. There were fewer of them than Johnny would have liked. Adler had been unavailable. Culver was out of the office. It wasn't like either of them to shun attention.

What did their absence signify? Everything meant something. He was beginning to see more and more connections wherever he turned.

She'd vanished. There were five entrances/exits in Change Alley. Alex explored every nook and cranny of the shadowy vennel. He felt like a rat in a laboratory maze. Had she led him down here deliberately?

A stray dog, truffling through garbage, made him jump. It was no good. He'd lost her. He'd try again tomorrow. The George and Vulture was round the corner . . .

He could smell her but not see her. A green scent hung in the air. Something earthy. What was it? Lemon? Vanilla?

A gloved hand gripped his shoulder. His heart lurched.

He turned round. It wasn't her.

CHAPTER
TWENTY-FIVE

The colours and angles were spectacular yet the title of the exhibition, *Fifteen Paintings of London*, and the name of the group of artists, the Euston Road School, had promised so little. Johnny had not been overwhelmed with enthusiasm when Rebecca Taylor had invited him. Nevertheless he'd accepted. He could always study her instead of the daubs.

The Storran Gallery, at 316 Euston Road, was a couple of minutes' walk from the station. Johnny, freshly showered, arrived there soon after seven thirty. The woman on the door had winced when he'd said his name.

"You're supposed to be a Green or a Brown."

"It's all right, Verity."

Rebecca appeared and pecked him on the cheek. "I'll look after him."

She handed him a glass of red wine. It was shockingly sweet.

"Half the guests were plucked from the Post Office directory. It's all part of their desire to make art accessible to the man in the street. Or woman."

"Truly?"

She giggled.

"Cross my heart. Their last show was titled *The Jones Exhibition*. Try keeping up with four hundred of them!"

The room was packed. It was impossible to tell who might be Green or Brown — everyone was red-faced. So far they had managed to stand in admiration in front of Graham Bell's café scene, *Forty-four Goodge Street*; Lawrence Gowing's *Mare Street, Hackney*; Claude Rogers's *Regent's Park*; and William Coldstream's *St Pancras Station*.

Johnny, as a wordsmith, considered himself an ignoramus when it came to art. It annoyed him that newspapers were happy to pay a premium for illustrations and photographs when the going rate for words was not even ten a penny.

The painstaking realism of these urban landscapes — images of places he knew — spoke to him far more than any pastoral scene. That said, the cynic in him wondered why they didn't simply use a camera.

The answer came in the form of Geoffrey Tibble's *Demolition of Verlaine's House*. Its composition was anything but composing: the jagged lines and vivid colours suggested violence and anger, yet the total impression was one of pathos. Passion destroyed by progress.

"A house of ill-repute," said Becky, rolling her eyes.

"Well, Verlaine would keep chasing Rimbauds."

She hit him to acknowledge the punchline.

"We can only guess what went on between the poets. No one will ever paint a picture of that."

"Don't be so sure," said Johnny. "Artists like to make a stir. The shock of the nude hasn't lost its power."

223

"It's still an act of vandalism to knock the house down. It's vindictive."

"The star-crossed lovers didn't stay in Howland Street for long. They moved to Camden, didn't they?"

"That's not the point. Great poems were written there — even if their subject matter is scandalous."

"What would you like the landlord to do? Turn it into a shrine? The place was falling down. He has to make a living. Money trumps art every time."

"If you say so." She didn't sound convinced. "Look, there's Eileen Agar. I must talk to her about her theory of womb-magic."

Johnny watched her make her way across the crowded room. She was in her element, surrounded by more women than men, radiant with excitement and love of painting.

"Barking up the wrong tree there, aren't you?"

Culver, by way of salutation, raised a glass of champagne.

"What are you doing here?"

"I was invited."

"By whom?"

"No one you know. Artists are always keen to meet moneymen. They cannot live on air alone. The muse must be fed."

"What did you mean about barking up the wrong tree?"

"Come off it, Steadman. Don't tell me the trouser suit didn't set the alarm bells ringing? Or d'you enjoy a challenge?"

"Rebecca is a free-spirited woman with an open mind. Unlike some folk here."

"No need to get shirty. It was an idle remark. How come you know her?"

"She was a friend of one of the murdered men."

"A close friend? Perhaps I was wrong."

"And you? Where did your paths first cross?"

"At Grocers' Hall. She's very adept at getting people to open their wallets. All in a good cause, of course."

Johnny, frowning at his red wine, nodded at the champagne. "Where d'you get that?"

"You'll have to buy one of the paintings if you want to find out."

"I see. Which one's yours?"

The Shark glided through the sea of spectators and stopped in front of a picture by Victor Pasmore. It wasn't what Johnny had expected. *The Flower Barrow* was a pretty street scene in pinks and greens.

"Why this one?"

His errant informant pointed at the man in black with a bunch of red flowers in each hand. "He's selling, isn't he? That's what I do. He's performing for the market, trying to attract buyers. And he's surrounded by ladies . . ."

"Every picture tells a story."

"Up to a point, Lord Copper. It's never the whole story. The framing is as important as the figures. What's left out is as important as what's left in."

"What am I missing?"

"Once upon a time wealth was only created from commodities: crops, currency, gold. Physical things.

Ideas and education — things you can't touch — were left to art. But ideas have intrinsic value too. So, as knowledge is power, it's essential to have access to these ideas and information. There's no real difference between commerce and art. There's an art to selling bonds just as there's an art to selling knowledge. The public is more than happy to pay for the knowledge of a teacher, a doctor or a lawyer."

"Such knowledge isn't beautiful, though. And you *can* touch a painting." Johnny put out his hand as if to stroke the canvas. "Once the exhibition is over, you'll pick up *The Flower Barrow* and take it home."

"True — but in the meantime the intangible skills of Mr Pasmore will have touched the public in their own unique way."

Culver, like the man in the painting, may have been a glorified barrow boy, but his wits were as sharp as his suit.

"Why did you abandon me at the baths this afternoon?"

"I had no choice. Still, by the looks of you, there's no harm done. I did try to find out what had happened. When the cops arrived and carted off a bloke who was out for the count I thought it wise to make a strategic withdrawal. Rubbed you up the wrong way, did he?"

"I never touched him."

"Who did then?"

"A friend of Quirk's."

"Who? I didn't know he had any."

Johnny hesitated. Knowledge was power. He'd tell him half the story and see what happened. "Rick Hollom."

The colour in Culver's eyes deepened from silver to platinum. He had heard the name before.

"You want to be careful of him."

The woman was old enough to be his mother. Smartly dressed, an expensive hair-do sheathed in a jazzy headscarf, the matron regarded him with a mixture of amusement and pity.

"Leading you on, is she? Playing hard to get? Well, this here's no garden path. Your waitress friend asked me to give you this."

She handed Alex a slip of paper that looked as if it had been torn off an order-pad. It bore a scribbled address.

"You'll find her there."

As they walked down Cleveland Street on the way to dinner they passed the end of Howland Street. Becky, still elated by the opening — and its free-flowing wine and beer — insisted on making a detour. There was nothing to see. The gaping hole in the terrace was only a dormant building site. A glimpse of things to come.

The Rendezvous was a typical French restaurant: candles stuck in bottles, strings of garlic, lithographs of lavender fields in sun-soaked Provence.

Shivering in the sudden warmth, they both ordered the set-price special: onion soup, coq au vin and apple pie. Plus a bottle of Côtes du Rhône.

"What's that?"

227

She nodded at the brown-paper package that he'd retrieved from his pocket when the maître d' took their coats.

"It looks like a book. Is it for me?"

"No, it's for the waiter."

She laughed and, like a little girl on Christmas morning, slowly undid the string. When she saw the title she laughed even more.

"*Rebecca*. How perfectly splendid!"

"It's had rave reviews. I cut out this one from the *TLS*. Thought you might like to see it."

He bought the periodical every week. The pile of back issues in his bedroom almost touched the ceiling. Du Maurier's novel had been published in August. At eight shillings and sixpence it wasn't cheap. He was hoping that she'd lend it him after she'd read it.

Like many women who picked up a magazine, Becky started at the back — or in this case the bottom. Her administrative skills made her cut to the chase. She quoted from the final paragraph of the review.

"*Rebecca is extraordinarily bold and confident, eloquent and accomplished to a degree that merits genuine respect.*"

"They could be talking about you."

"Flatterer! I'll have to read it now."

"I'm sure you'll like it."

The soup arrived.

"Where's the wine? I'm thirsty."

"Sorry, madam. I'll fetch it forthwith."

The waiter, shooting a meaningful glance at Johnny, hurried to the bar.

228

"Sure you haven't had enough?"

"Quite sure." She put down her spoon. "Just going to powder my nose."

While she was gone he took the opportunity to read the whole review again. One sentence struck a particular chord:

It is to the girl herself, whose portrait stands out in fresh and attractive pastel tints from the heavy gilt frame of the narrative, that the reader turns in sympathy.

From what he could gather, the novel was the story of an unhappy marriage, a ghost story in which those in the present were unable to escape the past. Why, though, was the girl in the frame never named?

Becky was pleased to see a full glass awaiting her. They spent the meal discussing their work — she explaining how the livery company supported good causes; he how he strove to expose wrongdoing wherever it occurred. She was shocked and enthralled by the events of his day. He didn't tell her everything. For her sake, some things had to be left unsaid.

Her maroon — almost chestnut — eyes glowed in the candlelight. As the Grenache took effect he longed to kiss her pillowy lips. She tapped the hardback that lay face up on the table.

"Why this particular book? It wasn't only the title, was it?"

"No."

He took a sip of wine to give him time to think.

"As the *Times Literary Supplement* says: it's *an ingenious, exciting and engagingly romantic tale.* What more could you want?"

"A straight answer."

Johnny squirmed. "It's also about the love between two women."

"And you thought I'd be interested in that?"

"Aren't you? You seemed very interested in the love between Verlaine and Rimbaud."

She leaned across the table. "And you're not?"

It was more of an accusation than a question. Once upon a time Johnny would have denied it.

"I find friendship of all kinds fascinating. It's more complex than sex."

"You can also sleep with friends." She spoke as if addressing a child. "Besides, the Frenchmen were lovers. There's a thin line between sex and friendship. When you meet someone new, you never know how things will develop."

"That's what's so exciting. Yet once you cross that line there's no going back. I've come to understand that it doesn't matter who the friends or sexual partners are: it's the fact that love exists between them that counts."

"I agree," said Becky. "True love is rare. Why restrict your chances of finding it?"

"Indeed." He smiled ruefully. "I thought you were more interested in women than men. Was I wrong?"

"Just as interested would be more accurate."

Johnny nodded to show he wasn't shocked. "Most men would have counted their lucky stars when they found out. Why didn't Walter? Was he a prig?"

230

"No. He was a bigot. He didn't stop seeing me because I like women." She stared into her empty glass. "It was because I'm Jewish."

Johnny was stunned. Had he got it the wrong way round? If the murdered men hadn't been Jewish, perhaps the killer was . . .

Becky was waiting for him to speak. Her cheeks coloured as she misinterpreted his silence as disgust. "Does it make a difference?"

"No! Not at all! Of course it doesn't. You should know me better than that." He took both her hands in his. "I was thinking about the murder victims, not your faith. As far as I'm concerned, it's irrelevant — but it could well be relevant to the case."

"I didn't tell you earlier because Walter's reaction was so extreme. I was shaken by it. You read about anti-Semitism in the papers, but it's completely different when it's literally in your face. He spat at me. Yaxley was equally vile."

"Walter probably hated himself for loving you."

"It wasn't love. It was lust. On both sides . . ."

They didn't talk much for the rest of the meal. Ravenous when the main course finally arrived, they concentrated on the food and merely made appreciative noises. Johnny, moreover, was busy digesting what he'd learned.

Before he cleared away their empty plates, the waiter poured the last of the wine.

"Another bottle, sir?"

"No, thank you."

"Coffee?"

Johnny looked at Becky, who shook her head.

"Nothing else." He patted his stomach. "That was elegant sufficiency."

Becky watched the waiter's retreating back. She took a deep breath.

"And you?" She lowered her voice. "Are you interested in men?"

He'd half-expected the question. He was glad she felt able to ask it.

"Just the one. I only realized it a couple of years ago. We've been friends since we were kids."

"And does he feel the same way?"

"Yes and no."

"Frustrating, isn't it?"

"Don't set me off. I love his wife too — and she loves me."

"There will come a time when you have to choose between them."

"God, I hope not. I'd rather die than hurt either of them."

He thought of Hugh Walpole, a novelist who'd run off with a married policeman, lying low in the Lake District. He'd never be so lucky. A lump formed in his throat. It had been a long day.

Becky picked up the book.

"I believe you." She signalled to the waiter. "That's why this is my treat. You can pay for the taxi back to your place."

Alex got off the bus at Holborn Circus. Prince Albert, still in the saddle and flanked by figures of Commerce and Peace, raised his Field Marshal's hat to the City. Bartlett's Buildings was a dark cul-de-sac to the south.

He couldn't believe his luck. She actually wanted to see him! He reproached himself for his cowardice. He should have asked her out. He had so much to tell her. His heart brimmed with emotion.

A row of shabby townhouses faced the side of a bank. Rectangular white tiles covered the first two storeys. Thereafter bare bricks took over. Pedestrians were not expected to look up. An arrow at the mouth of an alley pointed to Fetter Lane.

Most of the houses had been converted into flats. The door to number 7 was ajar.

"Hello?"

He entered a dimly lit lobby that smelled of Pelaw's floor polish — and vanilla.

A radio fizzed behind the nearest door. Instead of knocking on it, he tiptoed to the foot of the stairs. He cleared his throat. His mouth was dry.

"Hello?"

He gripped his hat. It occurred to him — too late — that he could have been lured here as part of a sick prank. He got ready to run.

"What do you want?"

The voice came from above. He peered up the gloomy stairwell. A single star burned through the skylight. It was her! Locks of her beautiful hair cascaded round her shoulders as she peered over the balustrade.

"I'd like to talk to you if I may."

"Talk? I can do that."

"I'm Alex Vanneck. We met in Lockhart's."

"I know who you are. Come on up."

He didn't need asking twice.

Becky pooh-poohed his suggestion of a cup of tea. They went straight to bed.

"Where's the zinc oxide?" she asked.

He passed her the tin.

"Lie down."

He did as she commanded. The bedroom was an icebox but her hands soon warmed up his naked skin.

"You've done this before."

"That would be telling."

He hid his smile in the pillow. He couldn't have imagined a better end to the day.

"Tell me this then. Why is female friendship so different to that between men?"

"Is it?"

"Women are nastier to each other. Always finding fault, gossiping about their so-called sisters. Men accept each other for who and what they are."

"You think so? Some of the most spiteful people I know are men. Keep still."

Her hands moved gently down from his shoulders to the small of his back and, after an agonizing moment, set to work on his buttocks.

"I always thought it was because women see each other as rivals."

"Of course. A woman must have a man to be complete."

His blood was flowing. It was becoming hard to concentrate.

234

"Don't you want to get married?"

"No," said Becky. "I don't. Single girls have more fun. Turn over."

He did so. There was nowhere to hide. He smiled as nonchalantly as he could. The cold air had made her nipples erect.

"Gracious!" She licked her lips. "See what I mean?"

She held the door open for Alex.

"I've been waiting for you. Let me take your things."

He handed her his crumpled hat and struggled out of his coat.

"Thank you."

She pointed to a lone armchair beside the feeble coal fire. Instead of sitting down he went over to the desk beside the sink. Dozens of bottles of different sizes lined the shelves above it. It was more of a lab than a love-nest.

"What are these?"

"Chemicals. Essential oils. I make perfumes in my spare time."

"Including the one you're wearing?"

"Yes. D'you like it? It's based on vetiver."

"Not sure." He smiled in embarrassment. "If it's not made by Coty I can't recognize pongs." He sniffed as if to emphasize the point. "I like you though."

"Glad to hear it. Drink? I've only got beer."

"Spot on."

While she was busy at the kitchenette Alex studied the room. There was no bed. It must be behind the other door.

"I wouldn't care if I never saw one of these again," said Alex. He pressed the spacebar on the typewriter. "Bloody instruments of torture, that's what they are."

She came over to him, a glass in each hand.

"Cheers!" Suddenly in need of Dutch courage, he took a great swig.

"Your very good health." Her smile made his balls tingle. He looked away.

"Hey! That's queer. Why's there a Z where the Y should be?" He pointed to the top row of keys.

"It was made in Germany. Come on. Don't you want me to sit on your lap?"

After five minutes they broke off for a breather.

"Why didn't you ask me out?"

"I thought you were too good for me." He stroked the hair off her face. "Did you know I was shadowing you?"

"Of course. A girl can't be too careful nowadays."

"You might have let on. I felt such a cad."

"What d'you take me for? I don't pick up men in the street." She poked his chest playfully.

"I still can't believe my luck. Why did you give that woman your address?"

"Are you fishing for compliments?"

"No, not at all. It's just . . ."

"You remind me of someone."

"Who?"

"It doesn't matter." She sighed. "Besides, it's too late now." She traced the outline of his lips with her forefinger then kissed them again. Her nails were blood-red. "Let's go to bed."

Alex yawned and yawned again. He couldn't help it. Talk about sending the wrong signals! They held hands as they walked into the other room.

She was standing at the foot of the bed, fully clothed.

"Why've you got dressed?"

He tried to sit up but realized his wrists were still tied to the frame of the bed. Not only that — his ankles were too. What had she got in mind now? His cock began to stir.

"I've got to pop out for a bit. Shouldn't be too long."

She buttoned up her coat.

"Don't go anywhere."

Alex laughed nervously, aroused and alarmed.

"How can I? What kind of game is this?"

"You'll find out. I promise."

She picked up a circular metal object that resembled a giant retractable measuring tape.

"What's that gilhickie?"

"It's called a Spiderline."

"What's it for?"

"Never you mind. Now be a good boy. Lie still and think about what I'm going to do to you when I get back."

She bent over to give him a farewell kiss. It was only then that he began to panic. He didn't even know her name!

He cried out when he felt the prick.

CHAPTER
TWENTY-SIX

Wednesday, 9 November, 6a.m.

He didn't know where he was when he opened his eyes. The room was unfamiliar. It felt and smelled differently. There was a faint whiff of cigars. Lizzie's father chain-smoked them.

It had been after midnight when he'd knocked on the door. He'd got nowhere in Bishopsgate. His questions had been met with feigned incomprehension and genuine truculence. They had better things to do than investigate a break-in during which nothing was taken. They didn't know anything about a missing membership list. Besides, fascists didn't deserve special treatment. Hext was a small-time crook unworthy of further attention. His colleagues at Snow Hill were right when they said he'd be wasting his time.

Her parents had been in bed for an hour. As usual they were not pleased to see him. They were of the opinion that their daughter had married beneath her. One of the first things they'd taught him was the meaning of *morganatic*. What was he doing here? Lizzie had returned to Bexleyheath earlier that evening. Her father, unabashed at having his lies exposed, suggested Matt speak to his wife. Both their loyalties lay with her.

Irritation at been given the runaround was mixed with relief that Lizzie was well — and that it was far too late to make the arduous journey across South London to see her. He wasn't sure what he'd say. Anyway, he was dead on his feet.

He yawned and turned over. Perhaps he could snatch another ten minutes. His back ached though. The mattress was too soft. He was alone.

The thought of being reunited with Lizzie, curling up with her in their own bed, stirred his loins. No. It was going to be a hard day.

He dragged himself out of bed and forced himself to do his daily press-ups. All thirty of them.

Johnny, waking up, was disappointed to discover that Becky had already left. He smiled as the events of the previous night came back to him. No wonder he'd slept so well. There was a note on the pillow beside him:

Gone to Manderley! X

His smile widened. It might be Becky — or more likely the ointment — but this morning he felt remarkably comfortable in his own skin.

He bought the *News* before he caught the bus at Islington Green. His exclusive had dropped down the front page. The lead story concerned the setting up of a round-table conference on the future of Palestine. Arab groups were objecting to the number of Jews arriving in the region. He was pleased to see that the passengers on the number 4 appeared to be far more interested in his article.

Adler was not pleased to see him. He brandished a rolled-up copy of the *News* in his face.

"So you're the story now? An attack on a *Daily News* reporter is more newsworthy than a campaign of hatred against the next Lord Mayor?"

The tide of grey-faced office workers eddied round them in King William Street. The half-day meant they had a great deal to do before they could take their positions on the pavement.

"I can't keep the story going if you won't tell me anything," said Johnny. "What d'you want me to do? Make it up?" He stamped his feet. They'd turned to blocks of ice in the short time he'd been waiting. "Five minutes. That's all I need."

Adler didn't break the silence until he'd reached the safety of his office. For someone who was about to become one of the most powerful figures in the City he didn't appear to be on top of the world.

"Let's talk numbers," said Johnny. "Five hundred million. That's some float. Do *you* think England is about to be invaded?"

Adler sat down at his desk. He ordered tea for them both.

"No, I don't. No harm in taking precautions though."

"Sure Canada is safe? The Czechs thought London was safe — and look what's happened to their gold. Who's to say the Canadians — especially the Québéçois — might not decide to confiscate the assets of their colonial rulers?"

240

"I don't know who you've been talking to, but I do know you'll never be allowed to publish such information."

"We'll see. If push comes to shove I'll give the story to one of my colleagues across the Atlantic."

Adler made a steeple out of his fingers. Perhaps he was praying he could come up with the correct combination of words.

"The truth can be a dangerous thing. Especially to a reporter who won't listen to advice."

"Are you taking the advice of the police? Letting a bodyguard ride with you in the coach?"

"No. I'm not going to be the mayor who overturns centuries of tradition. The route will be lined with dozens of cops — in and out of uniform. I'm not afraid."

"So you know best."

"Indeed." He sighed. "We got there in the end."

"Do you want your parade overshadowed by the news that the City is in cahoots with the Nazis? That's what will happen if you don't come clean."

"Come clean? I'm not dirty! You haven't a shred of proof that any of your information is correct."

"I'll simply repeat your denials and the damage will be done. Look, we're on the same side, aren't we?"

Adler raised his eyebrows. Johnny pressed on.

"All right then. Let's say the Germans are our common enemy. I'm not a traitor. I'll keep quiet about the £500 million if you fill me in on the Czech deal."

"So you want to enter the trading floor, do you? Bargain with me? Exchange information? Watch out for the trapdoor."

The tea arrived. Johnny sat down on the other side of the desk. He waited till the door was closed.

"I got the impression you don't like Montagu Norman. What was it you said? *He never tells the whole story.* As Governor of the Bank of England he has to take responsibility for the deal. What was your role in it? Are you trying to protect the reputation of the BIS?"

Adler stared at the blotter in front of him, his mind elsewhere. He was making rapid calculations, adding up the pros and cons.

"Believe it or not, I like you, Steadman. What I'm about to tell you won't do you any good though. Quite the opposite, in fact. It's entirely up to you what you do with this information but my advice would be to file it away for future use."

"Go on." He got out his notebook.

"There were two accounts. The National Bank of Czechoslovakia transferred fifty tons of gold to the Bank of England. The first account, in its own name, contained twenty-seven tons. The second, in the name of the Bank for International Settlements, contained twenty-three tons. They thought it would be safe there. However, when the Germans invaded Czechoslovakia they demanded that the gold be transferred to the Reichsbank account in London. Our government had already blocked Czech assets so the gold in the first account was protected, but Norman secretly took it upon himself to sanction the transfer of the gold in the second account. He insists that individual governments should not intervene in BIS business."

242

"What a crook! How much of the twenty-three tons have the Nazis given him?"

"You'd have to ask him that."

"Well, he'll have to resign — immediately."

"The BIS cannot be prosecuted under national laws. It's immune."

"Even so, Norman's position will be untenable when the news gets out. Perhaps the Nazis will headhunt him — if he hasn't already been lynched . . . Maybe you'd like his job?"

"How d'you think I became the new Lord Mayor?"

Johnny sat up. So that was how a Jew had got into the Mansion House. He was beginning to see the bigger picture.

"Silence is golden."

"I couldn't have put it better myself. Of course your cooperation would not go unrewarded . . ."

Johnny, in spite of his anger, had to laugh. He'd come here to blackmail Adler into talking. Now Adler was bribing him to keep quiet.

Adler, to his credit, almost looked embarrassed. Almost.

"I'll be able to achieve far more as Lord Mayor than in any other role — and I'll be able to look over Norman's shoulder. He's already tarnished the reputation of the BIS — which is, whatever you say, a force for good — but I'm determined to see he doesn't pull another stroke like this one."

"Would it be such a bad thing if he were to fall on his sword?"

"The City is jittery enough. Any suggestion of financial malfeasance at the Bank of England would

243

trigger a stock market crash. Neither it nor the country can afford for that to happen."

Johnny knew Adler was right. This was the story of a lifetime. If he broke it he'd be able to walk into any job in Fleet Street — and he'd be able to name his price. On the other hand, the story would damage the City in the eyes of the world. Which was more important to him? Career or country? The idea that Norman could get away with collaborating with the Nazis made him see red.

Adler was watching him closely. "What are you going to do?"

"I don't know."

The empty house hadn't surprised Lizzie. Like most men, Matt couldn't cope on his own. He'd probably gone to his parents — or stayed over with Johnny. Now there was a thought . . .

She was glad to be home. Even before Commander Inskip had warned her about the kidnapping threat — and the need for silence — she'd needed to get away. Her disappearance had been for all their sakes. She had done a lot of thinking — and some weeping — but she could see clearly now. She knew exactly what she was going to do.

Lila Mae, sensing her mother's improved mood, gurgled happily as she was laid in her new American pushchair, a present from her grandparents.

"We're off to see the Lord Mayor of London, aren't we, lambkin? Perhaps he'll have a pussycat like Dick Whittington."

If there were no good vantage points in Fleet Street she could take refuge at the *News*. Johnny would look after them.

She slid the envelope containing the photograph behind the baby's back.

Johnny found himself following the planned route of the procession: Poultry, Cheapside, St Paul's Churchyard, Ludgate Hill. It hadn't been a conscious decision. He'd simply decided to walk back to the office. It wasn't far and would only take fifteen minutes. Everything — apart from the traffic — moved faster in London.

He had other matters to think about. *Solvitur ambulando:* walk about to work it out.

It was too cold to dawdle. Shafts of sunlight, breaking out from angry clouds, raked the City. His mother had called them angel's torches. He very much doubted that Jesus would want him for a sunbeam. He searched for a more mundane image. That was it: the floodlights of Twentieth Century Fox. The show was about to begin.

Why did Adler say that he wasn't afraid? He'd been too complacent all along. He'd accused Johnny of creating a mountain out of a molehill. Far more important matters required his attention. What was more important than saving your own skin?

Adler knew more than he was letting on. That was a given. He'd come clean about the Czech deal more readily than expected. Why? England's gold reserves were more important, of course, but that didn't explain the wealth of detail that he'd provided. It was as if he knew it would never be seen in print.

Perhaps it wasn't Adler's life that was in the sights but his own.

However, Johnny wouldn't have lasted this long without a keen survival instinct. He was no fall-guy. Something else was going on. Why had Adler wanted him rather than the police to investigate the attacks? Was he concerned they might find a skeleton in his closet? Adler must be using the Czech deal to distract him. Once again the country was being sacrificed to protect people in power. If such dirty business were a sideshow, what was the main feature?

A few spectators had already staked out their claim on the pavement outside Hereflete House. A bobby who tried to move them on was shouted down as a spoilsport. They celebrated their victory with cups of hot tea poured from Dewar flasks. The constable grinned when he tasted the Scotch.

Johnny told the liftboy to take him straight up to the seventh floor. He waited impatiently for the red light to go out.

"No word from Whitehall yet," said Stone. "Probably got other things to worry about. Still, it's a good sign."

He put down the *Financial Times*. Johnny sometimes thought Captain Vic spent more time reading his competitors' pages than those of his own newspaper. *Know your enemies* was another of his catchphrases.

"You're looking a lot better this morning, if you don't mind my saying so."

246

"Not at all, sir. I'm about to make you feel better as well."

"Out with it then."

The more he heard the angrier his editor became.

"Write it up. Don't make any calls — we don't want to alert the authorities. There'll be plenty of time for them to express their outrage and issue categorical denials — which will keep the story alive. There's no point giving them the chance to bury the story before it's even seen the light of day. I'll speak to Patsel."

Johnny didn't envy him.

"There's something else, sir."

"Go on."

"The government is about to send £500 million in gold to Canada to keep it out of German hands. As Lord Vivis is already in the country . . ."

"I'll speak to him — but don't tell anyone else about this until I say so. Is that clear?"

"Yes, sir."

"Get a move on then. There's still time to get it into the first edition — if you're quick."

Patsel's throne was unoccupied. PDQ and Soppy were poring over some photographs, of what Johnny couldn't see. Dimeo was arguing the toss with an Australian colleague who wouldn't let him forget his country had retained the Ashes in July.

Johnny dumped his mail on the desk. He had no intention of dealing with it now. He ignored the ringing telephone. He had to place himself in the mental bubble that allowed him to work amid the din and distractions of the newsroom.

Tanfield looked as if he were fit to burst. The boy's eagerness brought out the paternal side of Johnny. His eyes shone with excitement. At least he hoped that's what it was.

"I can't talk, Timmy. They're holding the front page."

"I know," said his sidekick. "The police have found another body."

CHAPTER
TWENTY-SEVEN

The dirty money was still in his locker. He'd half-hoped someone would have swiped it. Personal property was always going missing.

Lizzie must have been determined to punish him for his selfish behaviour. Why else would she keep secret her whereabouts? She knew how protective he was — and how to hurt him. Zick's abduction of her two years ago had made him more fearful of her safety. And now there was Lila Mae too. He hadn't realized she could be so cruel.

Watkiss stuck his head round the door.

"Tyser requests the pleasure of your company in the murder room. There's been another one."

"Male?"

"Of course." He frowned. "Why? Expecting a dead female to turn up?"

"No," said Matt. "But I wouldn't be surprised if some firebrand flung themselves in front of the Lord Mayor's coach. *Peace not war! Save the Jews! Protect our jobs!* The whole world wants more than they've got."

"Don't be such a damper. It's going to be a great show."

Herbie's enthusiasm was almost touching. He was enjoying his secondment to the Detective Squad. Matt suddenly felt old.

Tanfield grinned at the surprised expression on Johnny's face. He thought he'd got one over on him. So be it. He'd let him labour under the misapprehension.

"Where?"

"Waithman Street. Alongside Ludgate Hill Station."

"Who told you?"

"No one. It came in over the wire."

"You better get over there then."

Tanfield grabbed his hat and coat. "Aren't you coming?"

"Need me to hold your hand?"

"No — but this has been your story so far."

"And it still is. It's only round the corner. I'll be with you shortly. Must get a couple of paras off first."

"About what?"

"Adler. It's his big day. We ought to mark the occasion. You know: point out the police have yet to arrest the ringleader. Ask what precautions have been taken. Raise the question of public safety."

"Quite right. I'll see you there."

The young pretender ran towards the lifts.

"That's not like you — letting someone else chase a corpse."

Dimeo, knowing full well that Johnny didn't like it, perched on the corner of his desk.

"I'm going after live prey this morning."

"Anyone I know?"

"I doubt it. He's our new Lord Mayor."

"Ow!" The point of a pencil penetrated one of Dimeo's buttocks. The sports reporter stood up. "That hurt."

"It was meant to. Now, if you'll excuse me, I have a deadline. Remember what one of those is?"

"I remember you asking for my help last week." He rubbed his behind. "It feels like you broke the skin."

"You've had worse injuries."

Johnny was referring to the time he'd knocked Louis out in the showers.

"I haven't forgotten," said Dimeo. They both knew he'd deserved it. "Did you ever find your treasure?"

"Yes, thank you."

"Well, leave my arse alone then."

He limped away.

Tesoro. Johnny repeated the word in his head. He'd found Hollom — but he'd never asked him what he'd been talking about in the backroom of Otarelli's. He was Anglo-Italian too . . . First things first. He'd think about it later.

Alexander Vanneck's eyes were open but he was blind to what was going on around him. He was still bound to the bed in Bateman's Buildings, spread-eagled and stark naked.

He'd had the time of his life.

She must have left him alone for at least a couple of hours but she'd made it up to him when she returned, even more excited than before. It had been well worth the wait.

251

She said she couldn't bear to let him go yet. She'd been searching for a man like him for so long. It felt as if they had met in a past life. She'd done things to him that no woman had ever done before. He would die if there were no encore.

And yet she refused to tell him where she'd been. The wait — his waiting for her — was what counted. The hopes and fears coursing through his body. The frantic machinations of his brain.

He daren't tell her that he'd fallen asleep soon after she'd left. That he'd only woken up when he heard the bedroom door creak open. That had been a tricky moment. If someone else had come in, he would have screamed.

He knew it was too good to be true. He didn't usually have this effect on women. He must be missing something. Something didn't fit. He didn't claim to know the workings of a woman's mind — perhaps that was why he'd never had a fiancée — but he suspected this waitress had a screw loose. God, though, she knew how to screw! She was cock-mad.

She said she was lonely. That she had lost someone close to her — she'd tell him the full story one day — and that she missed him with her heart and soul. That she often woke up crying. Dreaming about him, then realizing that it had only been a dream, was like losing him all over again.

There was no end to her grief. Sometimes she could taste her loneliness. Base metals. Bitter herbs. She had tried to bottle it. Would he care to smell it? He'd politely declined.

252

He'd lost count of the number of times she'd collected his essence. She said only sex silenced the silent scream in her head.

He was utterly drained when, an hour before dawn, she'd finally set him free — on the promise that he return that evening. They were made for each other. Wild horses wouldn't stop him . . .

A sheaf of rolled-up papers brought him back to reality. Wilderspin — what was he doing down here? — had struck him in the face.

"I telephoned three times. Where've you been?"

His bloodshot eyes scoured the cubbyhole. There was nowhere to hide.

"I've been at my desk since eight thirty, sir."

"You're a damned liar — if you don't mind my saying so."

"I do, sir."

"What's that?"

"I do mind. Very much so, in fact. Would *you* mind if I hit you in the mush? Give me those papers. Let's find out."

"Are you insane?"

"Quite possibly."

"Well, you can forget about the Lord Mayor's show. I want every one of these letters typed three times."

Vanneck shot to his feet. Wilderspin stepped back.

"That's right," said Vanneck, waving a fist. "Get out of my way, you pompous prick. Find someone else to correct your mistakes."

"I think you'll find you're the one making a mistake," said Wilderspin. "A big one."

Fleet Street had been closed to traffic. The road surface had been swept and scattered with a mixture of sand and sawdust. The bells of St Bride tolled eleven o'clock. Across the City at the Guildhall, the Silent Ceremony would be starting.

Waithman Street — named after another former Lord Mayor, a draper who did well for himself — was the first turning on the right in Pilgrim Street. Johnny emerged from Bride Court — the shopping arcade decked with bunting — and headed for the bridge directly opposite that would take him under the railway.

He spotted Matt straightaway. He was talking to Tanfield — and Simkins.

"Too late, Steadman. Timmy's got all the juicy details."

"When did you two get so palsy-walsy?"

Simkins laughed. "Wouldn't *you* like to know! What kept you?"

"Wait and see," said Johnny. "I suggest you invest in a copy of the *News*."

"Timmy?" Simkins's ebullience was waning.

Tanfield looked as if he was about to say something but thought better of it and shrugged instead. Johnny, Simkins and Matt — who was enjoying the situation — said nothing.

Tanfield reddened. "What? Johnny never tells me anything."

"You know that's not true. For instance, I told you never to trust Simkins. It's not my fault if you've ignored my advice. Been comparing notes, have you?"

"They had no choice," said Matt. "Neither of them has been admitted to the scene."

"Have you knocked on everyone's door?"

Tanfield nodded and glanced at Simkins.

"Not at the same time I hope," said Johnny.

"Of course not," said Simkins. "That's why we were sharing information. Now, if you'll excuse me, gentlemen, I have someone to see."

He blew Tanfield a kiss then strode off towards Union Street. The scent of sandalwood faded.

Johnny waited, savouring Tanfield's discomfort.

"So what have you learned?"

Tanfield raised his chin defiantly. "The victim's name begins with an aitch."

For a moment Johnny feared that Hollom had been exposed — and executed.

"Out with it!"

"Hext. Steven Hext."

"Any further details?"

Johnny glanced at Matt. His eyes were burning blue.

"Not many," said Tanfield, consulting his notebook. "Ran a stall in Finsbury Market, apparently. Fruit and veg. Unmarried, early twenties."

"Has he been mutilated like the others?"

"DS Turner refused to confirm the rumour."

"I'm confirming it now," said Matt. "You'd do a lot better by yourself, young man."

"I take it, Detective Constable, that you're not a fan of Henry Simkins."

"You could say that."

"Care to elaborate?"

"Shouldn't you be getting back to the office?" said Johnny. "You're in danger of missing the noon deadline."

Tanfield checked his watch.

"Crikey! You're right. D'you want to see the copy before I file it?"

"No. There isn't time — but don't make a big deal of the location. Trains haven't been stopping here for ten years. The killer must have come by pushbike."

Tanfield hesitated.

"Yes," said Johnny. "I'm pulling your leg. Now shift yourself."

Matt gave Johnny the once-over.

"What a difference a day makes. What happened? Strained your greens?"

"Is it that obvious?"

"Only to me. Anyone I know?"

He could have made some flippant remark about Lizzie but didn't. It wouldn't have been fair to her or Matt.

"Rebecca Taylor. Her given name was Schneider."

"That's interesting. Seeing her again?"

"Hope so. I really like her."

A police photographer came out of the house and began packing his gear into a van.

"Let's go up," said Matt.

He nodded to the constable on the door. They began climbing the stairs.

"Heard from Lizzie?"

"Not in person. She's been hiding out at her parents. Swore them to secrecy. She went back to Bexleyheath last night."

"Why her sudden departure?"

"No idea. I must have done something wrong."

That must be it. Lizzie couldn't possibly have found out about the bribe. She must have been giving him a taste of what would happen if he ever were to be unfaithful.

"You can't have been that naughty," said Johnny. "If she was intent on leaving you she wouldn't have returned home so soon . . ."

Hext had slept on a single bed in a tiny room under the eaves. He'd either been extremely untidy or someone had rummaged through his belongings. Had they been searching for the membership list too?

Matt pulled back the sheet. Nowadays it took a lot to shock Johnny — he felt he'd heard and seen everything — but he couldn't help recoiling.

"You might have warned me!"

There was blood everywhere. Not only below the waist but all over the body and the bed as well.

"He must have been conscious," said Matt. "Looks as if he fought like hell."

The hands and feet were grotesquely swollen, the ties that bound them cutting into the mottled flesh like cheese-wire.

"The killer's sliced off more this time — the cock and balls."

"I had noticed." The congealing gore turned Johnny's stomach. "They're losing control. It's as if they were in a hurry."

"Aren't we all?" said Matt. "Who d'you think Simkins was in such a rush to meet?"

"Zick?"

"Who else? I've discovered where he's set up shop. Hanging Sword Alley."

In spite of the dead man between them they couldn't help giggling.

"The nerve of the bastard," said Johnny. "Talk about rubbing our noses in it."

Thanks to Dickens, he knew exactly where the alley was in Fleet Street. Jerry Cruncher, bodysnatcher and porter for Tellsun's Bank, had a bolt-hole there in *A Tale of Two Cities*. Zick was something of a resurrection man too.

Matt checked nobody was eavesdropping, then confided, "It gets better. The establishment is called Cockaigne — with a K — Corner."

"Sounds right," said Johnny. "The land of lost content."

"At least we know where to find him now — should it be necessary."

"It's certainly convenient for Simkins."

"Too convenient," said Matt. "I had a brief word with him when he arrived. I got the impression he's as much under Zick's thumb as we are. He actually had the effrontery to thank me for my cooperation."

"What about mine?"

"For some reason he's still not sure about you."

"Splendid."

Johnny walked over to the open window. There was a magnificent view of St Paul's. The baroque cathedral soared above the soot and grime, the people and pigeonshit which surrounded it. Such beauty amid such squalor! There was more than one city in London.

Five floors below an alley cut through to Broadway.

"The door was open when we got here," said Matt.

"We?"

"I was with DI Tyser. He's dashed off to Old Jewry to brief Inskip."

"Because there's now a connection between the murders and the attacks on Adler."

"In more ways than one," said Matt. "It was Hollom who found the body."

CHAPTER
TWENTY-EIGHT

Lizzie got off the train at Farringdon and walked through Hatton Garden. It was strange being back. She was no longer the woman who had worked on the perfume counter in Gamages, the department store at the end of the road. The old Lizzie had been single, full of independent spirit, determined to make something of herself. Lila Mae had certainly sprung from her loins — well, the forceps had helped — but, in those days, a child was not what she'd had in mind.

Her parents doted on their first grandchild, but the unspoken belief that she had sold herself short still hung in the air between them. Running back to them had been necessary but impolitic — it reinforced their suspicion that her marriage had been a mistake. It wasn't. Matt was a good man. Then so was Johnny. She hadn't been pregnant, she hadn't been forced into the union. She had made her choice and now she had to live with it — and Matt.

She'd been given precise directions and located Ye Olde Mitre Tavern with surprising ease, even though it was hidden away. She had to take care that the pushchair didn't scrape the sides of the alley. It was a charming building, like something out a children's picture-book. A sweetshop under a toadstool.

She was not in the habit of entering public houses by herself. The landlord scowled when he saw Lila Mae — men came here to escape family life — but swallowed his words when Simkins appeared at her side and ushered her into the Bishop's Room.

There was a bottle of champagne in an ice-bucket on the table.

"Care for a pick-me-up?"

"No, thank you. I don't wish to be here a moment longer than necessary."

"Suit yourself. Odd that we've never actually met before, isn't it?"

He charged his glass, the silver bubbles threatening to boil over but, instead, merely bursting on the brim.

"Why? You're not the sort of person with whom I would choose to consort."

Lila, staring at the curious man, began to whimper.

"And yet we have so much in common," said Simkins. "Johnny, after all, is our mutual friend."

"He's not why I'm here."

Lizzie bent down to comfort Lila and extracted the envelope. She tossed it on to the table.

"Keep it," said Simkins. "There are copies. Your husband is magnificent *tout nu*, isn't he?"

"I'm glad you think so. You seem unaware, though, that I've seen the photograph before."

Simkins, the saucer in his hand halfway to his mouth, froze. "That's not possible."

"I admit I was deeply shocked the first time — it must be two years ago now — but why would you want me to see it? You don't appear to need money."

"Haven't you spoken to your husband?"

"No."

"Why contact me then?"

"To explain that your blackmail attempt won't work. There are no secrets between us."

"Oh really? How touching."

He slid another envelope across the table.

"Your husband told you about this, did he?"

Lizzie, suddenly afraid, withdrew the contents. The photograph was of Johnny, stark-naked, in a similar pose to Matt. She couldn't tear her eyes away. She'd often imagined what he'd look like without any clothes. Now she knew.

Simkins watched the colour spread across her cheeks.

"They make a pretty pair, don't they? Like to see some more? How about one of them together?"

He was bluffing. No such photograph had ever been taken.

Lizzie sat down. Lila, sensing the hostility in the room, started to cry. Her mother let her.

"Why are you doing this?"

"He has no choice."

She screamed in surprise. A hidden door in the wainscoting — that led to an upstairs chamber — opened to reveal her former abductor. Lila was now screaming too. Lizzie took her out of the pushchair and held her — to reassure herself as much as the baby.

Zick swept up both pictures and put them back in their envelopes.

"Don't be afraid, Mrs Turner. Once again, I have cause to regret my good nature. I never learn: it seems if you want anything doing properly, you must do it yourself."

"I say! That's a bit off," said Simkins.

"Pipe down, Henry. Give me some of that fizz. It's not spiked, is it?"

Simkins shook his head.

"Sure you won't have a glass, Mrs Turner. You look as if you need it."

He poured a glass and placed it in front of her. Lizzie sat down again. She knocked back the alcohol in one gulp.

Zick refilled her saucer and sat down opposite her at the table.

"A thousand apologies for my sudden entrance. I was hoping it wouldn't be necessary but — as usual — Simkins here is making a hash of things. I don't think he was expecting to see a child. He likes children very much, you see. Especially boys. Boys with scarcely a hair on their bodies . . ."

Simkins stood up. His head was only an inch from the low ceiling.

"Stay where you are," said Zick. "I haven't finished with you yet."

"Well, I'm finished with you. Get someone else to do your dirty work."

"Do as you're told and sit," said Zick. "What are you going to do, call the cops?"

263

"Something like that."

"There's no need. I'm sure we can work this out to our mutual satisfaction. Don't you think so, Mrs Turner?"

There was a knock on the door. The landlord stuck his balding head in.

"Everything hunky-dory? Thought I heard a scream."

"It was only the baby," said Zick. "Since you're here, Jubb, you might as well send in another bottle."

"Yes, sir."

The door closed.

"Is there anyone you're not blackmailing?" Lizzie wiped Lila's tears away with her hanky.

"I haven't come to an arrangement with you — yet," said Zick. "Although I'm sure you wouldn't like people to know that your husband and his best friend have been at it behind your back."

Lizzie glanced at Simkins. He maintained a Sphinx-like silence. His only movement was a single blink.

"What was this odious man supposed to make me do?"

"Nothing," said Zick. "I simply asked him to ensure that your husband and friend would not interfere with the running of my business."

"And if they did?"

"The photographs would be released to the press. They would, of course, never be printed but the damage would be done. Their careers would be over. I never told Simkins to send you the photograph."

He turned to his accomplice. "Why did you, Henry?"

"I panicked. I don't trust Steadman. It was meant to be a bit of extra insurance. If he couldn't persuade Turner to keep his mouth shut, then I was sure his wife could."

"There was no need," said Zick. "I'd made other plans. The Commander kindly suggested that Mrs Turner make herself scarce for twenty-four hours to remind her husband what could happen if he didn't toe the line."

"Toe the line?" Lizzie, starting at his unusually small feet, looked Zick up and down.

"Do nothing. That's all. Not too much to ask was it?"

"You always ask too much." Simkins, furious at being outwitted, was almost snarling. Zick ignored him.

"I wonder how Steadman will feel when he finds out he saved the life of a complete degenerate. Henry does so love a mystery."

Lizzie looked puzzled.

Zick smiled. "Such innocence! I'm not talking about detective stories — although the police are involved. In certain low quarters a mystery is what they call a young prostitute."

"He has footage of me with young boys," said Simkins.

"Then you deserve everything you get," said Lizzie.

"Are you prepared to destroy your husband in the process?" Zick shook his head slowly. "If I know anything about Henry, it's that he won't go quietly. So you see, my dear, everything depends on your silence. My business, Henry's liberty, the well-being of you and your husband — even your lover's job — all of them depend on saying nothing."

Lizzie looked even more puzzled. "Johnny's not my lover! Who told you that? A minute ago you were implying he was my husband's lover. Neither slur is true. You've been misinformed."

"Henry," said Zick. "I was under the impression you were a journalist. Didn't you check your facts?"

"One of Steadman's colleagues told me."

"Told you what?"

"That he'd seen her with Steadman."

"Doing what?"

"Yes," said Lizzie. "What were we doing?"

"Walking arm-in-arm — like a couple. There's no smoke without fire."

Someone rapped on the door.

"That'll be the champagne," said Zick.

He was wrong. It was Matt.

Alex, ignoring the queue, charged into Lockharts. The workers wanted to fill their bellies before fulfilling their roles as loyal citizens, freezing their balls off to cheer a fat cat who had got the cream.

There was no sign of her. He grabbed another waitress.

"Where is she?"

"Get your paws off me. Who the blazes d'you think you are?"

"A man in love. You know full well who I'm after. You spied on us enough."

"How dare you!"

She tried to slap his face but he caught her arm.

"Tell me or I'll ram my fist down your throat."

"She didn't turn up this morning. That's all I know. Probably gone down with something."

"Then why didn't you say so?"

The manager, noticing the contretemps, was heading their way. Loaded forks, dripping gravy, were poised in mid-air. Aware of the audience, Alex relinquished his grip and ran out of the restaurant.

If she was ill he needed to be at her side.

All they'd had to do was cross New Bridge Street — already blocked by diverted traffic — and a minute later they were outside Cockaigne Corner. If there was anyone home they were not answering the door. The windows were shuttered. No light escaped through the cracks.

Matt wasn't surprised.

"There's too much activity, too many cops about. Zick hasn't survived this long without knowing when to lie low."

"Let's break down the door then," said Johnny.

"On what grounds? How could we justify it?"

"Let me count the ways: prostitution, extortion, corruption."

"Nothing new there. Besides, Inskip would be less than pleased."

"I hadn't forgotten about the photograph."

"How could you?" Their eyes met. "Give us a gasper."

Johnny lit one for them both. "Come on. We'll share a taxi — if we can find one."

"Where to?"

"Saffron Hill. We need to warn Hollom. He could be the next victim."

"Unless he's the killer," said Matt. "He stole the membership list, so he'd have known where everyone lived."

"He works for the government though."

"And governments don't kill? He warned you off, didn't he? He was afraid you'd queer his pitch."

"Like you did for Hext."

Johnny felt guilty as soon as he'd said it. Matt was dismayed.

"I didn't know I was putting the little turd in danger."

"I'm not saying you did. Besides, his fellow fascists have shown no consideration for the safety of others. Perhaps that's why the government is bumping them off one by one — mutilating them purely to complicate the picture. A secret plan to pre-empt the group collaborating with the Germans."

"It makes sense to me," said Matt. "Even if it does sound rather far-fetched. You do let your imagination run away with itself sometimes."

"If you say so. Wouldn't it be good, though, if it were true? Anyway, there's only one way to find out. We'll ask him and see what happens. If he were going to kill me to guarantee my silence he'd have done it by now. He can hardly kill a cop and a journalist in broad daylight. He's supposed to avoid unwanted attention."

268

"I ought to inform Tyser."

"Well, there's a police box in Hatton Garden. If Hollom's not at Otarelli's we might find him in the Mitre."

Zick, a look of sheer terror on his face, bolted for his upstairs hidey-hole.

"Stay where you are, Mr Zick. Can't stay away from my wife, can you? I must say I've been waiting for this moment for a long time."

He turned to Lizzie. "Hello, darling. Am I glad to see you."

What on earth was she doing here? She was flushed but, apart from that, appeared to be well. Had her disappearance been down to Zick after all?

Lila, hearing her father's voice, tried to speak. Matt tickled her under the chin. The happy gurgling made his heart swell.

"And how's my little angel? I've missed you both so much."

"Sorry," said Lizzie. "I'm so, so sorry."

"Not now, dear. We'll talk once this sordid business is completed."

Simkins, who had watched the exchange with amusement, stood up.

"Worthy of a weepy, I'm sure." He picked up the envelopes. "However, I must tear myself away and get back to the office."

"The only place you're going, Mr Simkins, is Snow Hill."

"You can't arrest him," said Zick. "You're not in the City of London. The land you stand on belongs to the see of Ely and as such is under the jurisdiction of its Bishop."

"The last person to question my authority is currently lying in the mortuary," said Matt. "However, should you wish to turn yourself over to the Bishop rather than the Lord Mayor you have the right to do so. Of course, Commander Inskip will be powerless to help you if you do."

Zick sat down without a word.

"Henry Simkins, I'm arresting you for the attempted blackmail of Elizabeth Turner and John Steadman . . ."

"Where's your proof?"

Matt pointed to the envelopes. Simkins dropped them.

"They're not mine — they're his!" He pointed at Zick.

Matt knew this was true. Arresting him would still hurt Zick though — and help Johnny.

"He likes little boys," said Zick. "I can show you the film, if you wish."

"No, thank you. I don't want to see images of any kind."

"Not even the ones of your good self?"

Simkins managed to combine a sneer with a leer. "They've given a lot of pleasure to a lot of people — including your wife and Johnny."

"That's not true!" Lizzie, still holding Lila, struck him across the face. "You poisonous ponce! Johnny saved your life. Is this how you repay him? Why are you trying to destroy him?"

270

"Not sure," said Simkins. "Boredom, I suppose. I'm actually rather fond of him."

"You've an odd way of showing it," said Matt.

"Loyalty seems to be a rare commodity these days," sighed Simkins. "I look forward to telling you all about Zick's various ventures."

"What will your father say? And his political allies?" Lizzie was fascinated by his loathsome self-interest.

"That's what I'm looking forward to most of all. Knowing my luck, he'll succumb to apoplexy before the whole story comes out. He hates me and I hate him."

"You never did know when to button it," said Zick.

He pulled out a pearl-handled pistol.

A miasma of misery always seemed to hang over Saffron Hill. The ghosts of Fagin's pickpocketing catamites still lurked in the network of narrow alleys that connected the hotchpotch of workshops and laboratories. Toxic fumes from furnaces and refineries added to the fug.

Hollom was not at work. He had gone to watch the Lord Mayor's Show and would be back around two o'clock. Was the secret agent expecting an attack on Adler? Had the EFF planned something special? Hollom would know. The procession was about to start.

Johnny trotted down Hatton Garden. A taxi with its flag out had stopped at a pedestrian crossing. The flashing amber globes of the Belisha beacons made him see the light. Adler wasn't the victim in all this: he was behind the campaign. That's why he hadn't been concerned for his safety. He knew what was coming — at least he thought he did . . .

The driver's delight in picking up a fare soon faded when Johnny told him the destination.

"You'll be lucky! The City's chockablock. This ain't a magic carpet."

"Prefer me to get out? Thought not. As near to the Mansion House as you can, please."

Leslie Hore-Belisha, the Minister of Transport who'd introduced the lights, was half-Jewish. Dimeo and Hollom were half-Italian. Becky danced at both ends of the ballroom. Life wasn't black and white like the pole of a Belisha beacon. It wasn't a question of being one thing or the other. Light was both a particle and a wave. Two opposites within one form. Good men did bad things and vice versa. Adler had two faces. He was a double-dealer.

The two stories he was working on were somehow linked. Everything meant something and everything was connected in London's giant web. If Hollom was involved in both cases then Adler had to be too. That's why he'd wanted Johnny, rather than the police, to investigate: he was buying time. For what though? For more crooked deals to go through? For the gold to reach Canada? Or for Hollom to get the last man on the list?

Gresham Street was as far as the cabbie could go. Gresham's Law: bad money drives out good. There was no such thing. Money was a concept — without morals, without intrinsic value. Midas learned this lesson the hard way. He starved to death.

Johnny didn't wait for his change. He started running.

Alex was so wound up he'd walked all the way from Fenchurch Street to Holborn Circus. Most pedestrians seemed to be heading into the City, not out of it. Yet again, he was swimming against the tide.

He bought a bouquet of red carnations — that he could now ill-afford — from a barrow outside the bank and hurried into Bartlett's Buildings. He couldn't wait to see her. Would she be pleased to see him?

Standing on the threshold, he realized he was shaking. Anger with Wilderspin? Nervous exhaustion? He hadn't slept a wink last night. Sexual anticipation? All three most likely.

He knocked gently. She might be in bed. He knocked again, harder this time. Still no reply. Slowly, he turned the knob. The door was locked.

He took out his wallet and extracted a nail file. Lovers shouldn't have secrets.

Matt immediately placed himself between Lizzie and Lila and the gun.

"If you fire that thing you might as well shoot yourself. Even Inskip won't be able to cover it up."

"He hasn't got the balls," said Simkins.

"Hark who's talking!"

"Shh!"

Matt could tell Lizzie was more livid than afraid. She held Lila tightly, glaring at Simkins not the gun.

"Don't do it," said Matt. "He'd rather die than face public humiliation."

Lizzie couldn't help herself: "Johnny will so enjoy covering the court case."

Zick lowered the pistol but stepped back and raised it again when Matt moved to take it from him.

"Stay where you are. How do I know you won't arrest me too? You're clearly not a man to let bygones be bygones."

"You'll have to trust me," said Matt.

Simkins laughed.

"There's no one more honest than my husband," said Lizzie. "I should know."

Matt looked at her in a new light. He wasn't sure what impressed him most: her loyalty or bravery. Was he still honest though? The money remained in his locker.

Lila Mae, wanting to join in the game, held out her arms to her father.

"In a minute, Angel. Daddy's busy."

"He's scared what might come out in court," said Simkins. "Oh, the stories I could tell . . ."

"I went to great lengths to keep you happy," said Zick.

"And silent."

"Very true," said Zick, and shot him.

The Lord Mayor's coach — a fantasia in red and gold — emerged from Prince's Street by the Bank of England and turned, groaning on its leather straps, towards Poultry. Adler, leaning out of the window, doffed his

274

cocked hat to the dignitaries assembled under the portico of his new home, the Mansion House. The ostrich feathers on his hat rippled in the chilly breeze.

The cheering crowds that packed the pavements did nothing to scare the horses. Pairs of mounted policemen protected the coach at the front and rear. The floats that followed were also mainly drawn by horses, whereas others relied on another form of horsepower. It was one of these that stalled. The actors portraying Sir Francis Drake and his fellow bowlers staggered as the truck coughed then lurched to a stop.

The theme of this year's show was physical health. Everywhere banners proclaimed FITNESS WINS! Dancers, boxers, golfers and rowers continued to demonstrate their moves.

The plaster of Paris mountain being climbed by the alpinists started to emit smoke. Johnny watched in disbelief. No one climbed an active volcano.

The army jeeps and wagons of the auxiliary fire brigade rolled on. They were on parade, not on duty.

As soon as a gap appeared in the procession, Johnny pushed through the crowd lining the route and crossed Cheapside.

He weaved his way through a maze of penny-farthings, unseating a couple of the riders. Their companions, cursing loudly, wobbled precariously but somehow remained upright and continued to pedal. Some of the spectators started to boo.

A few members of a marching band, distracted, fell out of step. The loss of rhythm was accompanied by an unscored clash of cymbals. The catcalls got louder.

One of the police outriders craned his neck to see the cause of the commotion. Calling to his colleagues, he turned his mount around and headed towards Johnny.

Adler, arm aching from waving to his devoted citizens, stuck his head out of the left side of the coach. Below him, on a painted panel, Mars, god of the City of London — and not, as many assumed, Mammon — pointed to a scroll held by Truth. What was going on?

His molehill had become a mountain.

Johnny, surrounded by coppers, indicated the flames on the back of the float. They ran towards it.

Hollom emerged on the other side of Cheapside and headed for the coach. Was he going to kill Adler too?

Before he could do so Johnny rugby-tackled him. It was like head-butting a tree. Both men fell to the ground and scrabbled in the sand and sawdust.

More cops ran towards the melee. Jeers, whinnying and whistles competed with the faltering brass. Johnny glimpsed wheels, hooves, running feet. He smelled Hollom's garlicky sweat, felt his enormous strength. He didn't have a chance.

The last thing he saw was Watkiss — half-shocked, half-amused — bearing down on them.

The City's bells — including those of St Olave's, St Margaret Pattens', St Swithin's London Stone, St Mary's Woolnoth and St Bride's — continued to ring out the good news.

Hollom's fist met his chin. The whole world exploded.

CHAPTER
TWENTY-NINE

Simkins didn't bite the bullet — he swallowed it.

At first Matt thought Zick had missed him altogether. Simkins, clutching his throat, fell backwards. A chair toppled over as he met the floor with a crash. He didn't move.

Neither did Matt. The explosion roared in his ears — as if the confined space had instantly filled with hot water. It was hard to breathe.

Lizzie and Lila Mae both had their mouths open in silent screams. Zick dropped the gun and disappeared behind the hidden door. Matt let him go.

Black blood pooled behind Simkins's head. His chestnut curls glowed against his blanching skin. His eyes were open but for him the picture was over.

Jubb peeped round the edge of the door.

"Call Snow Hill immediately," said Matt. His voice sounded odd. "Ask for DI Tyser and Commander Inskip. Tell them Henry Simkins has been shot dead."

The landlord stared at the cooling corpse. Simkins had been one of his best customers.

"I don't suppose you'll be needing the second bottle now."

"Keep it on ice," said Matt. "Go on then. Shift yourself!"

Matt closed the door against a huddle of excited drinkers. He picked up the gun, wiped Zick's prints off it, and pressed it into Simkins's right hand.

Lizzie watched in horror.

"What are you doing?"

"If anyone asks, *I* shot Simkins with his own gun." He took it out of the dead man's hand. His prints now overlaid those of the "assailant". It was about time Simkins was the fallguy. "It will be far simpler this way, believe me."

"I do."

Matt held his wife and child in a wide embrace. They were safe. They were all safe.

"My ears hurt," said Lizzie. "God knows what damage has been done to Lila's."

She was shaking, but her voice, as far as he could tell, was steady.

"We'll have them checked. In the meantime you need to get out of here. If my bosses learn you've been here, there'll be hell to pay."

"What about you?"

"I'll keep the ghouls at bay."

"Where should I go?"

She was at a loss what to do. Were they safe now or in greater danger?

Matt kissed her on the forehead. He stroked Lila's silky hair.

"The *Daily News*. Johnny'll look after you. There'll be a good view of the parade from his office. I'll collect you from there as soon as I can. We'll go home together."

"That will be nice."

Embarrassment and pride could be glimpsed in her fleeting smile. Matt thought she'd never looked so beautiful.

They both jumped as another door in the wainscoting opened. Jubb had clearly been listening at it.

"This way, madam. That mob ain't going nowhere." He nodded towards the bar. "I'll show you to the back door — you'll be able to slip out into Farringdon Road."

"Thank you," said Matt.

He kissed his girls goodbye. As soon as they'd followed the landlord out Matt, burning the envelopes first, threw the photographs on the fire. His and Johnny's naked bodies writhed in the flames. He stared into the hearth long after the images had gone.

The landlord reappeared. "The birds have flown."

"Thank you. That's one thing less to worry about."

"What about him?" Jubb pointed to the ceiling.

"Is he still here?"

"Indeed. Awaiting instructions."

"Tell him he can go too — by the same exit, if you please. We know where to find him."

"Is he in lumber?"

"Of course — but he seems to like it this way."

"Pity," said Jubb, scratching his bald patch. "Zick and I go way back."

Matt shook his head. He wasn't surprised. He was trying to clear his muffled hearing.

"If I were you, I'd keep quiet about that."

Johnny woke up in gaol. He was lying on a narrow shelf that ran round a windowless cell. A similar one opposite was unoccupied. Previous inmates had scratched names and curses into the slime-green paint that covered the walls. There were no doors, only floor-to-ceiling bars. His head hurt. It felt like someone had stamped on it.

Footsteps echoed down the subterranean corridor.

"Sleeping Beauty awakes!"

"You're no Prince Charming."

"Don't be like that." Watkiss sniggered. "You're in the Birdcage. They used to keep female prisoners here. The other one was for the men."

"Where am I?"

"The Magistrates Court."

Johnny had sat upstairs in the press gallery many times but he had never been down here. He knew a tunnel led to the Mansion House next door to protect the Lord Mayor from angry mobs.

"What time is it?"

"Why? You're not going anywhere."

Johnny, stiff all over, got to his feet and went over to the bars.

"If it wasn't for me, you wouldn't be here." He patted his pockets. "My possessions seem to have been confiscated. Why?"

"Why d'you think? You tried to attack the Mayor."

"As if! I was trying to save his life. Where's Hollom?"

"Who?"

"The chap who clobbered me."

"He's not here."

"Well, who is?"

"No one. I'm holding the fort. The court, for obvious reasons, isn't sitting today. We're all alone."

"Let me out then. I can't be under arrest because you can't arrest an unconscious man."

"True. You're being held for questioning."

"On whose say so?"

"Commander Inskip."

"Why here rather than Snow Hill?"

"It was the closest place of safety."

"What happened?"

"A bomb went off. Fortunately, it was only a small device. Adler would have been injured if you hadn't slowed him down."

"So I'm a hero."

"That remains to be seen. I'd say you deserve a cup of tea though."

"Haven't you got anything stronger?"

Five minutes later Watkiss returned with two steaming mugs. It was cold in the cells. Johnny could hear the thud of pedestrians passing overhead.

Watkiss handed him both mugs. He opened the gate and locked it behind him. He took one of the mugs and sat down beside Johnny.

"A couple of spectators were hurt in the crush but, thanks to your intervention, the only real damage was to the float. The show could go on."

"Nothing must be allowed to impede City business."

"You can say that again."

The younger man was looking at Johnny in a different way. He didn't recognize the expression because it was one of admiration.

"How did you know the Mayor was in danger?"

"I received a tip-off."

"Anyone I know?"

"Quirk."

"But he's dead."

Johnny, in spite of his sore jaw, couldn't help laughing. "He wasn't when he told me."

"Why d'you think that big feller was about to attack Adler?"

"Call it a hunch."

"He didn't half lay into you."

"So I'm discovering. What did Hollom — his name's Hollom — do afterwards?"

"He got into the coach. Adler's face was a picture."

"Of what? Fear? Outrage? Recognition?"

"Fear, mostly. Then indignation. He made him lie on the floor so no one could see him."

"The police didn't try to get him out?"

"No. They were too busy throwing a cordon round the burning lorry. They ensured the parade rolled on. Some of the spectators assumed it was all part of the show."

"Why were you in Cheapside?"

"Keeping an eye on Adler. Making sure nothing happened to him."

"I reckon, all things considered, you succeeded."

"Well, I knew you weren't a threat."

"Thank you — I think." He drained his mug. "One sugar next time."

"I made it extra-sweet to counteract the shock."

"I'm not in shock."

"Not yet," said Watkiss. "Henry Simkins is dead."

★   ★   ★

It wasn't Johnny who came down to the foyer. A beefy young man, at least a foot taller than him, approached her. She'd have said he was a rugger player if it weren't for his shyness.

"Mrs Turner? Tim Tanfield." He held out his hand. "We have met before."

Lizzie said nothing. It would be rude of her to say that she didn't remember him.

"How d'you do. Where's Johnny?"

"I think the correct phrase is *he's been unavoidably detained*. Do come up to the newsroom though."

He smiled at Lila Mae who seemed dazzled by the sunburst ceiling.

"I'm sure this cherub would like to see the rest of the parade. It's much warmer and we can have a little chat there."

"What about?"

"Henry Simkins."

It wasn't difficult to appear shocked — she was surprised how fast the news had travelled. She reproached herself for her naivety. Alcohol loosened tongues even when gunfire wasn't involved.

She could see Tanfield was excited. His grey eyes shone. He had a lead on a fatal shooting and Johnny wasn't around to steal the headlines. She wasn't going to tell him anything.

He led her over to the lifts.

"The death of one of our own — especially in the line of duty — is always upsetting but what makes Henry's so personally shocking is that we only had lunch last week."

"You were friends?"

"I wouldn't go so far as that. *Colleagues* would be more accurate."

"Not rivals?"

"Not in this case." He looked away, shifting uncomfortably. "He certainly lived up to his name. Out in India, champagne is known as Simkin. Something to do with how the locals pronounce it, apparently."

"I suppose that's the only way it touches their tongues."

He seemed even younger when he laughed.

"I can see why Johnny likes you."

"And I like him."

Tanfield nodded, as if in possession of secret knowledge. "He and your husband are very close."

She was about to ask him what that was supposed to mean — had Simkins said something? — when the lift-doors opened and an elderly woman tottered out. Before they could enter, two gentlemen in handmade suits shoved past them.

"Don't mind us," said Lizzie. "What happened to women and children first?"

The older of the two, suave yet thuggish, held out his hand to prevent anyone else entering the car.

"You're not in any danger, madam. Yet."

He turned to the liftboy, who instantly wiped the grin off his face.

"Mr Stone's office — and no stopping on the way."

For a moment he felt nothing at all. They had been through a lot together — most of it unpleasant — but saving a man's life bound you to him just as much as it bound him to you. If he had to describe the emotion

284

that was slowly dispelling the numbness he would say it was relief not grief.

Watkiss was enjoying the effect his bombshell had created. "Say something! It's not like you to be lost for words."

"How did he die?"

"He was shot." He licked his lips. "Matt shot him."

Like a man on the scaffold, Johnny could feel the trapdoor swing open.

"He must have had a good reason."

His gaoler let him stew for a moment before responding. "Self-defence was what I heard. Simkins pulled a gun and Matt managed to grab it off him."

"Hoist with his own petard."

"What?"

"Nothing. Where was this?"

"Ye Olde Mitre Tavern."

"Who else was there?"

"Not sure."

Footsteps — more than one pair — could be heard coming down the stairs.

"Why don't you ask him yourself?"

Matt, unscathed and unsmiling, appeared at the bars — closely followed by Inskip.

"What the fuck are you doing in the cell, Watkiss?" Inskip held out his hand for the keys. "If we weren't so overstretched I'd leave you in overnight. You don't fraternize with prisoners."

"He's no longer a prisoner, though, is he, sir?" Matt injected the honorofic with as much contempt as he could muster.

"That remains to be decided. Get back to the station, Watkiss. DI Tyser needs all the help he can get."

"Yes, sir."

Watkiss flinched as he made his exit, half-expecting the Commander to clip him round the ear.

When he was certain the three of them were alone, Inskip sat down and gestured for Matt to follow suit.

"You've got your friend here to thank for your immediate release, Steadman — but don't go thinking that we're now on the same side. We may have certain shared interests, but that's as far as it goes. Your sort are nothing but trouble.

"Saved your bacon though, didn't I?"

Johnny took the envelope Matt was holding out to him. It contained his watch — Ah! It was nearly four — wallet, cigarettes and loose change, but not his notebook.

"If Adler had died, you'd have had to fall on your sword."

"He's very much alive — and according to Hollom — kicking. It seems he doesn't like sharing the limelight."

"Were you aware of his investigation?"

The Commander hesitated, as if deciding whether or not to tell the truth.

"No. It's nothing to do with the City of London Police."

"It is if he's been eliminating fascists in the Square Mile. Wouldn't you like my help with that?"

Matt glared at him to make him shut up.

286

"What?" Johnny felt the noose tightening round his neck.

Inskip pulled out Johnny's notebook and riffled through it.

"You're delusional, Steadman. You see conspiracies everywhere. If the governor of the Bank of England isn't a closet Nazi, a government agent is a contract killer. What happened to checking your facts? Your front-page splash today has made you a whole new set of enemies. Still, it's not my job to silence you this time. I've got a multiple murderer to deal with."

"What makes you so sure Hollom isn't a killer? Or, for that matter, Adler? He could have planted the bomb himself."

Matt put his head in his hands. Inskip stared at Johnny as if he were genuinely mad.

"Perhaps you're suffering from concussion, or nervous exhaustion or full-blown paranoia. Whatever the problem, I suggest you let Turner here look after you in future. If you're not careful, someone less understanding than me might have you carted off to the booby hatch. You know, once you've been admitted it's almost impossible to get out . . ."

Johnny snatched his notebook out of Inskip's hands.

"What don't I know? Why do I feel I'm a hanging man?"

Inskip stood up. "I'll let you do the honours, Turner. My driver's waiting. Don't take too long about it. Tyser needs you."

Johnny needed Matt. He had always taken care of him. They waited until Inskip was out of earshot.

"What's happened? Is it to do with Simkins?"

Matt put a hand on his shoulder. "No. He's no longer a problem — for either of us. Zick shot the bastard. Inskip's overseeing the case. The story is that Simkins pulled a gun on me and Zick. He got hurt in the struggle."

"Why would he pull a gun on you?"

"Zick was threatening to expose him as a child molester. A botherer of little boys. He says he has film of him doing it."

"I knew Henry was capable of almost anything — but I never suspected him of that. I thought he was after me."

"Maybe he was."

"I hope he refrained after I saved his life."

"No doubt Zick will be able to tell us."

"So he's got something else on us now, besides the photographs."

"Forget about the photographs. They're gone. Simkins's final act placed me in a far more compromising position. Let's just say I'm now well and truly in Inskip's pocket."

He would tell Johnny about the money later. There was further information to pass on.

"You need to get back to the *News*. There was another murder this afternoon. Neither Hollom nor Adler could have done it. In fact, Hollom could have been the next victim."

"What proves their innocence?"

"They both have an alibi."

"Have they been checked? Perhaps they're in it together. They might have an accomplice."

"Johnny, Johnny, listen to me. It's over."

He couldn't believe it. He knew in his bones that Adler was up to no good. He'd already admitted that he'd blackmailed Montagu Norman. Perhaps it was true that morality played no part in business.

"They might be in cahoots — which would explain Adler's fury at being seen with Hollom. What was he doing at the show? What did he say to Adler? They could be in league with others. Something, something of paramount importance, must have happened that made it imperative for them to talk — even during the parade."

"Johnny, Johnny, listen to me. It's over. We've arrested the killer."

The rope reached its full extent. However, it wasn't his neck that snapped but his patience. Matt waited for the stream of invective to dry up.

"Tanfield is at the scene now."

Johnny opened his mouth to start cursing again. Before he could do so, Matt put a giant hand over it and laughed when he tried to bite him.

"Don't you try to silence me as well!" Johnny was beside himself. "I will not be gagged."

"Keep your hair on. Inskip, in a token gesture of gratitude, has agreed to let you interview the killer so you'll still have an exclusive at the end of the day."

"Thank you. I know it's you I should thank, not him. There's not enough time though. I've got to write up how I saved the life of the Lord Mayor — and how a man whose life I saved has been killed by a wicked policeman."

Johnny was correct. He was wicked.

"I think you'll find that Tanfield has both stories covered."

"But he doesn't know what I know."

"That's true — which will make your follow-ups seem all the better. Now, do you want to come face to face with the killer of six men or not?"

Matt, none too gently, pulled Johnny to his feet.

"You're going to have a black eye."

"Good. It'll make for a striking picture. Hollom really went for me."

"You'd disobeyed his orders. Made him break cover."

"Not deliberately. Not in this instance. He never mentioned Adler."

"Well, Hollom was the one who insisted you were locked up."

"Did he say what he was doing in Cheapside?"

"No. As soon as his identity was verified, he made himself scarce."

"I need to talk to him."

"First things first. The killer awaits."

"What's he called?"

"She. A true femme fatale. So far we've only got a first name out of her — Rebecca."

CHAPTER
THIRTY

Lila Mae was hungry. They both were. She had enjoyed watching the marching soldiers and pretty horses through the open windows but now needed a feed. However, Lizzie wasn't leaving without Matt. They had been apart for too long.

Lila's angry cries attracted disapproving glances even amid the office din of frantic typewriters and unanswered telephones. The newsroom was no place for a woman.

An athletic man with Mediterranean features — olive skin, eyes black as Whitby jet — sauntered over to them.

"May I fetch you anything?"

"No, thank you. Although you might show me the way to the Ladies — if you don't have a deadline."

"All done. Not much happens on a Wednesday at this time of year. Follow me."

Tanfield, flushed and panicky, brushed past them. He threw off his hat and coat and was flicking through his notebook before his backside hit the chair.

"Louis. Where are you taking Mrs Turner?"

"Upstairs, if that's all right with you. Baby Dumpling's tum-tum is empty."

"She's a girl, not a boy."

Lizzie was grateful for the fact. Males were so transparent. Most of them, anyway.

"Whoops! My mistake."

Dimeo, unabashed, bent down and kissed Lila Mae. Tanfield envied him his nonchalance.

"Okay. I'll let Johnny know where you are. He shouldn't be much longer."

After the Lord Mayor's show came the dustcart. Gaiety gave way to squalor.

From the back of a cab, Johnny watched an army of men shovelling horseshit, collecting litter and sweeping away the sand and sawdust from the streets. He had his own mess to clear up.

Matt filled him in on the way to Snow Hill. At one o'clock that afternoon a report came in that a naked man had fallen through a top-floor window of a block near Holborn Circus. Not *from* the window — which could be explicable — but through its panes of glass. He'd died at the scene.

Shortly thereafter, as police entered the house, a woman was seen abseiling down the front of the building that backed on to it in Thavies Inn. She was using a safety device, known as a Spiderline, intended to aid escape in the event of a fire. However, its spool had jammed and left the woman dangling in mid-air. On seeing the cops she had tried but failed to slice through the line with a sharp knife.

Tyser, sweating and stubble-chinned, emerged from the interview room in triumph.

"She's told us everything. Made a complete confession. Says she wants to die."

He held up a jar containing what looked like dried rose petals. Shrivelled flakes of brown and red.

"What d'you think these are?" He opened the lid. "Have a sniff. Go on!"

Matt declined but Johnny, true to form, stuck his nose in. They smelled musty — nothing like roses.

"Foreskins!" Both men laughed as Johnny recoiled. "She was going to bind a book with them — when she'd collected enough."

"She must be insane," said Johnny.

"Perhaps," said Tyser. He stopped laughing. "Then she's every reason to be. You've got ten minutes — and not a second longer."

He held his breath as Matt opened the door. A handsome, dark-haired woman sat at the stained wooden table. It wasn't Tooting Becky.

Matt told the constable to wait outside.

"Right, you're on your own. I've got a couple of things to do, then I'm off to meet Lizzie."

"So she's turned up?"

"Indeed. I don't have all the answers yet. I'll tell you the full story tomorrow. This bloody business should be completed by then."

"I'm glad," said Johnny. "For both of you."

She waited until the door closed behind him.

"Are you glad? Reporters aren't supposed to tell lies."

"I'll ask the questions, if you don't mind. There isn't much time."

This short but pneumatic woman had killed six men and yet for some reason he wasn't afraid. Her eyes — black flecked with amber — were full of hurt rather than hatred. He felt as though she could see deep inside him.

"Thank you for speaking to me. I appreciate you don't have to."

"It's not as if I have anything else to do. Besides, it's what's not said that means the most."

He opened his notebook.

"Make sure you spell my name correctly. R-E-B-E-K-K-A-H. Rebekkah Maslow. M-A-S-L-O-W."

"And the man you love?"

She smiled. A beautiful smile of lost joy and long regret.

"Kaspar Fortgang — with a K."

"That doesn't sound Jewish."

"He wasn't. They killed him for wanting to marry me."

They had spent the day walking in the Grunewald. Five members of the Schutzstaffel interrupted their sunlit idyll and demanded to see their papers. When they didn't like what they saw they ordered them both to strip. She thought she was going to die — especially when they unleashed the Alsatians. However, they set the dogs on Kaspar.

The young men held her, groped her, forced her to watch as the snarling animals sank their teeth into her lover's flesh, tearing off his penis, biting him all over his body, while their aroused handlers jeered.

"I can still hear his screams. In my head he is always screaming."

Her cries for help were either unheard or ignored. She could do nothing but stare in horror. Kaspar fought for his life as long as he could before, lapsing into unconsciousness, he slowly bled to death, the demented dogs slavering over the corpse.

However, Rebekkah's ordeal was only beginning. The blond boys took it in turns to rape her again and again. In her mouth and *tukhus* too.

"They could have killed me — but they wanted me to suffer, to live in shame and grief. Day after day after day."

"When did the rage begin?" Johnny was furious on her behalf.

"Immediately. As soon as I was alone. I wanted to tell Kaspar how I felt but — of course — I could not."

There were so many things he needed to know. Her background, how she came to England. He fought to control his emotions and organize his thoughts.

The murders had to take precedence.

"Five men attacked you. Why did you keep on killing after your fifth victim?"

"I wasn't going to kill Alex. He wasn't, as far as I could tell, a fascist. I liked him — but he betrayed my trust. When I found him in my rooms, uninvited, whatever was between us vanished. I took him to bed and told him exactly what I'd done and what I was going to do to him. He didn't believe me at first until I told him about Kaspar — and showed him the jar of offcuts. He was in a blue funk — and I'd locked the door — so, when I produced the handcuffs, he flung himself out of the window. He didn't hesitate in the slightest . . . The *bris* doesn't hurt that much!" She sighed. "I rather enjoyed being a *mohel*. The look in their eyes when they knew they were going to die — I saw it in Kaspar's eyes too. The moment of ultimate knowledge . . .

"I don't care what happens to me. I haven't since the day he died. My intention was to keep on bloodletting for as long as possible. If I hadn't met Alex, I wouldn't have been caught. My only mistake was to like him. He would have made someone happy. Affection is a weakness. I should have killed him as soon as I knew he was following me."

"But you didn't. He wasn't on the list."

"Neither are you, Mr Steadman, but I could grab that pencil and stab you in the eye before anyone could save you."

Johnny sat back quickly.

"Why? You want your story to be told, don't you?"

"That's why you're still alive. I want the whole world to know what's happening in Germany — even if they don't want to hear it."

"I'll do my best. I promise."

He meant it. This was the twentieth century yet Hitler and his henchmen seemed intent on ushering in a new Dark Age.

"How did you get the list of EFF members?"

"I broke into the office and stole it. Neither was hard to find."

"You used a Spiderline?"

"Yes. I've never been afraid of heights."

"And you simply started at the top of the list?"

"More or less. As a chemist I was trained to be methodical. However, as a Jewish woman, I could only get employment as a pharmacist in Berlin. Still, the little I learned about toxins proved useful."

"Why begin with the Bs though?"

"It was a question of geography. All the As lived out of the City. I'd have got to them eventually."

"Did you meet them at work?"

"No. Why d'you ask me that? I met Alex at Lockharts, but no one else."

"Both Bromet and Broster had the same stomach contents: boiled pork and pease pudding."

"We're allowed to take home any leftovers from the restaurant. That's what made it so easy to poison the fools. When a man is offered sex *and* food he rarely says no. I would offer to cook them a meal at their place and, knowing they would soon be unconscious, return later with my tools. This allowed me to establish an alibi, should one ever be required."

She sounded proud of her modus operandi.

"Why enter through the windows though?"

"It was more discreet. Few people are in the habit of looking up. Londoners keep their heads down, especially at night. I'd open and close the window before I left to ensure I could get through it."

"Wasn't it difficult, getting back on to the roof?"

"Not at all. The winding mechanism works both ways — up and down. Besides, if necessary, I could have climbed the line like a rope."

Johnny was using shorthand yet still struggled to keep up with the torrent of words. She may have been bragging but she was also relieved to be able to finally share the information.

"Did you follow the same routine each time?"

"More or less. Alex unsettled me though. I sensed the end was near. If I didn't kill five fascists Kaspar would remain unavenged. Hext was a last-minute substitute. I'd actually chosen a man called Hollom to be the next victim. He was close by in Hatton Garden but he didn't appear to sleep at his given address and this made me suspicious."

"A shop called Otarelli's."

"Indeed. You know the man?"

"I've met him. In fact he almost broke my jaw today. He works for the British government. In some strange way I think you and he must be on the same side. He's infiltrated the EFF but I'm not sure why yet. At one stage I thought he was the killer."

"I am glad that I did not kill him. He has had a lucky escape."

"It's more likely that he would have killed you."

"One way or another your government will have its way with me."

Johnny paused. She would have made an excellent secret agent. He glanced at his watch. There was one minute left.

"Hext apart, did you have sex with all the men?"

She glared at him. Johnny gripped his pencil.

"I'm not a whore. I did what I had to do, pandering to their pathetic fantasies so I could tie them up. I had sex with Alex, that's all. He reminded me of Kaspar. I think it's the way he gave himself to me straightaway. He didn't hold back. Such vulnerability now terrifies me. Kaspar was my soulmate. Maybe I was Alex's — but it would never have worked out. You can only have one secret sharer."

The sudden silence made Johnny look up. She was studying him.

"The blond detective. Maybe he is your soulmate?"

She had been more than truthful. He owed her one straight answer.

"Yes."

"I knew it. You hide it well, Mr Steadman, but your eyes give you away."

"It doesn't matter," said Johnny. "I've never said the words but he knows it."

Matt popped into the Robin Hood on their way back from the station. Lizzie didn't say a word. He bought a bottle of Mackeson for her as well. They both needed a drink.

They put Lila Mae — already in dreamland — to bed. Matt got the fire going in the parlour while Lizzie prepared a light supper of bacon and eggs. They ate in silence. Lizzie knew she would have to be the one who broke it.

She waited until he'd finished wiping his plate with a slice of bread. She could hear her mother tut-tutting.

"You got the murderer then?"

"Yes. It was more to do with dumb luck than detection. A German woman out for revenge."

"For what?"

"The Nazis killed her fiancé. He was fraternizing with a Jew."

"What will happen to her?"

"If she's lucky, she'll stand trial in England. If not she'll be sent back to Germany."

Lizzie shuddered. The latter would surely be a fate worse than death.

"What were you doing at the Mitre?"

Matt met her gaze. "I could ask you the same question." He stood up and held out his hand. "Come on."

They sat holding hands in the firelight.

"I was trying to locate a government agent who seemed implicated in the murders."

"And did you?"

"Not straightaway. Turns out he was thumping Johnny in Cheapside."

"Is he all right?"

"He'll live. Should I have been the one landing the punch?"

"No. Of course not! Tanfield deliberately misled you. Why didn't you say anything when you came to collect us?"

"No need. As one of Simkins's spies he'll be interviewed in connection with the blackmail attempt. We won't be able to prosecute him, but the shock should make him appreciate the value of discretion."

"I was going to tell you about Zick."

"When?"

"When I'd resolved the matter."

"And how would you have done that if I hadn't turned up? You could have been shot!"

"So could you. My only concern was that Simkins didn't let the photographs fall into the wrong hands."

"I'm sorry you had to see them."

"In a way I'm glad I did. We shouldn't have secrets from each other." She squeezed his hand. "Someone sent me the ones of you two years ago."

Matt resisted the urge to leap up. He'd done his utmost to keep her in the dark about the assault and yet she'd known all along.

"Who?"

"I don't know. I destroyed them."

"Didn't you wonder how they were taken?"

"I assumed the same way as the ones of Johnny were."

"They weren't taken at the same time."

"It doesn't matter if they were. It's clear that neither of you were conscious."

"Did Johnny tell you what happened to him?"

"Not in so many words. I've a fair idea though. We've never talked about it — just as I've never talked about this with you before."

Matt was furious with Zick — it had to be Zick; he'd broken his promise to destroy the negatives — but at the same time he was relieved the sordid saga was finally out in the open. Zick, at Inskip's insistence, had already given up Timney. A small price to pay to save his neck. The photographer would never make another nudie.

He hugged his wife. "Thank you. I don't deserve you. A lesser woman would have walked out."

"I thought I had."

She laughed at Matt's look of panic.

"I'm teasing you, Matt. Commander Inskip suggested it would be safer for us all if I did so."

So that was it. The apparently well-meant warning was designed to exert greater pressure on him. He dreaded to think what would have happened if he hadn't taken the money.

"I should have told you I was going to my parents, but I was angry with you. I was at the end of my tether. I felt taken for granted, bored and frustrated. I hate your job for changing you, for taking you away from us so often. There has to be more to life than this, but I'll never do such a selfish thing again."

Matt listened carefully. He would make it up to her somehow. All he'd ever wanted to be was a cop. What else could he do though? War was coming. It was his duty to protect her and Lila. His well-being depended on theirs.

"I thought Zick was behind your disappearance. That's the thing about blackmail, it leaves behind a taint, a sneaking suspicion that never goes away. When you think about it, he's at least partly to blame. You can't tell another soul this, Lizzie, but Inskip is in business with Zick. I realize now that I can't possibly escape their clutches without ending my career. They have too many so-called friends. I took thirty pieces of their silver to get them off my back. That's why Simkins's death won't be a problem. They think I'm on the same side as they are. I suppose we are now. I'm as corrupt as they are."

For a moment Lizzie, staring into the flames, said nothing.

"You aren't like them. Not a jot . . . Does Johnny know this?"

"Not yet."

"Don't tell him."

"Why not?"

"It will destroy him," said Lizzie. "You know how he looks up to you. You're his hero."

"And d'you know how he feels about me?"

"I've always known."

"Aren't you jealous?"

"Do I have any reason to be?"

"No. You should know me better than that! If I'm being honest, though, I do envy the closeness between you. The way your minds think alike is unnerving — and strangely intimate."

Lizzie kissed him, long and slow, drinking in the heat and taste of him.

"Well, detective," she said, slightly out of breath. "Consider the evidence. We love the same man."

It was only later that he realized the "we" could refer to Lizzie and Johnny or Lizzie and him.

This time he'd been expecting recriminations as well as congratulations.

Johnny stood in front of the vast desk while Stone raged at him.

"Your theories turned out to be pure poppycock! Adler and Hollom are entirely blameless. They haven't killed anyone. Now I've got the Ministry of War breathing fire down my neck."

"That's because the story about the gold is true."

"It's been classified as a state secret — so we have to publish both a recantation and an apology."

"Why? Regulations can't be introduced retroactively. What was true yesterday will be true tomorrow."

"The Emergency Powers Act covers a multitude of sins. We're about to go to war. The usual rules do not apply."

"Your brother-in-law could back us up."

"And why would he do that?"

"We'll reveal the Bank of England's part in stealing the Czech gold if he doesn't."

"Aren't you listening to me? The first casualty when war comes is truth."

"Maybe in America. What does LV say?"

Stone, living up to his name, froze. He regarded his idealistic reporter impassively.

"You haven't told him, have you?" Johnny was mystified. "Why not? Who are you trying to protect? It better not be Adler."

"I don't need to explain myself to you, Steadman. Take it from me: the Lord Mayor is beyond reproach — or soon will be."

"What's that supposed to mean? Who's got to you? I thought we were on the same side."

"Choose your words carefully or you won't even be on the same newspaper."

"I always do. I presume you've heard the *Chronicle* needs a new crime editor?"

"Tanfield has written an excellent account of Simkins's death. You trained him well. He also enjoyed reporting on your arrest this afternoon — as well as the final murder. He's had a busy day in your absence. What were you thinking?"

"I wasn't arrested, so you'd better correct his copy before the late edition. And Vanneck jumped to his death, so technically it wasn't murder. I thought your brother-in-law was in danger. Hollom, after clouting me, got into the coach. Did you know that? I see Tanfield didn't mention it. Or did you censor his copy?"

Stone appeared genuinely surprised.

"Is this true?"

"Yes. There must be dozens of witnesses. Why would Hollom do such a thing? What was so important that he would break cover to speak to him?"

"Let's ask him."

Stone told his secretary to get Adler on the line. While they were waiting, Johnny related his exclusive interview with Rebekkah Maslow.

"So the EFF provided the victims, not the culprit?"

"In five cases, yes. But don't forget it was the EFF that firebombed the synagogue. They must be behind the attacks on Adler too. A single conversation with Hollom could clear this up."

"I think your shiner says it all. He lets his fists do the talking. You're not to approach him in any way. Is that understood?"

"Yes, sir."

If truth was no longer paramount then lying was not important either.

One of the telephones rang.

"It seems he's unavailable," said Stone. He didn't like being thwarted. "Probably out celebrating his ascent of the greasy pole. I'll try him at home later. Something doesn't add up. In the meantime, bash out the interview. Two thousand words as quick as you can. I'll tell them to remake the front page." It was after nine when Johnny filed his copy. The expense of holding the presses would be more than offset by the extra copies sold. The Lord Mayor's show disrupted, the fatal shooting of a journalist, a sixth death plus an interview with the Jewish woman responsible: it would be a remarkable, collector's edition.

It wasn't only the crime desk that was working late. The foreign desk was buzzing. There was no sign of Patsel. Reports were coming in of another night of violence in Germany. Across the country Jewish businesses were being attacked, synagogues burned down. In Berlin well-dressed people had applauded as Hitler Youths beat Jewish people senseless with lead piping, their screams aped by crowds of laughing spectators. Some women even held up their children so they would have a better view. The streets were strewn with so much broken glass that it was already being called *Kristallnacht*.

Johnny's heart ached as much as his head and jaw. He feared this was only the start of something, something truly evil. How could people — citizens of a Western nation — behave like this?

306

He looked at the bottle of champagne Matt had left, a gift from Ye Olde Mitre, courtesy — if that was the word — of Zick. No, he wasn't in the mood. He was exhausted but knew he wouldn't sleep if he went straight home. Tanfield, wisely, had scarpered — probably to toast his perceived successes. It was too late to call Becky and, by now, Matt would be back in Bexleyheath with Lizzie.

He'd take a leaf out of Dickens's book and walk through the City at night. Rebekkah Maslow had been arrested in Thavies Inn — mentioned in *Bleak House* — and it was on the way back to Islington. Besides, he wanted to see where she had lived and Vanneck had died.

Fetter Lane provided the most direct and safest route. Hollom was obviously still furious with him. He had tried several times to contact him on various numbers without success. He didn't fancy taking a chance and negotiating the maze of dark alleys behind Fleet Street. He was fed up with being a punch-bag.

He turned right into High Holborn. The corner of a poster for Frank Capra's latest film, *You Can't Take It with You*, starring Jimmy Stewart and Jean Arthur, fluttered in the river-breeze. Perhaps Becky would like to see it.

Bartlett's Buildings was, as expected, dirty, gloomy and ghastly. There was a dispensary at the end of the cul-de-sac that might have supplied Maslow with her narcotic additives. A boarded-up window was the only evidence that something untoward had happened that day. Tomorrow, thanks in no small part to the *News*, it would become a short-lived tourist attraction.

It was only when he saw the offices of Cobden-Sanderson that he remembered he'd been to Thavies Inn before. He'd attended a book launch there — the title of the book in question escaped him — but he'd wanted to see where the *Criterion* had first been published. He still felt guilty about filching a copy of the quarterly magazine. There'd been so much hoo-ha about *The Wasteland* he'd wanted to study it. He hadn't understood a lot of the poem but some lines had stuck in his memory as soon as he'd read them: *I had not thought death had undone so many.*

Gamages, across Holborn Circus, made him think of Lizzie. She must have come to her senses — or at least made up her mind. It was the right choice — for all of them.

Was Maslow right when she'd said affection was a weakness? Love gave you the strength to do many things. The prospect of enduring a time of war unattached was terrifying — but wouldn't worrying constantly about the safety of a lover be equally hellish? There was only one way to find out. Becky was lovely but she'd said she wasn't the marrying kind. He was. Nevertheless, they must make the most of however much time the two of them had left.

He didn't make a conscious decision to enter Hatton Garden. Again, it was the most direct and best-lit route. The shuttered shops gave no hint of the treasures that lay securely within. *Tesoro.* What had Maslow said? Hollom didn't sleep at Otarelli's. What was he doing there then? As an undercover cop he couldn't give the EFF his real address but his given place of work must have some significance.

The shop sold scientific instruments. Was the firm working on some secret project for the government?

He turned left into Charles Street. The front of the building was in total darkness. He might as well check round the back.

He continued along the empty street. Leather Lane was at the end but before he reached it he came to a covered passage on the left called Robin Hood Yard.

He'd once enjoyed the adventures of the outlaw who seemed to change character more often than he changed his clothes. He was never seen in anything other than his ridiculous outfit of Lincoln green. Hood was portrayed as an aristocratic friend of the poor, a political agitator, a critic of the church and, on one notorious occasion, even a gelder of monks. Simkins had suffered a similar fate to that of the sybaritic brothers but, after today's news, Johnny wished he'd suffered greater torment. He wouldn't be the last person to escape justice by means of a bullet.

The passage, the width of a single vehicle, opened out into a large dead-end that gave access to the rear of a terrace on Hatton Garden as well as a few buildings on Charles Street — including Otarelli's, where a bare bulb burned in an attic room.

Johnny strained his eyes to see how things fitted together. The shop was actually connected to the premises of one of the largest and most successful businesses in Hatton Garden. Over the centuries it had gradually absorbed more and more properties in the terrace that Johnny was now behind.

The furnaces of Purchon & Moy never went out. The company specialized in refining precious metals, melting down everything from unloved or out-of-date jewellery to the most microscopic of filings and sweepings that were zealously collected by local craftsmen at the end of each working day. When it came to gold and silver, nothing was allowed to go to waste.

The foundry cast a baleful glow on the surrounding jumble of outhouses and sheds. Vapours curlicued in the cold. Acrid fumes from vats of chemicals, by-products of the smelting process, percolated the night air. Johnny stifled a sneeze.

It was just as well he did. Somewhere — in a flash of yellow light — a door opened and two male voices broke the silence.

He recognized both of them. They belonged to men who were avoiding him. Furthermore, he had been told to stay away from each of them. He crept closer to the sounds of conversation.

"The bomb has been traced to the EFF."

"How so soon?"

"Leask coughed. Once he realized he wasn't going to die, he decided to make life easier for himself. I believe you've met."

"He's lying. What reason could I possibly have for meeting someone like him?"

"The same reason you agreed to meet me when our paths crossed today. When I stopped you being savaged by your pet hack."

"And what reason would that be? As I told you, I had nothing to do with Hext's death."

"You knew Hext though, didn't you? Shared his love of money. Or should I say gold?"

Johnny peered round the corner of a coal bunker in time to see Hollom fling a large leather purse at Adler.

"That's the latest haul. Came through yesterday's diplomatic bag from Berlin. Go on, take a look."

The Lord Mayor loosened the drawstring.

"Excellent."

"The watches and jewels have already been sent elsewhere. This lot's for the melting pot."

"I still don't see why we had to meet tonight."

"Last night would have been infinitely preferable, but the balloon hadn't gone up then — the bomb hadn't gone off. Someone like you should never have become Lord Mayor."

Adler took a step forward.

"Someone like me? You mean a Jew?"

"That's right, keep playing the part till the end. If you're so proud of your Jewishness, why are you hand-in-glove with the Germans? Why help them dispose of your people's belongings when they get sent to the work camps?"

"I don't know what you're talking about."

"I'm not only a member of the EFF. I'm a member of the Secret Intelligence Services too. We know you've been bankrolling the EFF in return for their orchestrating the campaign of fake anti-Semitic attacks."

"I thought it was rather clever. Who would suspect a Jew? We're no more virtuous or sinful than anyone else.

Perhaps we're better at exploiting each other, but isn't that a definition of business? People are commodities too. Believe me, those in the camps won't be coming back. I'm simply cleaning up."

Hollom shook his head in disgust.

"You're not as clever as you think. There had to be some other reason why you were being targeted apart from becoming Lord Mayor. Most Britons don't parade their prejudices in public, they prefer to hide them. It didn't ring true. You didn't divert attention away from your financial skullduggery, you alerted us to it."

"Montagu Norman was responsible for the theft of the Czech gold, not me. Ask him."

"We have. He's already signed an affidavit saying you blackmailed him into the mayoralty. He can't help you. The government may have decided to turn a blind eye to the despicable deal but there's no way it can ignore this. You're on your own. Norman accepted your outrageous terms to safeguard the good name of the City. However, there's only one way to bury this repugnant scandal now."

Adler scoffed at the implication.

"You can't kill me. There'd be an international outcry. How would my death protect the reputation of the City?"

"As you know, dead men tell no tales. You were quite prepared to kill to save your skin."

"I haven't killed anyone. Hext killed Quirk. I only found out last night. Prison walls have ears. The little shit agreed to keep silent in return for an early release, but he soon broke his word."

"I believe he spoke out of conscience rather than greed. Imagine that! A fascist with a sense of guilt . . . By the way, thanks to Leask, we've found your secret lab. Fond of petrol, aren't you?"

"It's cheap, quick and painful."

"I wish this could hurt more. You deserve worse."

Adler was dead before he knew it. In one seamless move Hollom produced a revolver and fired a single bullet into his forehead. The back of his skull disintegrated as the explosion echoed round the yard.

Johnny gasped. He'd witnessed a summary execution by an agent of His Majesty's Government. If he couldn't write about the gold — from Czechoslovakia or Britain — he would expose how Nazi tactics were now being used on this side of the North Sea.

His heart leapt as a large hand gripped his shoulder.

"Fancy seeing you here. Lurking in the shadows again. You never learn."

Commander Inskip didn't let go. He'd lied when he said Hollom had nothing to do with him. He dragged him into the light. Adler's sightless eyes gazed up at the stars.

Hollom didn't seem surprised to see Johnny. He was cleaning the gun. He didn't say a word. His work was nearly done.

No one knew where he was. He was an innocent bystander, but that wouldn't save him.

Johnny knew the game was up.

AFTERWORD

The entire newsroom was silent. Everyone — apart from Patsel, who had quit — stood with heads bowed. The telephones, thanks to the Hello Girls on the ground floor, also remained still. No one, not even Tanfield, about to jump ship to the *Chronicle* — but not as a replacement for Simkins — remained untouched. Death, especially on this day, was in all their minds.

Johnny's chair was empty. His desk was just as he'd left it. The battered typewriter, unemptied ashtray and untidy piles of papers were testament to a life lived at full speed if not complete fulfilment.

Acres of white crosses, each marked *A British Soldier*; blasted trees in no-man's-land; snaking lines of wounded men trudging through the mud: everybody had their own image of the Great War, the war to end all wars.

Even though his father was one of the hundreds of thousands of men who had not come home, Johnny did not approve of Armistice Day. The dead should be remembered every day, not once a year. The tank brought back from the Western Front twenty years ago still stood guard outside the British Museum. The way things were going it would soon see service again.

He was glad to be in Stone's office instead of the newsroom. Men were not supposed to cry — even though, in private, many did.

The radio crackled. King George VI; Prince George, Duke of Kent; and Neville "Umbrella" Chamberlain — watched by fur-clad members of the royal family — had laid their wreaths at the Cenotaph in Whitehall. The Empire was paying its respects to those who had done their duty.

A cannon shot signalled the end of the two-minute silence.

Stone sank down into his chair. All four telephones started trilling. He ignored them.

"So you won't change your mind?"

"What's the point, if I can't tell the truth?"

Hollom had given him a stark choice. Do his patriotic duty or die. In other words, say nothing. It would be simple enough to frame him for the murder of the Lord Mayor. He was bluffing, though. Johnny could see that such an atrocious crime by a prominent figure would never be acknowledged officially. Why go through the rigmarole of a trial? He'd simply disappear like his alleged victim.

Inskip, only too aware of what Turner would do should any harm befall Steadman, had urged him to make the right decision for all their sakes. So, in a sense, Matt had saved him once again.

Adler was at the bottom of a tank of nitric acid, his bones being cleansed by the same liquid that had purified the stolen gold. Dissolved shins rather than absolved sins. Johnny assumed that Stone had known what was going to happen to him — which was why he'd warned him off — but was too embarrassed to discuss the scandal afterwards. His attempt to contact his brother-in-law on Wednesday afternoon proved Adler had kept him in the dark.

Stone stared at the telephones with malice.

"At least think about it. Compromise is an uncomfortable but essential part of any successful career. And, no matter what you think, you've had a great couple of weeks. The EFF has been disbanded and you came face to face with a multiple murderess."

It had been announced that Rebekkah Maslow had hanged herself in her cell. In spite of what she'd done, Johnny felt genuinely upset. Few people could ever recover from such an ordeal. It was no mean achievement to make someone care about your death.

Fascists were obsessed with foreigners, afraid of being invaded, but the blind fools had let their minds become infiltrated, infected, by ugliness and hate. The real danger lay within. Perhaps every human was his or her own worst enemy.

Stone had indulged him long enough.

"Lord Vivis is delighted with your efforts — even if we couldn't publish all your findings. Neither he, nor I, wish to lose you. I'd offer you more money if I didn't think you'd start screaming about bribery. Haven't you always wanted to be Chief Reporter? Anyway, the offer remains on the table. Discuss it with your friends and give me your answer on Monday."

* * *

Dimeo was perched on the corner of Johnny's desk when he got back. Blenkinsopp pretended to be far too busy to watch.

"There you are!"

Dimeo pointed to a column on the lower half of a page devoted to country pursuits and pastimes that appeared each Friday. Reporters despised it, although it was popular with readers. It was headed: *Can Quail Poison? No*.

Johnny was puzzled. He didn't eat game, let alone go shooting.

"You owe me a quid," said Dimeo. He held out his hand.

"Don't you see?" Tanfield couldn't help looking smug. "It's an anagram of *colposinquanonia!*"

Ironic laughter rippled round the office. Steadman had come unstuck — again.

"So it is. Close but no cigar. The letters are all there, I grant you, but not in the right order. Half wrong is still wrong. Tell you what, I'll give you ten shillings."

"Done!" said Dimeo. They shook hands.

There were times when it seemed the whole world was on the take.

He'd already talked it over with Matt. They'd met the night before in the Coach & Horses.

"Why refuse your heart's desire? The only person who will suffer if you don't take the promotion is you. What good are principles if they do you harm? Nice chaps finish last."

"Maybe — but someone has to speak up for the man in the street. The voice of ignorance is always loudest."

"That's why we have to soldier on. We can't let the sods get away with it."

"Can't we? Zick seems to have done pretty well out of this. In more ways than one he's made a killing."

"His day of reckoning will come," said Matt.

Johnny attributed his newfound optimism to his rapprochement with Lizzie. And who could blame him?

Matt, groaning, got to his feet. "One for the road?"

Johnny watched him leaning on the bar, chatting to the landlord.

He was right. Adler was already yesterday's man. Rumours of a nervous breakdown, suicide and even German spies were galvanizing the City. Sir Frank Bowater, not Adler, would be presiding over the Lord Mayor's Banquet at the Mansion House on Monday. If the wheels of commerce continued to turn, why shouldn't he go on? What else could he do? Besides, he'd seen the perfect Crombie for him in Gamages: green and gold herringbone.

It wasn't Matt's parting words — "you're a good man" — that Johnny remembered from that evening. It was something he'd said earlier, when he'd been rabbiting on about Tanfield's obsession with train stations and his hopes for him and Tooting Becky.

Matt, once more looking like his old self, had, for no apparent reason, fallen silent.

"Johnny?"

"What?"

"Don't ever change."

318

BIBLIOGRAPHY

The following three books proved invaluable:

The City of London: Volume III — Illusions of Gold 1914–1945 by David Kynaston (Chatto & Windus, 1999)

Diamond Street: The Hidden World of Hatton Garden by Rachel Lichtenstein (Hamish Hamilton, 2012)

Bombardiers: A Novel by Po Bronson (Secker & Warburg, 1995)